CHAFFEE OF ROARING HORSE

Ernest Haycox

ROUNDUP LARGE PRINT
HAMPTON, NEW HAMPSHIRE

Library of Congress Cataloging-in-Publication Data

Haycox, Ernest, 1899-1950.
  Chaffee of Roaring Horse / Ernest Haycox.
    p. (large print) cm.
  ISBN 0-7927-1859-3. -- ISBN 0-7927-1858-5) (softcover)
  1. Large type books.   I. Title.
  [PS3515.A93C4393   1993]
  813' .54--dc20   93-32209
                                                        CIP

Copyright © 1929 by Doubleday, Doran & Co.
Copyright renewed 1957 by the Estate of Ernest Haycox.
All Rights Reserved.

Published in Large Print by arrangement with the
Golden West Literary Agency by Chivers North America
1 Lafayette Road, Hampton, NH 03842-0015.

Printed in the United States of America

To Mother and W.J.H.

CHAPTER ONE

JIM CHAFFEE TAKES A LOSS

When Jim Chaffee walked out of his homestead for the last time in three long years of struggle, it was with his senses sharpened to the pleasantness of the place he was losing. The cabin sat on the south bank of a small creek that crossed the desert diagonally from the white and hooded peaks of Roaring Horse range to the dark, dismally deep slash of Roaring Horse Canyon. Cottonwoods bunched about the log house, the lodgepole corrals, the pole-and-shake barn. The morning's sun, brilliant but without warmth, streamed through the apertures of the trees; the sparkle of frost was to be seen here and there in the shadowed crevices of the creek bank. Standing so, Jim Chaffee could look up along the course of the creek and through the lane of trees to see the distant bench fold and hoist itself some thousands of feet until it met the sheer and glittering glacial spires of the range. A solitary white cloud floated across the serene blue; the broad, yellowing cottonwood leaves bellied gently down around him, and there was the definite threat of winter in the sharp air, reminding Jim of the nights he had spent beside a glowing stove, listening to the blizzard howl around the stout eaves, dreaming his dreams. He could never step inside the cabin again; those three years had gone for nothing.

Before closing the door he ranged the room with a last wistful glance, a last reluctant appraisal of those household gods with which he had lived for so long a time. Everything was neat and clean on this eventful morning; the dishes were washed and stacked in the cupboard, the floor swept, the fire drawn. Nothing was out of place, nothing removed excepting one small article, a bright blue-patterned mush bowl that he carried under an arm. Even the bed was made up. All this he studied, as well as the pictures tacked to the walls—pictures cut from old magazines—and the odds and ends of furniture that he had so laboriously created. He looked at these things gravely, regretfully, and then closed the door, turned the lock, and dropped the key in his pocket. As the lock clicked his lips pressed together and his face settled; from the moment of discovery Jim Chaffee had liked the location above all others. Within its area he felt contented, somehow controlled by the conviction that he had struck roots into the very soil. Nor had he ever gone away from it without turning restless and wishing soon to be back. Three years of himself was in the place; a part of his heart was there.

His horse stood saddled and waiting. Jim swung up and turned out along the trail. A hundred yards away he stopped to look for the last time. The cabin was half hidden in the creek's depression, a faint wisp of smoke spiraled from the chimney; he had seen this picture a thousand times, yet to-day it affected him strangely. For to-day at noon his notes fell due and he hadn't as much as a solid dollar to pay on them. Real property and chattels belonged after that hour to the bank, and he became what he had been in the beginning, an errant cow-puncher with a horse beneath him and the sky above. Nothing more. Three severe winters and a falling market had wiped him out.

He looked to the peaks and shook his head. They stood out too clearly, they seemed too close; and around the tips was a faint, contorted wisp of a cloud that inevitably augured the fourth successive hard winter. He lifted his gun from the holster, fired a single shot, and whirled about, galloping rapidly away.

"By the Lord I hate to go!"

For a moment rebellion and bitterness made a bleak battleground of his cheeks; then the expression was gone. It couldn't last long, for he had seen disaster coming many months before and had braced himself for this final scene. It wasn't hard to lose money or labor, but he knew he would never again find a piece of land lying watered and sheltered and snug like the piece he was leaving. Even if he did find it he wouldn't feel the same somehow.

"A man," he murmured, "nourishes a picture a long while and gets sort of attached to it. No other picture will do. Not even if it's made identic. Well, we're free. Now what?"

He studied the question over the even miles of desert. Studied it with a somber leisure, sitting slack in the saddle and ever now and anon sweeping the horizons with long, closed-lidded surveys. He made a splendid picture as he swayed to the dun beast's progress—a tall man built in that mold so deceptive to the casual eye. He seemed to have no particular claim to physical strength. His shoulders were broad yet rather sharp at the points, and his chest was long and fairly flat; on this frame his clothes hung loosely and so concealed the springs of his power, which were muscles that lay banded along arm and shoulder like woven wire. A stiff-brimmed Stetson slanted the shadows over a face lean almost to the point of gauntness. It was bronzed by the sun and without furrows or wrinkles to mark the labor he had put behind him. His chin was cleft, his mouth was wide, but his lips were thin, and constantly under the guard of his will. Deep within protecting wells his eyes were apt to remain fixed on some distant point for long intervals of time; and from the expression in them it was evident they had the power to draw the rest of his face into a mask or to fill it with buoyancy and humor.

"The answer," he said to himself after the homestead faded in the distance, "is sort of plain. A man can win or he can lose. I lost. But a man can always try again. I guess I'll muster up some cash and buy me a set of traps. There's a piece of country away up on the bench by Thirty-four Pass. By gosh, we ain't had time to take in this sight for quite a spell."

Horse and rider had reached a fence. Five feet beyond the fence the desert dropped into the black and profound gorge of the Roaring Horse. It was not wide, this gorge. Fifty yards would have covered the entire width. But except at nooning the sun never touched the buried water. And the sound of its booming, turbulent progress was all but lost in the depths. Jim Chaffee got down and crawled through the fence, advancing to the edge of the rim. He had no particular reason for doing this, but there was something about the Roaring

Horse that always struck a responsive chord in his nature. The same lure lay in the distant peaks, or in the soft smell of sage carrying across the desert, or in the sight of a fire gleaming like a crimson bomb over the plain at night. So he stood watching the river boiling away its terrific temper far below. Presently he was asaddle and riding off.

"That gives me a thought," he mused. "I'll be buckin' old lady fortune again. I'll be tryin' to make a go of somethin' else. But why not take a little vacation? Why not lay in the sun like a snake and soak up a heap of laziness? I've been countin' the pennies till I ain't hardly a white man any more. I've been worryin' and schemin' and muckin' till I'm all shriveled up inside like a last year's potato. I ain't had a drink, I ain't gambled, I ain't danced, I ain't grinned—since when? Good gravy, I dunno how long. Why too long, anyhow. I'm the original old man from the hills. Nobody knows me any more; nobody remembers what I used to be. I'm in the habit of talkin' to myself; I can see a sort of glassy look in my eyes when I shave. If that keeps up I'll bite somebody and be put in the dog pound. It's time to relax."

He traveled faster, aiming away from the rim of the canyon. He had a chore to perform before hustling into town; he had to see Miz

Satterlee at the Stirrup S and give back the blue mush bowl. Once upon a time she had sent it to him filled with homemade fudge. So he drawled soberly at the dun horse and left the miles behind him. All this was Stirrup S soil—Satterlee range. The sun swung up, the air was racy with autumn decay; and he laid his course by a remote windmill. Once upon a time he had been a Stirrup S rider and mighty proud of it. Maybe he'd tackle it again, after he had taken his justly earned rest. Thinking thus he at last came to the sprawling home quarters of the ranch, threaded a series of collars, skirted the enormous bunkhouse—Stirrup S was a large outfit—and drew rein before the porch of the big house. Miz Satterlee rocked herself thereon, as she had been doing for thirty years. She looked up at him, smiling briskly.

Miz Satterlee was a character in the land—a small and sprightly woman with snapping black eyes and a head of hair that even now showed no gray. She spoke with a terrific frankness when the spirit moved her, and her charities were numberless. It was a mark of Dad Satterlee's character that Miz Satterlee had publicly said her husband was smart enough to be governor. She was smart enough to be governor herself, and she knew a good man when she saw one—even if it was her own husband.

"Hello, Jim. When were you away from your ranch last?"

"Couple-three months I guess, Miz Satterlee," drawled Jim, hooking a leg over his saddle horn.

"I bet you're down to bacon rind and bran biscuits. Most men are foolish like that."

He bent over and laid the mush bowl on the porch. "I'm returnin' it with thanks," said he. "I won't be eatin' out of it for some time."

She bit a thread and raked him with a birdlike glance. "Times a little bit hard up your way, Jim?"

"Oh, so so. Guess we're all in the same boat this year."

She spoke with an admirably offhand air. "I was telling Dad last night he ought to get you to do the wood haulin' this fall. Somebody's got to do it and you know how high spirited these young hands of ours get when anybody mentions manual labor. Haul wood—it'd insult 'em."

For no reason at all he grinned, and it changed his looks so completely that even Miz Satterlee marked the transformation. It took five years from his face and added a quality of good-humored handsomeness. "Don't worry none about me, Miz Satterlee. I locked my door a little while back. I'm deliverin' the key to Josiah Craib at the bank. What's left out of the wreck you see on the humble person before you."

"Jim Chaffee! Busted? Why, you darn fool, didn't Dad Satterlee make it a point to say he was behind you any time?"

"A keg without a bottom ain't much of a keg at all," said he.

"Fiddlesticks! Men are darn fools. Always were, always will be. Satterlee's the only one I ever met that wasn't." She abandoned her sewing and rocked vigorously. "Now what are you aimin' to do?"

"Not sure."

"I know," decided Miz Satterlee. "You go put yourself back in circulation awhile. Play some cards, drink some. Not too much, but some. Go back to some of that devilment you used to worry the county with. Let the girls see you again, Chaffee. They'll fall head over heels to invite you around to eat, and you'll get some decent cookin' for a spell. You need it—pulled down terrible. Maybe some of them won't mind bein' kissed a couple times. Scandalous advice, but it'll make you feel a heap better."

"Sage words," murmured Jim Chaffee. "All except the kissin' part of it. I'm pretty bashful, Miz Satterlee. Who'll I start with?"

"Go 'long, don't you try to fool me. Start

with the girl you kissed last."

"She's married," said Jim cheerfully.

"Whoever she is," countered Miz Satterlee with promptness, "you could of married her first. Bashful! Don't tell me that. I know your reputation. There's six or seven girls who'd have been tickled to death to've kept house over on your place. You made a mistake, Chaffee, in not takin' one of them. Any one. You wouldn't be broke now if you had."

"I wouldn't ask any girl to work that hard," said he, not so cheerfully. And the shadow of his long battle settled in his eyes for a little while.

"What's a woman for, Chaffee? You're just as foolish as the rest of the men. You all seem to want some frilly little picture of a female. You get one with a good sound head and a good sound body, and then make her pay for her keep."

He changed the subject. "Where's Dad?"

"In town. He's to be judge of the rodeo to-morrow. Went early to arrange things. That's what he said, but I know Satterlee. You'll prob'ly find him in the Gusher playin' poker."

"Ain't you afraid of him gamblin' like that?" drawled Jim, smiling again.

"Why should I be?" parried Miz Satterlee. "He always wins."

Chaffee gathered the reins. "Imagine me forgettin' it's rodeo time. I'm the original old man from the hills. I reckon I'll have to introduce myself all over again. So long, Miz Satterlee."

The mistress of the Stirrup S watched him canter through the yard, her bright eyes raised against the sun. And she sighed. "Chaffee don't know how good lookin' he is," she opined to herself. "Well, it's nice to be humble about yourself, but it ain't nice to be downright dumb about it. They'll be some girls sprucin' up their caps from now on, I vow."

The rodeo in Roaring Horse town explained the empty Stirrup S yard. Everybody would be crowding the county seat, primed for the morrow's excitement. Jim Chaffee grew eager to be among old friends again as he paced down the broad and hard-beaten trail. Left and right lay the leagues of Stirrup S range. In the foreground browsed a scattering of Dad Satterlee's white-face cows—feeder stuff drawn in to weather the winter. The trail was the same, all down its winding length; far off was the outline of Melotte's Circle Open A home quarters; the twin pines still guarded the bridge by Chickman's creek; Roaring Horse town threatened the southern reaches, sharp building points breaking the sky. And about three of the afternoon he entered the place, stabled his horse, and set forth toward the bank to wind up the last sorry details of his bankrupt homestead; and feeling a great deal like Rip Van Winkle coming back to a different world.

He had called himself a stranger. Yet twenty times or more in the short interval between bank and stable he was called by his name and stopped to swap gossip. He was struck resoundingly on the back; he was hauled about and threatened with violence if he refused to enter and tip up a convivial glass; he was called the sort of names that are not carelessly passed around except among fine friends. The gravity left his lean face, and a sparkle invaded his deep eyes. Down by the Gusher's front he bumped into a solid delegation of Stirrup S hands, all old-time cronies, and they closed about him hilariously. One shrill, united yip split the street.

"Hi—look at this lean slab o' bacon!"

"Don't talk to that damn' nester. It's him what's been butcherin' our beef!"

"How could a man eat fat Stirrup S beef and still be so peaked around the gills?"

"Well, mebbe he's been eatin' mutton, then."

Jim Chaffee built himself a cigarette and

grinned at the pack. "Boys," said he when a lull arrived, "take the advice of one that's a father to you all. Never stray far from a steady pay check. Honor your parents, cherish the little red schoolhouse, speak respectfully of all our great institutions—and don't try to run a jack-rabbit ranch like me."

"Feel poor?" demanded one of the party.

"No, I'm too dumb to feel poor," drawled Jim. "I'm froze out. I'll be back toppin' horses for the outfit when I get rested up. Where's Mack Moran?"

"Somewhere lookin' for a scrap. You know Mack. He's been a-mournin' yore absence, Jim. Yuh know how he mourns, don't yuh? It makes him so weak he's got to have a brass rail to rest his foot on and a bar to lean his elbows against."

"He'll mourn my presence," said Jim, grinning with anticipation.

"Goin' to ride in the rodeo, Jim?"

"Forgot how."

A terrific clamor met this. Then a woman's voice, clear and musical and slightly amused, said: "If you please, gentlemen." Stirrup S, to a man, moved convulsively off the sidewalk. Jim Chaffee, wedged in the center of the group, looked over the shoulder of a friend to see a vision passing by. Her face was half hidden under a gay and wide-brimmed hat of the period; but her hazel eyes met him for a moment with a kind of curiosity in them, seeming to ask him: "What kind of a man are you that all these punchers should make so much noise about you?" The next moment she was gone, and he saw the flash of her dress down by the entrance of the hotel. Something happened then and there to Jim Chaffee. He muttered, "I've got to go, boys. Let me out of this stampede."

"Theodorik Perrine's in town, Jim. He's ridin' to-morrow."

They had all been rollicking and easy humored. Now they were very sober, watching Chaffee with the close inspection that a friend is alone able to give another friend. Jim Chaffee's attention centered on the speaker. His lids drooped. "That's interestin'. Maybe I will ride. Now I've got to hustle off to the bank. See you later."

He shouldered through and walked past the hotel. The girl was at that moment climbing the lobby stairs. One quick sidewise glance told him that. Going on, he entered the bank and tried to maintain a cheerfulness of countenance he was by no means feeling. Mark Eagle, the teller, raised a full-blooded Umatilla Indian face to Jim and spoke pleasantly. "Hello, Jim. I saw Mack Moran two-three minutes ago on the street. He was wondering if you'd come in."

"I'd better find him before he tears something apart," replied Jim Chaffee. "You're puttin' on fat, Mark. Better take some time out hunting. Craib in his office?"

Mark Eagle ducked his round cheeks. Chaffee walked to a far door and opened it without knocking. Josiah Craib sat stooped over a plain pine desk, his finger trailing along a small map; he looked up with the air of a man about to speak disapproval. But that changed when he saw his visitor. Jim said, "Hello, Craib, I'm surrenderin' the last legal relic o' my ranch. Here's your key and God bless you. I'm busted."

Craib's bald and bony head glistened under a patch of light slanting through a high side window. "Shut the door, Jim. I'm sorry. Sit down."

"Why be sorry?" countered Jim, throwing the key on Craib's desk. "A banker can't afford to be sorry, can he?"

"I would like to give you another year—" began Craib. But Jim Chaffee broke bluntly into the other's talk.

"I'd be just as poor next year as this one. It takes three seasons to get a herd started. I banked on that. I lost. It would take me another three to get back where I began. I can't do it. There's another tough winter hidin' up behind the peaks."

Craib seemed a clumsy figure for his profession. His lank legs were too high for the space beneath the table; his spare chest towered above it. Everything about him was bony—fists and cheeks and nose. He owned a narrow, overlong face, across which the skin lay tight, holding his features in a kind of cast. And because of this physical peculiarity he was an enigma in Roaring Horse county after twenty years' residence. Sometimes, as he strode along the street with his chin tucked against his chest and his clothes flapping on the awkward frame, it appeared as if he was a man smothered beneath solemn thoughts. From season to season there was not a shade of variance in the set expression; he talked very little, he had no friends and no family. The country made up strange and contradictory stories about him—he was as hard as flint, he was just; he was fabulously rich, he was poor and on the verge of bankruptcy; he was credited with a scheming, brilliant brain that lusted after power in the county, and at the same breath people spoke of him as nothing more than a dull and plodding man who never rose above the pettiness of penny shaving. Nobody fathomed him, and now as he faced Jim Chaffee there was nothing on his parchment face to indicate what he felt about the former's misfortune.

"I would like to give you another year," he repeated, as if not hearing Jim. "But unfortunately I am not in a position to do so. This has been a bad season. I cannot afford to hold paper. I've got to take yours over, Jim, and realized on it."

"May the Lord have mercy on you," drawled Jim. "I don't know how you'll get anything out of it. There she lies, idle and profitless."

"I have a man who is buying it," said Craib in the selfsame, even, expressionless tone.

That stirred Jim's curiosity. "Now who's foolish?"

"I'm bound not to say," replied Craib.

Jim got up, smiling. "The man must be ashamed of his lack o' discretion. All right, Craib. Sorry I've been a poor customer. But I'll be tryin' again somewhere and sometime. After I get a rest." He opened the door and looked out, wistfulness clouding his eyes. "By George, I hate to lose that little place. Won't ever find another like it."

Craib rose, knocking back the chair by the force of his unwieldy legs. "Can't loan you any of the bank's money, Jim," he said, "but if a personal loan of a hundred dollars will help any I'll be glad to let you have it. No note, no security."

It was so unusual a proposal, coming from Craib, that Jim Chaffee was plainly astonished. "Well, that's handsome of you, Craib. Maybe I'll take the offer. Let you know later."

"All right," grunted Craib, busy again with his map.

Jim left the office, nodding at Mark Eagle. The teller's eyes followed the rangy cowpuncher all the way to the street. And long after, Mark Eagle tapped his counter with an idle pen, squinting at some remote vision.

Within twenty paces Jim Chaffee confronted three entirely dissimilar gentlemen whom he knew very well. Mack Moran, Dad Satterlee, and William Wells Woolfridge, who owned an outfit adjoining Satterlee, broke through the crowd. Mack Moran threw a hand over his face at sight of Jim and appeared to stagger from the shock of it. "Oh, look at the stranger from the brush! Mama. there's that face again!" He came forward, Irish countenance split from ear to ear. "How, Jim!"

"You're drunk."

"I ain't drunk," was Moran's severe retort. "I ain't even intoxicated. Been lookin' all over hell's half acre—"

Satterlee, a stout old fellow with iron-crusted hair rumbled an abrupt question. "When did you get in?" Woolfridge contented himself with a bare nod and found something else to interest him. Jim shook hands with his old boss and before he could answer the question Satterlee shot another at him. "Enterin' the buckin' to-morrow?"

"Shore he is," chimed Mack Moran. "And there goes yore hundred dollars first money."

"I don't know," said Jim. "Ain't rode for an awful long while, Dad."

"Get in it," urged Satterlee. "Theodorik Perrine's ridin'."

All three of them watched Jim with considerable gravity. He reached for his tobacco, quite thoughtful. "I have heard the name before," he murmured. "Maybe I'll ride." Satterlee grunted and moved on with Woolfridge. But Mack Moran had, as he said, found the answer to a maiden prayer and placed a great hand through Jim Chaffee's arm.

"We'll settle this right now. Yore ridin'." He took off his hat and rubbed a tangle of fire-red hair; he looked up to Jim—for he was a short and wiry bundle of dynamite, this Mack Moran—and chuckled to himself. "I been like a chicken minus a head all day. By golly, I'm glad to see yore homely mug. Let's do somethin', let's drink somethin', let's rip up a few boards."

Jim stopped, attracted by a fresh sign painted on an adjacent building front: "Roaring Horse

Irrigation and Reclamation Corporation." He pointed at it.

"How long's that been there? What is it?"

"I dunno. Some new fangled outfit come in here a few weeks back. They's a dude in charge that calls himself secretary. In plain words, a pen pusher. What's behind it I ain't able to state. They been buyin' land and doin' a good business at that. Tough year. Small folks are sellin'. What does the aforesaid corporation want with land that ain't worth four bits an acre? I dunno. Here's where you sign up."

He led Jim into a hardware store, where all the contestants applied for places in the next day's rodeo. Jim signed. But when then gentleman in charge asked for the customary ten dollars he stared rather blankly at Mack. "I forgot that. Ain't got ten dollars."

"I have," said Moran, and peeled the sum from his pocket. He slapped it down. "And I'll state I'll bring a hundred iron men back with it to-morrow night."

The gentleman behind the counter accepted the ten but not the comment. He looked curiously toward Chaffee. "Theodorik Perrine's ridin'."

"The name," replied Jim, "is not altogether strange to me."

The partners went out. Mack suggested it

was time to humor the inner man, and they started through the crowd, bound for the restaurant. "Jim," was Mack's abrupt question, "have you seen Theodorik yet this aft'noon?"

"Ain't had that pleasure for a great many months."

"Well, he's ornerier than ever. If you could cross a skunk, a grizzly, and a snake you'd have a combination half as mean as Theodorik. Most men stop growin' when they get of age. Theodorik just keeps gettin' bigger and meaner."

"Be interestin' to see him again," drawled Jim. His head snapped upward, and he gripped Mack Moran's arm so tightly that the latter jumped. "Walk slow," breathed Jim fiercely. "Walk slow like you was just wastin' time."

"Yeah, but—"

"Shut up!"

William Wells Woolfridge came toward them; beside him walked the girl Jim had seen earlier in the afternoon. She had a parasol raised against the late afternoon's sun, and her white chin was tipped toward the man. She was talking gayly, while her free hand made graceful gestures that seemed to flow into her words and add life to them. Chaffee, venturing one direct glance, saw the robust freedom about her and the assured carriage she owned. Every piece of clothing and every step stamped her as belonging to a world remote from this dusty old cattle town. He muttered a word to Mack. The latter, puzzled by the sudden change in his friend, blurted out an impatient phrase loud enough to wake the dead. "Don't mumble thataway. What was it yuh tried to say?" The girl walked by, head erect and attention straight to the front. She hadn't seen Jim Chaffee. At least that was the impression he gathered.

"Who is that girl?" he demanded, far removed from ordinary calm.

"Great guns, don't bite me in the neck," grumbled Mack. "Her name's Gay Thatcher. She's from the territorial capital, takin' in our rodeo as a sorter pilgrim."

"A bright spot in this gay street," murmured Jim. "A thoroughbred. Gay. Ain't that a pretty name, Mack? Ain't it pretty now?" He turned to his partner, glowering. "Any relation to that coyote Woolfridge? The son-of-a-gun looked like he owned her. Any relation?"

"How do I know?" protested Mack. "Don't think so. She come with a party of society folks on the special stage caravan. Town's full of them. La-de-da ladies and slick-eared gents. They's to be a grand ball at the Gusher tomorrow night. Woolfridge is the high card dude around these parts with them people. You and me is only rough, rude cow persons. But Woolfridge ain't only a common rancher, my boy. He's got connections in genteel families down-territory. He's rich, he uses lots of big words, and he knows the difference atween pie fork and meat fork. I heard somebody say that. What is said difference, Jim? Since when has a fellow got to use two forks to eat his vittals? Hell, I ain't used any, and it don't seem to impair my appetite none."

"Gay—by George, that's a pretty name. Mack, I've got to meet her."

"Ha!" snorted Mack, and considered that a sufficient answer. He started to pull Jim into the crowded restaurant. Josiah Craib's gaunt frame stepped around the pair. The banker had his hands clasped tightly behind him, and his long face bent forward like that of some droopy vulture. He drew Jim's attention by a slight jerk of his shoulders.

"About that personal offer, Jim. I spoke a little prematurely. I will have to withdraw the offer. Sorry."

"That's all right," said Jim soberly. "I don't—" But Craib was gone, plowing a straight furrow through the multitude.

"He's crooked as a snake's shadder," grumbled Mack. "What's he talkin' about?"

"Nothing," replied Jim. "I've got to meet her, Mack." They passed into the restaurant.

Jim Chaffee thought she hadn't seen him. But she had clearly discovered the excitement simmering in his eyes as she passed by. And he would have been immensely interested if he had known that later in the night she stood by the window of her hotel room and looked across the street to where he stood. The Melotte family was in town; Lily Melotte and a pair of other girls had cornered Jim in front of Tilton's dry-goods store. His hat was off, and he was smiling at the group in a manner that for the moment made him quite gracefully gallant. Lily Melotte touched his arm with a certain air of possession, and at that Gay Thatcher drew away from the window and lifted her sturdy shoulders.

"They tell me he is a lady's man," said she to herself. "It would seem so. Yet I have never seen a finer face. He carries himself so surely—and still without swagger. I wonder if he will try to meet me again?"

With that feminine question she crossed to the table and began to write a letter to the governor of the territory. It was not a social letter; it was one of sober business with the words sounding strangely like those of an equal to an equal. Gay Thatcher was in Roaring Horse ostensibly to attend the rodeo; in reality her presence was for the purpose of finding certain things about certain people. Dress, manner, and beauty might be feminine, but beneath her dark and quite lustrous hair was a sharp mind and a store of experience surpassing that of many a man. Gay Thatcher was a free lance.

CHAPTER TWO

A SECRET MEETING

William Wells Woolfridge was not an impressive man in the open air; in fact he was apt to take on a neutral coloring when surrounded by neighbors. It required four walls and a little furniture to draw him out. With a desk in front of him and a few sheets of business to trap his attention, he slowly acquired a distinct personality and threw off an atmosphere of authority that his subordinates were quick to sense and even more quick to obey. There is no autocrat like the man who feels himself lacking in outward command.

Perhaps it was his face that made him seem negative. It was a smooth and pink face, suggesting freckles. He wore riding breeches and cordovan boots, and all his clothes matched in shade and were scrupulously pressed. His hair ran sleekly into his neck, his hands were like those of a musician; he had the air of eating well, and indeed his ranch kitchen was stocked with victuals the rest of the country never heard of, nor would have eaten if they had. He was thirty-five and seemed younger; he looked like an Easterner, which he once had been; he looked like a business man, which he was; he looked nothing at all like a cattleman, but he owned more acres than Dad Satterlee, hired thirty punchers in season, and sported a very modern ranch house appointed with Filipino boys in white jackets. The rank and file of Roaring Horse never quite got used to him; but they didn't know, either, the extent of his power nor the far-reaching sources of his fortune; his forefathers had done very well in many lines and many places.

About nine o'clock in the evening William Wells Woolfridge entered the hotel and walked as inconspicuously as possible up the stairs, letting himself into a room occupied by two other gentlemen. One was a visitor from down-territory, the other Josiah Craib. After a few preliminary words, preceded by an adequate measure of rye, the gentleman from down-territory, whose name was on the register as T. Q. Bangor, came to the issues.

"Fortunate thing, Woolfridge, that this rodeo gave me an excuse to come up here and see you. The less of fuss the better. Written correspondence won't do at this stage. It may interest you to know that our engineers have given me some rather favorable estimates."

"Good enough," replied Woolfridge. Though a fortune hinged on the statement he took it with urbane calm. "But why not use words that bite a little deeper?"

At this point Craib rose, gaunt body casting a grotesque shadow against the wall. "You don't need me. I'll go back to my office." With a nod to each of them he went out, closing the door softly behind him, and down the street; as he marched through the crowd, hands clasped across his back and his eyes dropped to the sidewalk, there seemed to be a deep and somber fire burning within the man. Once, when he passed into the bank, he looked at the stars above. That was a rare thing for Craib to do.

In the room Bangor proceeded. "Your banker friend gives me an uneasy, insecure feeling. What does the man think about?"

"God knows," said Woolfridge. "It doesn't matter. He's tied to me. Go on."

"I didn't put the specific case before our engineers," explained Bangor. "I made it an arbitrary and theoretical proposition to keep them off the track. Until the big news breaks we want no leaks. But they assure me of this point—to divert enough water from the proposed power dam for irrigation purposes will be all right. It depends on the following factors—that the number of acres to be irrigated does not require more than so many acre-feet of water, that the dam is high enough and the back basin great enough to take care of a set minimum for the generation of electrical current. I have all the figures with me. It checks all right with the reserves we will be carrying when the Roaring Horse project goes through. I'll give you the sheets to run over. But there are a lot of angles to this thing, and I wish you'd talk to me straight out. I want the picture in your head."

Woolfridge pulled a map from his pocket and unfolded it on the bed. It covered the Roaring Horse country between peaks and western alkali wastes, between Roaring Horse canyon and town, and it had been especially drawn by surveyors for Woolfridge. He laid a finger on it. "All you see here is desert grazing land. Intrinsically worth whatever you've got to pay for it. Fifty cents an acre, ten dollars an acre. All as dry as a bone except for drilled wells and two small creeks. The Roaring Horse absorbs everything. At present this land is good for nothing but cattle. Less than eleven inches of rainfall a year on it. That's the first fundamental proposition.

"The second proposition is that this land is astonishingly fertile; it will grow absolutely anything if irrigated. I've tested it. The third proposition is that we have had three bad cattle years with another in prospect and the ranchers discouraged and willing to sell. I have quietly bought a lot of range through my dummy company next door. I will continue to buy until I have an almost solid strip along the canyon within easy irrigating distance. The control will be absolutely mine. I will irrigate it, divide it into small farms, and sell. Ten dollar range land with water on it is worth, in this district from fifty to a hundred and fifty dollars."

"Yes, but Woolfridge, have you given enough attention to the cost of installing an irrigating system? One unforeseen item can lay you flat on your back."

Woolfridge smiled, still the mild, soft-fleshed man. "Let's check the items of expense. First, the dam. You are building it for a power dam—doesn't cost me a penny. You will charge a nominal sum for the use of the water later, but that falls on the homesteader, not me. Second item is the main ditch. And outside of one small piece of digging, about three hundred yards, that won't cost anything, either. Look on the map here."

He traced a shaded line that started on the upper end of the Roaring Horse canyon and worked parallel to it, though angling away slightly as it traveled. "That's a gully which in prehistoric days was a good-sized creek. Its mouth comes within three hundred yards of the rim, and that piece had somehow been overlain with soil. It travels down grade with the general contour of the country for ten miles, sliding gradually away from the rim. When your dam is built that gully, shoveled out, will tap your basin, take the water and carry it by gravity those ten miles. Soil is hard underneath, no porous sands. And there is my main ditch."

Bangor shook his head. "You are a very lucky man, Woolfridge."

Something of the mildness went from Woolfridge. His eyes cooled, the smooth cheeks became distinctly hard. All at once he was a different individual, aggressive and slightly overbearing. "Not lucky, Bangor. I have been studying this five years. One more item—the lateral ditches. They will go in as I sell the ranches. I've got a mechanical digger in mind that will slash them out of the ground in no time at all. There is the cost of it. Advertising will mount up, of course. Buying out the present ranchers will cost. But the whole sum is nothing when compared to what I expect to make. There is a quarter or a half million in this one angle."

"We are the means, therefore, of supplying you with a very nice fortune," said Bangor, not overenthused.

Woolfridge had been watching his man closely, gauging the latter's reactions. The coldness became more pronounced, his speech snapped more crisply, more rapidly. "I expected some such reply, Bangor. I am prepared to meet it. I said I have studied this five years. It depended wholly on somebody building a dam on the Roaring Horse. A power dam with excess water for irrigating purposes. Otherwise it couldn't pay. Your company had to get a site. I called this to your attention—an ideal location from every point of view. Moreover, when you got in trouble with Bi-State Power I saw to it my block of stock was instrumental in giving you a position that was not assailable. I helped you. I expect help in return."

"Your help had definite strings attached," Bangor reminded him. "It still has strings attached."

"I believe in protecting myself," was Woolfridge's quiet answer. "This isn't charity. You will make money from the deal. Not only in water rent but in the development of a whole new region. Personally I've got controlling interest in the bank, in a warehouse, and shortly will also have bought the major store here. All through the dummy corporation. I expect to build up a marketing organization in time. Long after I take my first profit there will be a steady, year by year percentage of the general prosperity coming my way."

"You let nothing past you."

"I have studied it a long time," said Woolfridge. "There is yet one difficult barrier to cross. I have got to buy out Satterlee or the whole thing falls to pieces. His land slices my project in two. The ditch runs across it; and the man would let his fingers be hacked off before he'd see the cattle range split into homesteads. So I have got to take him out of the game."

"From what I saw of him," suggested Bangor, "he looks both prosperous and stubborn."

"Both," agreed Woolfridge. "But all men have a price. Somewhere up the scale I'll find his. Now, we must work quietly and let nothing get out. You don't know how cattle land hates the smell of small farms. They'd block me if they understood. The name of my dummy—they wonder who is behind it—sounds like a big joke to them. They can't understand how this country will ever get water. Moreover, they don't want it."

"Who is in with you on this deal?" question Bangor.

"Nobody. When I want a thing done I do it myself. I never let another man see my hand if I can help it. And the rewards I keep alone, having well earned them."

In saying that the core of his nature broke through the neutral wrapping and lay exposed. His round cheeks were flushed and hard; there was a slanting, oriental cast to his eyes that defied Bangor's power of analysis. Bangor saw part of Woolfridge's underlying coldness and a part of the man's acquisitive will, but there was still some latent explosive force beyond sight. It was to him an uncomfortable moment. He broke it quickly.

"We should have an answer to our application in Washington. That's only formality. It will go through. And so will our business with the territorial engineer. You had better get your necessary legal business in order as well."

"I am taking care of that," said Woolfridge. Bangor had the disquieting sensation that the man had taken care of a great many things. He knew Woolfridge very well; he knew his approximate wealth and connections. Yet from time to time Woolfridge surprised him by producing still another weapon out of the case;

stock, a friendly official, some secret control.

"Well," went on Bangor, "when you are ready to break the news let me know. I'll hold off until then. By the way, the governor is preparing to lay a series of distinctly radical reforms before the ensuing legislature. I don't like it. But we'll beat them."

"Give the governor my regards," was Woolfridge's ironical comment. "Two years from now I'll send him back to private life."

"How?" was Bangor's startled question.

Woolfridge shrugged his shoulders and motioned to the bottle. The interview was over. They drank in silence, and Woolfridge prepared to leave. By the door he turned for a last word. "See you in the morning. You are sitting with me. It will be very interesting. Watch a man named Jim Chaffee. It will repay you. He has a terrific reputation for ability in these parts." He seemed to thaw and drop back to his inconspicuous rôle. "By the way, Gay Thatcher is an extraordinarily charming lady. Where is she from?"

"Don't know," said Bangor. "She's been socially up around the capital this fall. Her past seems to be entirely her own business, but she walks through the best doors."

"I should think so," murmured Woolfridge, and let himself out.

Bangor waited a spell. Then he pulled off

his shoes and stared a long, long interval at the wall. His thoughts seemed to displease him, and in the end he spoke a short piece. "How did he get that stock in the first place, and how did he know we were battling for a place in the sun? Now he talks to me as if I were a secretary. Me! And I'd like to throw him overboard but don't dare. He's playing his own cards, which may not be mine. Where does he think he's going to get the power to defeat the governor? That man is a profound mystery."

William Wells Woolfridge went down the plush carpeted stairway of the Gusher and paused in the lobby beneath a crystal chandelier. The Gusher was not a modern hotel. Its frame dated back to an ancient army post. But recently unknown capital had taken over and remodeled the place. It glittered cheerfully of a night, its walls were loaded with murals, and its woodwork ran to fancy scrolls and jigsaw figures. Each room on the lower floor opened grandly into another—lobby, dining hall, ballroom, and gaming parlor; and each room was differently colored and took name from that color. Most appropriately the gaming parlor was called the Gold Room, into which Woolfridge sauntered, seeming pleased at the comfortable crowd gathered there. It should have pleased him. It was his hotel, though this was another under-cover possession, and the Gold Room was his idea. It netted him money; it furnished a cosmopolitan air to the town and public sentiment in no wise disapproved. The Gold Room, according to his own rigid directions, was thoroughly genteel, and women sometimes stood at the doorway looking on. There was a bar beyond a partition, but not a drop of liquor entered the precincts of this room; men went to the bar if they were athirst.

The playing had started, but he found Dad Satterlee leaning idly against a wall, talking politics to French Melotte, looking for all the world like a man who had absolutely no interest in the click of chips or the shuffle of cards. Dad was an inveterate poker player, but he went about it cagily. Woolfridge tapped him on the arm and nodded toward the lobby. Satterlee followed, his red, blunt face shining honestly against the light; his hair was the color of iron and his eyes were like disks of steel; but Satterlee liked to laugh, and the echo of it rang strong and free wherever he was.

"Nice crowd," said Dad, scanning the lobby.

"That's right," agreed Woolfridge. "About that proposition of mine—"

"Oh, hell, I thought you had somethin' to

tell me about the rodeo. Don't pester me with any more offers."

"I will meet any reasonable price you set, Satterlee," insisted Woolfridge. "I'm serious."

"Yuh? Son, if I set a price it wouldn't be nowise reasonable. And that's likewise serious. What would me and my wife do with a lot of money and no place to go? Shucks, you ain't talkin' to a poor man."

"Now you're trying to draw me into something else," said Woolfridge mildly. "I don't care what you do with the money. Buy a battleship and tour the world. It may sound like nonsense to you, but I need your range worse than you do. I want it bad enough to pay a stiff price. And I have always found a man could buy anything if he wanted it sufficiently. I have also found all men will sell at a price. I'm trying to find yours."

"Great shades!" snorted Dad. "You got the dangdest way of dickerin' I ever heard tell about. Same as sayin' I can keep on talkin', but you'll get my land by and by."

"I'm trying to find your price."

"Well, I'll set a price high enough to keep you off," said Dad. Immediately he checked himself and looked into Woolfridge's face with a sharp, shrewd penetration. "No, I won't let you run me into any corral like that, either.

Might take me up. You're foxy, but you ain't got good sense tryin' to extend your range in a bad year. Not when you got to pay boom prices. What's in the back of your coco, anyhow?"

"Just what I told you," was Woolfridge's patient answer. "I want to be the kingpin in this piece of country. If a man can afford to nurse his vanity, why not?"

Satterlee bit into his cigar and became mellow. "Now, listen. I was born here. I courted my wife here, and I buried three kids out yonder on a green little knoll. I made money here, and I've sorter put my roots way down deep. Don't you talk dicker to me any more, son. I'm finished. All you and me can discuss is horses and buckers to-morrow. Believe I'll sit in a judicious game."

He left Woolfridge, eyes sparkling with the robust anticipation of battle. Woolfridge watched him settle up to a vacant table and crook his fingers at sundry prospects. There was one particular man who seemed on the verge of joining this new game; but Woolfridge caught that man's eyes and held it for a fraction of a moment. He turned into the street and walked through the shadows. In a little while somebody drew abreast, obscured. "What was it, Mr. Woolfridge?"

"Before you sit in that game with Satterlee,"

murmured Woolfridge, "I wanted to tell you to tighten your play all around. Tighten it up, Clyde, understand? Play for Satterlee and let the others win or lose, but play for Satterlee."

A moment's silence. "You told me when you brought me into this country, Mr. Woolfridge, I was not to turn a crooked card."

"So I did and so you have. And you have built up a reputation for being square. Which is exactly what I wanted you to do. Now go back there and do as I say. I have been nursing you along for this particular time. Use all the tricks in your bag, Clyde, which are manifold. That's all."

"How much have I got behind me to do this?"

"You are free to sign I O U's to twenty thousand. I'll privately protect them. I'll protect any obligation—so long as you whittle down Satterlee. Boost the play high. Dad's feeling good. Now go back there and work."

"All right—"

Behind them was the smashing of glass and one sharp explosion. They turned to see a saloon door erupt a vast, towering form. Down the street came a mighty wailing cry, weird and full throated and savage; a cry that seemed possible only to some enraged beast. It poured along the thoroughfare, striking a chill into the holiday humor of the crowd. Clyde the gambler swore and made nervous gestures with his slim fingers.

"Great God, what's that?"

Woolfridge lifted his thin shoulders. "That is Theodorik Perrine twisting his own tail for to-morrow's battle."

CHAPTER THREE

A DUEL OF THE ARENA

The flag was up; the cowboy band had finished the last bar of the national anthem; the crowd in the grandstands settled back; a pistol cracked at the far turn of the track; and a dozen ponies came battering down the main stretch on the opening relay of the rodeo. Excitement roared from one end of the field to the other; the crowd was up again and yelling encouragement to the riders swirling through the dust. Yellow and red flashed in the sun; there was a sudden mêlée at the opposite turn of the track, and a pony went down, rider swinging through the air. A sigh like the passage of wind swept the onlookers; then the race was over, and the spilled rider sat up and waved his hand at his departing horse. Again a pistol cracked; the show was under way.

The rodeo hands were in the center of the field with the first of the bucking horses, each brute snubbed up to the hand's saddle horn. Blindfolds were on, and men went about the ticklish business of saddling. Jim Chaffee stood at one side of the arena, smoking a cigarette and looking over the fence to some far distant point of the horizon. His long legs were spread slightly apart, his blue neckpiece fluttered slightly to the wind, and his up-tilted hat let the sun fall fully on his lean, bronzed cheeks. His eyes were half closed, the cigarette drooped from a corner of his thin lips. It was a splendid picture of a man relaxed and indifferent; he seemed entirely forgetful at the moment of the part he was about to play. And in truth he was. Looking northward, gravely wistful of features, he was seeing in his mind the cabin by the creek and the tall surrounding cottonwoods. It didn't seem right that so cheerful and tucked-in a place should be lying tenantless. There ought to be a fire in the stove, and somebody ought to be out fixing that broken corral pole. And he was saying: "I never will find another like it. Not in a thousand years."

Gay Thatcher saw him there and stored the picture in her memory. Leaning forward from the foremost box in the stands she drew the attention of William Wells Woolfridge. "Is he riding to-day?"

Woolfridge was one of the three judges; at present he sat on his horse beside the other two, French Melotte and Dad Satterlee, waiting for the rodeo hands to get the buckers ready. He turned at her question. "Who? Chaffee—yes he's riding, Miss Gay. He has some reputation for that sort of thing in his country."

"He looks—picturesque," said Gay, and then inwardly protested at her own use of the word. It sounded exactly like what a tourist would say. She wasn't a tourist and she hadn't meant that. "I mean, he looks exactly like a Westerner should look."

Woolfridge smiled. "Perhaps there's a little grandstand gesture in that pose. Most of the boys like to show off before the crowd."

Dad Satterlee had his attention on the field, but he caught that last sentence and turned suddenly. "What you talkin' about, son? Chaffee don't play to the crowd. He ain't built that way. Never was, never will. He wasn't even figurin' on competin' this year. That ranch of his sorter ties him down."

"He no longer has it," corrected Woolfridge, amused. "He lost it. That bank took it over yesterday."

"Oh," said Gay, instantly sorry.

Satterlee's bulldog face showed disbelief. "What's that? You're kiddin' us, Woolfridge. He'd come to me for help first. He'd told me right off."

"I happen to know," replied Woolfridge. He was so quietly positive about it that Dad Satterlee's red cheeks grew crimson.

"Of all the dumb fool things! By Jupiter, if I don't tear the hide offen him! Three years work gone up the spout, and he's too doggone proud to ask me for a boost! Wait till I lay a tongue on the young stiff-back!"

Gay's attention was attracted elsewhere. "Who is that enormous man coming through the side gate?"

All three judges looked; all three exchanged glances. "His name is Theodorik Perrine," said Woolfridge, voice changing.

"What a mountain he is," breathed the girl. "What a peculiar walk!"

Theodorik Perrine marched slowly into the field; and the crowd, seeing that his course took him directly in front of Jim Chaffee, fixed its attention upon the pair and grew silent. Every soul in the Roaring Horse country understood the antagonism, bitter and profound, that lay between the two. It had existed since the first meeting years ago, and through those years the Roaring Horse country had seen the breach widen, had witnessed the tentative crossing of wills, the duels each staged at the rodeos, the slow piling up of temper in the men, auguring some tremendous and terrific struggle that one day must surely come. It was ordained. Somebody behind Gay whispered: "Those boys are pointed t'ords each other again. Some day there'll be an almighty big explosion. It can't last much longer like this." Gay, unconsciously doubling her small fists, leaned forward and studied Jim Chaffee's fine lean face.

Chaffee had his back to the approaching Perrine. Yet he caught the silence coming over the crowd and he felt Perrine's presence. He took a final draw on the cigarette and tipped his head to the distant horizon. The cigarette veered through the air and Jim, all muscles seeming slack, turned casually about, thumbs hooking into his belt.

The man behind Gay drew a deep breath, exclaiming: "Look how slow and easy he does it. Those fellows don't make any quick motions when they meet. By the Lord, Jim Chaffee's a sight to watch. Now hold on to yourself."

Theodorik Perrine advanced, boots sliding across the soft earth with that particularly sinuous motion so much a part of him. His knees buckled with each step as if the weight of his body pressed him down, and his hands traveling back and forth were turned so that the palms brushed thigh and thigh at every swing. Theodorik Perrine was a Tennessean, of that class of mountain folk who trace their ancestors back without a break or flaw to the England of the Thirteenth Century. Yet from the hairy reaches of his mighty neck to the crown of his head his skin was burned to a brown that suggested some darker blood; and Theodorik Perrine's features were all bold and rounding and supported by massive bones that seemed too thick to be broken. His Stetson was lowered, with a braided rawhide passing from it under his chin; and his eyes were a dull, slate-colored pair of windows that clouded up and concealed the fires burning within the recesses of his vast being. Yet the plain physical impact of his glance was like a blow. A brooding, sullen, and unfathomable man with a wild record behind him.

Jim Chaffee's lids drooped and his lips pinched in until they made a thin line beneath the swooping nose. And he waited while the lumbering giant came to a stand five yards away. Seldom did either man come closer to his own will. Perrine poked a thumb against the brim of his hat and shot it upward, clearing his face. He didn't immediately speak; first he took a leisured chew of tobacco and ground it solidly between his teeth, collecting one by one the exact words he wanted to use. In the end they came out of him, freighted with a world of cold belligerence.

"Got to buck again' you this year, uh?"

"I reckon, Perrine."

Silence. The summoning up of more words. The same mutter and rumble, the same dead and stony look. "I'm takin' first this year, Chaffee."

"Maybe."

"To hell with yore mebbe," said Theodorik Perrine, boosting the words truculently across the interval.

"I'm repeatin' the same word," drawled Chaffee.

"I'd go a thousand miles to lick yuh."

"I wouldn't go that far, speakin' for myself," said Chaffee.

"Yore trail runs too close to mine. Some day they'll cross. Ever think of that, Chaffee?"

"It's marked in the calendar," said Chaffee solemnly.

All activity seemed to have halted around the arena, the crowd was quite still, and even the three judges tarried a moment. For this was a scene that engrossed Roaring Horse, that gripped every man's imagination. One spark flashing along the bright cold morning's air and touching the explosives. Perrine's towering shoulders squared and his chest rose.

His slate-colored eyes cleared for a moment, and Jim Chaffee saw the volcanic fire flickering far down. Then Theodorik Perrine moved and walked on across the arena, circling and placing behind the man he both hated and respected more profoundly than any other.

Gay Thatcher's fists ached with the pressure she had unknowingly put on them. Her throat hurt. She heard the man behind release a long held breath and at the same moment speak in a high-pitched accent. "Not this time. But blamed soon. This can't go on much longer. Chaffee's lightin' a cigarette, and I'll bet his fingers ain't shakin'. I'd gave a million dollars for his nerves." Gay leaned forward, looking to Dad Satterlee. "What is it—why is it?"

Satterlee gathered his reins. "Two kinds of men—poison to each other, ma'am. Both at the top o' the heap. And in such case they ain't room for but one. Come on, boys. Time for the ball to roll."

A rider was up, high against the sun. Before the girl could adjust herself Satterlee's gun cracked and the ride was over. Action swirled out there in the bright oval. Another puncher was up and then down in the dust while hoofs flailed across his body. Pickup men streamed away, new buckers came in. Conversation boiled around her as she sat forward, chin cupped in one hand, still watching Jim Chaffee. Presently her attention was recalled by the mention of Perrine's name, and she saw the man's vast frame settling into a saddle. The judges were spreading out, each to command a different view of that ride; the horse surged away, breaking in two, it seemed to her. Yet, above the pounding and the spurts of dust and the dynamic thrusts of the brute, Perrine sat like a rock, heels roving fore and aft, one arm free, voice sounding over the field and striking away back in the stands. Nothing, it appeared to Gay, could ever move that giant. Partisan spirit took hold of her and she wondered how Jim Chaffee would fare. The man behind was volunteering more information.

"Chaffee up on Lovey-Dovey. There's a tough one. Perrine made a nice ride. Always does. Jim's gotta show well on that double-jointed brute. Now watch the difference in style. Perrine bears down, Jim does it fancy."

Gay thought Chaffee looked directly at her, but the sun was in her eyes and she couldn't be sure. He threw away his cigarette, long arm rippling outward, and turned toward Lovey-Dovey. From that moment Gay neither saw nor heard anything around her. Chaffee's rangy body was beside the horse, and his hands were roving along the cinches. Lovey-

Dovey struck with venom and danced away, dragging the anchor horse a yard along the arena. The rodeo hand bent, saying something to Chaffee and Gay saw the latter look up and shake his head. He was unsmiling and again he touched the cinches and seemed to be soothing the animal. A foot went cautiously into the stirrup. He was up in one lithe, graceful pull. He was looking down at the stirrups and settling his feet into them; he had the reins in his hand, free arm taking up the slack and moving sinuously here and there about Lovey-Dovey's head. Gay gripped the stand railing, feeling the suspense of that long interval. It seemed a long while to her, yet in reality it was but a moment; then Jim Chaffee's arm was far above him and Lovey-Dovey had reared on its hind feet and launched the fight. Thereafter her eyes were filled with a piece of weaving, raw beauty. Man and horse were one. Jim Chaffee sat securely, yet swaying to each immeasurably violent jolt. Silver flashed in the sun, the brown dust came jetting up. She saw Chaffee far over, she saw the horse curling, and then she thought the man was gone. It was a trick of eyes burdened with those swift and continuous flashes of action; Chaffee was yet riding, matching rhythm with rhythm, still touching neck and flank with his spurs. Lovey-Dovey's four hoofs were off the ground and Chaffee was on a lonely seat above the wings of the dust. Gay caught that picture and never thereafter forgot it—Jim Chaffee with his long arm above him, black hair gleaming, rein arm crooked rigidly, and his lean face looking down between the ears of Lovey-Dovey with the expression of a man whose whole will was thrown out to battle.

"Why don't they fire the gun!"

She thought somebody else said that. But she said it; nor did she know that she was on her feet, leaning far over the rail. The gun broke the spell. Pickup men streamed in and lifted Lovey-Dovey's head. Jim Chaffee slid neatly out of his perch and across a pickup mans' horse to the ground. Gay watched him stride over the dirt, legs far apart and body still weaving a little from the fight. But he was smiling. The sharp, almost severe lines of his face were gone, giving him a reckless and exuberant air. He passed through a side gate without turning his head, leaving Gay Thatcher a little less interested in the succeeding rides. Already another man was up. The talkative individual behind her offered somebody a bet.

"It'll be the same as last year. Perrine and Chaffee battling it out this afternoon for the money. Don't he put on a pretty show?"

Shortly before noon the girl slipped away

and went back to the hotel. As she turned in she happened to glance on down the street and saw Jim Chaffee staring up at a building wall. She wondered what drew his interest. There was nothing on the wall but a sign: "Roaring Horse Irrigation and Reclamation Corporation."

Directly after dinner Mack Moran ran into Jim Chaffee with a message. "Dad Satterlee wants to see you now at the Gusher. Where you been?"

"Investigatin' that new-fangled corporation," said Jim Chaffee, and let it ride at that. They walked down the street and found Dad Satterlee on the hotel steps, surrounded by the other two judges and lesser town dignitaries. Satterlee broke away from the conversation to survey Chaffee with a certain truculence. "You're ridin' Mixup and Fireball this afternoon."

"I'm obliged for the news," drawled Chaffee.

"Mebbee you won't be later," grunted Satterlee. "We are givin' you these horses to spike any gossip about favoritism." He grew redder and homelier. "I hear you lost your ranch."

"Nothin' spreads like bad news."

"Yuh darn, skittle-minded fool!" bellowed Satterlee. "What did I tell you away back in the beginnin' about help? Ain't I yore next-door neighbor?"

"Charity is a noble thing," replied Jim Chaffee.

"Who said anything about charity?" roared Satterlee "There's some more of yore doggone pride. You always was a stiff-brimmed idiot. I take this affair as plumb unfriendly on your part, Jim. What's a neighbor for? Roaring Horse has got to a hell of a pass when it abides by the rules of seven per cent mortgages. I'm goin' down to the bank and settle that myself."

"No. Too late, Somebody's already assumed it."

"Who?"

"Craib wasn't in a position to reveal the said person," said Jim.

Satterlee revolved the information angrily around his mind. Once his eyes roamed down the street toward the sign of the Irrigation and Reclamation Corporation; then he directed his glance at William Wells Woolfridge. The latter was listening to all this and offering no comment. He met Satterlee's unspoken question with the same bland and neutral countenance. The owner of the Stirrup S moved his shoulders as if irked by an unseen pressure. "This used to be a white man's land. Looks like it's changin'. Well, Jim, you're comin' back to my outfit as peeler again. Don't consider that charity, do you?"

"I'd reckon not," answered Chaffee, smiling. "That's hard work."

Chaffee turned away with Mack Moran. They traveled leisurely and silently back toward the arena and settled down against a pile of baled hay adjoining the corrals. Cigarette smoke curled into the bright crisp air. Mack Moran was not wholly pleased.

"Mixup and Fireball. Two loads of grief. Why don't they give Theodorik Perrine one o' those monsters? Looks 'sif you got to ride all the outlaws to make a place. Mixup is bad enough, but this Fireball brute is unhealthy distinct. I'd ruther steal a hundred dollars than fork him to win."

"Who do you figger is behind this irrigation corporation doo-ratchet?" asked Chaffee, idly scanning the azure sky. Mack only grunted.

"It's peculiar," went on Chaffee. "I walked in to have a look. They's a fellow in charge. But he ain't the main push. Why? He wears a white collar, but they's a hole in it. I got a look at his shoes, and they're run down at the heels. He ain't no capitalist. He's a dummy. I've got a feelin'."

"What kind?"

Chaffee drew a long breath of smoke, his eyes narrowing. "Something's goin' to happen around here pretty soon. There's that corporation. A mystery. Why should anybody want to go about buyin' land so doggone devious? Same applies to whoever bought my little piece. Now there's this half dude Woolfridge. Tryin' to buy Satterlee out of the country."

"Shucks, I didn't know that!" interposed Mack Moran in surprise.

"I just discovered it. But that ain't but half the kernel in the peanut. Notice the sky limit on the poker last night? That lily-fingered fellow kept boostin' Satterlee till the cowbells rang. Took considerable money away from the old gent at that. Maybe will take some more to-night. Satterlee's hard to beat, too, in a level game. Mack, that lily-finger dude is bent in several places."

"Uh?"

"Crooked. I'm goin' to watch a little closer to-night. And here's Theodorik Perrine in town, howlin' like a dyin' wolf. He's come to fight me, as usual. But what's his gang doin' here with him? This town never did tolerate the presence of Sleepy Slade before. He's outlawed. But here he is, big as life. And the sheriff ain't doin' anythin' about it. Any time before this Sleepy and most of the rest of Theodorik's crude assassins would be in the clink, writin' poetry on the walls. Consider that in your wheat papers." He leaned forward, growling tremendously earnest. "Mack, things are linin' up around here. Unbeknownst to us. And there'll be one roarin' time when the lid's pulled off. I'm feelin' it in my bones. I *know* it."

"I wouldn't mind a little excitement," said Mack Moran, and his white teeth flashed.

"You'll get it," was Chaffee's grim answer. "Time to ease into the field." He rose and walked around the corrals, casting one sharp glance at a solid buckskin horse crowded against the bars. "I got a lot of respect for you, Mister Fireball."

The stands were filled, the buckers coming out. This afternoon the riders were fewer, for the morning's bucking had eliminated the unskilled. Within the hour the second rides would be over and the choice narrowed down to the three best men. And in the third rides would emerge that individual who had proved himself entitled to first place. Roaring Horse ran its rodeo somewhat differently than other cattle towns. There was no stagecoach marathon, no fancy display of lariat work. One free for all pony race opened the day, and a short bit of steer roping filled in an interval; the rest was bucking.

Dust rolled afresh along the ground and the roar of the crowd beat across to where Jim Chaffee stood. A man was down, the lists narrowed by one. A great yell sailed high up and far out and the announcer's voice struggled against the washing currents of sound. "Perrine at the left end—up on Vesuvius. Watch out!" Chaffee didn't watch Theodorik Perrine; it was his habit never to watch another man on these afternoon rounds. But he knew from the crowd's reaction that Perrine had done well. Perrine always did well. He moved out to the center, hearing his own name. And as he went through the routine of inspecting cinches and hackamore, and of rubbing his hands dry of the sweat that always cropped out on his palms the moment before swinging up, he threw a short look toward the grandstand. The girl wasn't in her seat. After that and for some fifteen seconds he forgot her, as well as all other things not connected with Mixup. He rode and dropped off, shaking his head to clear away the fog. The announcer kept on with the interminable droning, from rider to rider as the afternoon crept forward and the shadows began to cut patterns along the arena's side. Jim leaned against the fence, nerves slowly tightening. It always happened thus before the final ride; a man fought the worst part of the battle before he touched the stirrups. Hell was due to pop some of these days in Roaring Horse. Things were lining up secretly, somehow throwing a premonitory shadow across the face of the land. And Fireball was a tough horse. There must be no cocksureness, never an instant's relaxing; Fireball never gave a rider a chance once that rider was so much as a hair's breadth off balance. The brute had uncanny perceptions. Jim heard the announcer.

"Jim Chaffee at the right on Fireball. Ladees and gents, watch and pray!"

CHAPTER FOUR

THE STORM BREAKS

Chaffee turned and walked to the far side of the arena; and, though he glanced toward the grandstand to find the girl, his vision became clouded and the crowd was to him but a vast blur of faces. Something was happening inside of him; all his vital forces were mustering at one point, shutting off unnecessary drains of energy. But he did see Theodorik Perrine crouched by a track post, black face turned toward this scene; and from that he knew the man had made the third ride. This was the last duel, the deciding fight, the end of a long day. Fireball was in front of him, stepping around the anchor horse. The brute's long jaw hauled against the rope and his muscles rippled uneasily across his haunches; when Jim Chaffee's hand touched him he stopped moving on the instant and froze, all four feet spread into the soft earth and ready to make that first terrific lurch and lunge that was a part of his history.

The rodeo hand muttered: "Rig suit yuh, Jim?" and Chaffee nodded. The pickup men were drawn in, watching wary eyed. Chaffee ran a hand under the cinch, studied the stirrups and hackamore. The bright sun slanted across Fireball's magnificent withers. Jim rubbed his hands along his shirt front, swept by a cold current. He stepped softly into the saddle and let his weight come easily down; he took the reins, running his hands along them time after time from a purely nervous reflex, and he kicked his heels lightly against the stirrups until he felt them take a sure and certain seat; nor did he ever know, as he raised his free arm in signal and lifted his chest, how cold and tight an expression he carried on his lean face. But Gay Thatcher, returned to the grandstand railing, saw it and marveled. "All right," muttered Jim. Rope and blindfold were whipped away; the anchor horse vanished. Fireball's ears swooped toward the ground, and Jim Chaffee rose high to the bright sky.

The crowd marked each move of Fireball's frenzied battle, but Jim Chaffee didn't consciously follow the movements of the bucker. With him everything was instinct, everything was feeling. Through the years Jim Chaffee had trained himself for a duel like this, hardening himself to the punishment, disciplining his nerves and senses to work along a set pattern without deliberate bidding. There was little time to think; thinking was too slow. All that he had learned was called in now to be unconsciously applied. His sense of rhythm and balance had to serve him while his mind grew black with the riot of blood; a hundred previous lessons had to prompt his muscles to do the proper thing. Shock after shock ran along his body; his neck was being pounded by great sledges. He tasted his own blood; he felt his vitals strain at their moorings as Fireball sought to tear him apart and leave him on the ground, rolling in agony; and two dim flashes of knowledge found a path into the congested cells of his brain—he was raking the brute as per regulations—it wasn't good for a man to take very much of this kind of punishment. His stomach was afire. There was a point beyond which he couldn't go. No horse had ever hurt him like this one. Then, after what seemed an age, he heard the gun; wind rushed full into his face and his thighs were being crowded by pickup men. Fireball's head was up, the horse was running away. Somebody shouted, "Crawl off, Jim! Yuh've had aplenty!" He vaulted over the back of that man's horse and struck the ground with both feet. And he stood quite still until the curtain of black rose from his face and the fine fresh daylight came into his eyes.

His hat was on the ground twenty feet away. He went over and got it. Perrine still crouched by the post, the judges were riding abreast toward the grandstand railing, conferring together; once more all things were distinct, and Jim Chaffee saw Gay Thatcher sitting in her place. She had seen that ride. He grinned and built himself a cigarette. The sun went westering, and it was a wonderful world to be in, to feel the clear air in his lungs and to see the carved beauty of the late shadows creeping around the arena. The crowd had ceased its murmuring; the judges were ranked together by the stands.

"Chaffee — Perrine — McIver — front an' center."

The three contestants marched toward the mounted judges. Dad Satterlee looked somberly at them and let the moments build up a suspense. Finally he ducked his chin toward Jim Chaffee. "It's yours. Perrine second money. McIver third honors."

Chaffee looked beyond the judges and directly at Gay Thatcher. No more than six yards separated them; across this narrow interval these two people, absolute strangers to each other, exchanged glances. Not casual glances, but the deep and intent measuring of worth. The girl had seen him three or four times in the last twenty-four hours, yet at none of those times had he appeared as he was now. The marks of the recent punishment still cramped his face, and his eyes were a profound, inky blue. She had known other men whose eyes changed color like that in stress of anger or trouble.

Chaffee nodded to the judges. "Thanks."

Theodorik Perrine wrenched his overwhelming bulk around so that he half faced the judges and half confronted Chaffee. Wrath blazed from his features and worked his great jowls. "Thanks be damned! This rodeo was framed! The result was signed an' sealed afore Chaffee stepped on a horse! King Solomon couldn't win a ride in Roarin' Horse if Chaffee was buckin' against him! I'm gettin' tired o' this favorite son business! You dudes are blind in one eye and don't see well from the other!"

"I will observe," replied Satterlee with an extraordinary and frigid politeness, "though it ain't incumbent on me to do so, that the decision was unanimous. The charge of favoritism is the squawk of a tinhorn sport. The judges decided to spike it aforehand and gave Chaffee the worst horses to ride."

"Yeah?" roared Perrine. "Well, why didn't yuh give me one o' them horses, so's I could make a showin'? All I get is a bunch o' distempered brood mares!" He raised a fist at Satterlee, dividing the threat of it equally between that rancher and French Melotte. Jim Chaffee, abiding by the range etiquette which told him to mind his own business, observed that Theodorik Perrine entirely disregarded William Wells Woolfridge. And he filed that fact away in his mind. "Yuh have been runnin' this country too long. It stinks!"

"You lie," said Satterlee. "Open yore mouth again in front of me and you'll never ride in another rodeo hereabouts."

Perrine stepped back a pace, his rage condensing to a far more dangerous stage. "Let me tell you somethin', Satterlee. Yore days o' rule are about done. They's a time comin' when yuh won't have no high horse to perch on. And when that time comes I'll settle my grudges, along with a lot of others. Remember it."

"Get off the field."

"You'll eat that remark soon enough," said Theodorik Perrine with a swift snapping of his heavy lips. He threw a hard glance at Jim Chaffee. "Yore days of glory are about done, likewise. I'm sayin' it."

"Any time," drawled Chaffee.

Theodorik strode across the dirt, knocking a field hand out of his path with a swoop of his arm. Chaffee turned toward the gate. Gay Thatcher watched him go, holding her seat while the rest of the crowd milled around her.

"He walks straight," she murmured to herself. No, there isn't an ounce of display or false spirit about him. But he walks as if he was the equal of any man on earth. All unconsciously. And he is. I wonder if he will try to meet me again?"

William Wells Woolfridge dismounted and gave his horse to a puncher; he climbed over the railing and bowed to the girl. "It was a good show, wasn't it?"

"Splendid."

He took her arm and let her through the crowd. "Now, I can't think of you leaving so soon. This is a beautiful country. You must stay over and let me show it to you. The doors of my ranch house are wide open. Really, I insist on it."

She threw a small, shrewd smile at him from beneath the brim of her hat. "If you are so insistent, perhaps I will."

The Gusher blazed with lights and the dining room had been cleared for the ball. Jim Chaffee and Mack Moran stood on the porch and listened to the music. Mack was content to be where he was and no closer to what seemed to him quite a glittering and imposing affair. But Jim Chaffee saw Gay Thatcher through the door, waltzing with Woolfridge, and he was restless. Mack Moran mistook the reason for the restlessness and became somewhat scathing.

"That hundred dollars burnin' holes in yore pocket already?"

"Mack, I'd like to go in there."

"Huh. Jim, was you borned thataway or did it sorter grow gradual? You and me belong down on the dark side o' the street. Let's go there and get some hiccup syrup."

"No, I—"

"What's this—Perrine on the prod—watch out!"

Perrine it was, coming down the street on horse with ten men riding abreast and behind him. Guns roared into the night, the sidewalks emptied of traffic immediately. Punchers broke by the partners, ducking into the hotel. Glass shattered as the cavalcade swept past, each of the band weaving recklessly in the saddle and firing at random. They stopped at the street's end, gear rattling; they came thundering back. The dust rolled up as a heavy fog, and Theodorik's harsh command rang like a trumpet when he hauled around and confronted Moran and Chaffee. He had been drinking, his eyes were shining like those of some creeping night animal, and his breath rose and fell in great gusts.

"I'm a wolf, Chaffee! I'm a howling, crazy wolf! Who runs this town? I do when I'm of a mind to! Yore time's comin'! So's Satterlee's! I'm about at the end o' my rope! The man that tries to lay hand on me to-night dies!"

"I reckon the marshal and the sheriff are within hearin' distance," drawled Chaffee. "I guess they ain't interested—to-night."

"You interested?"

"It ain't my town, Perrine. Don't own a nickel of it."

"I got a notion to ride through that dance hall and scatter them dudes to hell an' gone."

"I guess not," murmured Chaffee.

"What's that?"

"I said I guess maybe you wouldn't care to," repeated Chaffee, spacing his words more deliberately.

Perrine shifted his weight and stared down upon his ancient enemy. The man was struggling with his impulses, so much was visible.

The angry light simmered and was shut off by that slate curtain. "Yeah, mebbe," he decided morosely. "Play yore game heavy while yuh can, Chaffee. It ain't lastin' much longer." He pulled his horse around and went galloping away. And presently the town heard his wild, nerve-racking yell emerge from the Red Mill saloon at the western end of the street.

"He's loco," grunted Mack.

"He's twistin' his tail to make himself mad," replied Chaffee. "I know Theodorik. Pretty soon he'll pull off somethin'. I'd be pleased to know what. Mack, I'm goin' inside."

He walked through the door and across to the arch of the ballroom. The music, which had ceased at the height of Theodorik Perrine's raid was about to start again. Right inside the arch he saw Gay Thatcher seated, with Dad Satterlee and William Wells Woolfridge standing before her. Satterlee discovered Chaffee and ducked his head; Chaffee grave and casual, yet with a spark of excitement glimmering in his eyes, closed up.

"What did that renegade say?" rumbled Dad.

"The usual compliments."

"What's he up to, Jim?"

All three were looking at him; Gay Thatcher's hands were folded sedately in her lap, and there was the faint hint of a smile lurking in the corners of her mouth.

"Feedin' himself raw meat," drawled Jim Chaffee. "About ready to go on a rampage."

"Huh," grunted Dad, and changed the subject. "Suppose you're too prosperous now to work for me. Money burnin' your hands pretty bad?"

"Be at the Stirrup S in the morning." He looked from Satterlee to Woolfridge. Neither of them seemed to catch what was in his mind. The music started, and a third gentleman, some visitor from down country, come over to claim his dance with Gay Thatcher. She rose, and with a fragment of a glance at Jim Chaffee whirled away.

"I will be—" muttered Chaffee. "Ain't you boys schooled in introductions none?" He turned his back to the crowd and contemplated several things. Woolfridge went farther down the hall; Dad Satterlee crossed to the Gold Room for a session of poker. After a few minutes Jim Chaffee decided to follow and sit in. On the verge of leaving, a light voice struck a chill right up the middle of his back.

"Are you getting discouraged?"

Gay Thatcher was beside him, her partner lingering a few yards distant. Jim took off his hat, and a slow smile spread around his eyes. "I have known folks to introduce themselves."

"It might save time," said the girl. "Your name is Jim Chaffee. I believe I've heard it before. My name is Gay Thatcher."

"Yes ma'am. I know it."

"Well, we're introduced. I liked your ride."

"I'm obliged. I wish I could ask the favor of a dance."

"People," said she irrelevantly, "have said you were a man of courage."

"You don't know what sort of a dancer I am," he replied. "I'd better leave good enough alone."

"This is none of my business, Mr. Chaffee, but I overheard your friends say that you had some trouble with your ranch. I wanted to tell you that I'm sorry. Really."

"I kind of hated to lose that place. It's right by a creek and there's cottonwoods around it. I built a log house right where I could see the peaks. Sort of hate to lose it. A man gets his heart set on something. "But"—and he raised his arms Indian fashion—"I've always been able to earn wages."

"You're not going to try it again?" she asked, almost severe.

"Next spring, higher on the bench." He switched the subject. "Ma'am, is it just a visit you're makin'?"

"Oh, yes. I am going back."

He looked down, marking the beauty of her

dark hair and the rose color of her cheeks. He had never seen a woman with so clear and expressive a face; nor one so intelligent. "I'm sorry," said he. "My luck runs bad in bunches."

She saw that her partner was moving restlessly, so she started away. A rare smile came to her eyes. "I am going back. But I've decided not to go right back; I'll be in town for a week. Or else on Mr. Woolfridge's ranch."

"Well," he began, and didn't know just exactly how to finish.

"Well," she said, mimicking the sound. Then she was down the hall, dress flashing in the mellow light. At the turn she looked back and smiled again, a brilliant figure in the crowd. Jim Chaffee went toward the Gold Room, dissatisfied. "I didn't say at all what I wanted to say. What's the matter with me?"

Dad Satterlee was deep in a game and at the moment hoisting a bet made by the glum and pallid gambler who had the previous night played so heavily. The strain seemed to be bothering his nerves, for his long, slender fingers drummed the table. But Dad Satterlee was as stolid as a rock, his red and homely face puckered over the cards. He called and lost the bet to the gambler; and relaxed, appearing amused. Woolfridge shouldered through the crowd and bent over Satterlee, whispering.

"No—no, I told you I ain't going to be bothered any more with that nonsense. I ain't got a price to set. Never did have one, never will. Cut it out, son."

Woolfridge reared back and went rapidly from the room. Jim Chaffee turned to watch Woolfridge; at that instant there was a smashing report at the table. He jerked about and saw Dad Satterlee's whole countenance suffused with anger, his big fist covering the cards. He pawed through them, lifted one and another to the light and set his eyes close against the backs. The pallid gambler was half out of his chair. Satterlee took the whole deck and threw it full in the man's face. And he knocked everything aside in the bull-like uprisal.

"I thought you was crooked! The last five decks you produced are all marked the same! Yore a damn tinhorn gambler, mister!"

"I resent that!" cried the pallid one.

"Resent?" roared Satterlee. "Listen! This is a white man's country! Gentlemen play poker hereabouts, not card sharps! Get out of this place, get out of my sight! I've been watchin' yore style plenty long and I've plumb paid for the privilege o' exposin' you! You be out of this country by to-morrow mornin' or I'll personally see you run out!"

"I resent that!" repeated the man. "I will

not allow any man—"

"Get out!"

The gambler looked about him and found no comfort. The crowd, without inspecting the cards, instantly took Satterlee's words; for Satterlee was a blunt and certain man. So the gambler, as white as death and quite shaken, disappeared into the bar. Satterlee growled like an angry bear. "Who invited that sharp to play in this hotel?" Then he saw Jim Chaffee. "I'm goin' home, Jim. You ready to ride?"

"Yeah."

"Meet you here in ten minutes," muttered Satterlee. He cruised through the lobby and to the street. Jim idly followed. What had happened to the gambler? On the porch of the hotel he pondered a moment, shaking his head. Suddenly he sprang to life, running toward the stable where Satterlee had gone for his horse.

"I'm a blamed idiot for leavin' him—"

A shot roared out of the stable's mouth; a shot and a solitary cry. Jim Chaffee raced onward. Men poured into the stable before him. A lantern bobbed through the air. And before he got to the place he heard a single, gruff sentence. It hit him like the impact of a bullet and left him with a sensation of physical sickness.

"Satterlee. He's dead."

CHAPTER FIVE

JIM GETS A JOB

Jim Chaffee's thoughts shot far ahead of the catastrophe; out of the recesses of his mind came pouring all those stray side lights, all those significant gestures and stray words and puzzling circumstances that had caught his attention during the last twenty-four hours in town. Mack Moran raced by him, bound for the stable, gun half raised and crying: "Come on, Jim, we got to get the—" The rest of that sentence was passionately lurid. Yet Jim Chaffee remained rooted. Mystery and vengeance beat heavily along the dark reaches of the stable. Maybe the gambler Clyde had killed Satterlee in the heat of a quarrel but a few moments gone. Maybe, but there were others in Roaring Horse to be accounted for as well. Accounted for now, instantly. He doubled back to the hotel, shouldering roughly through a gathering crowd. He ran across the porch and into the Gold Room. Nobody there; but when he reached the doorway leading to the hotel bar he found the gambler downing a stiff glass of whisky. The man's face was as pale as ivory, and his eyes were wide and brilliant against the light. He shoved the empty glass across the bar, knuckles white with pressure. He was fighting his nerves, Chaffee saw that. And when the gambler discovered Chaffee watching him he threw back his head like some cornered animal.

"Where you been?" challenged Chaffee.

"None of your damn' business!" snapped the gambler. "You're not putting me on any cross!"

"He came in here from the side door like a shot out of a gun," accused the barkeep, heavy and foreboding. "What happened?"

The gambler turned away and went rapidly up a set of stairs leading from the bar to the second story of the hotel. "You better get that dude now if yuh want him," warned the barkeep.

But Jim Chaffee was already leaving the place. "He'll be there when we want him. He can't get out of the hotel." Down the street he ran, aiming for the Red Mill saloon. Everybody seemed to be collecting in the stable; inside the Red Mill was but one man—the owner.

"Callahan, was Theodorik Perrine in here when that shot was fired?"

The owner shifted a cigar in his mouth and studied Chaffee with a surly regard. "Why should I be tellin' what my customers do?"

"I'm askin' you once more," snapped Chaffee. "Your reputation ain't any too sweet to buck this affair."

"I ain't beholden to you!" cried Callahan. "I ain't beholden to the Stirrup S outfit none whatsoever! You go plumb straight—"

Chaffee smiled bleakly. "I'll give you a last chance. Come across quick or I'll tear this contraption apart. I don't bluff, Callahan! Was Perrine in here when that shot was fired?"

"No," grumbled Callahan.

"Was he here five minutes before the shot was fired?"

"Yes, and I ain't answerin' no more of yore questions, see? I'm protectin' myself."

Jim Chaffee left, crossing to the town's other large saloon, Ruby's Pet. As elsewhere, the place was deserted save for the man behind the bar.

"War Perrine here when that shot went?" demanded Chaffee.

"No, he wasn't, Jim. A couple of his gang was, though. But they sifted out pritty damn' quick when they heard it. Who's dead?"

Chaffee told him, striding through the swinging doors. Where was Perrine? Earlier in the evening he had noted the big man's horse, along with those of the rest of that gang, huddled by the Red Mill hitching rack. All were gone now. If they had all left town it had been done hurriedly and quietly. Debating a moment on this he saw a part of the crowd at the stable break away and rush down upon the hotel. He understood the meaning of that and, not exactly sure of his part in this piece of retribution, followed. Every Stirrup S puncher, with a scattering of others, rushed into the place. Mack Moran was issuing orders. "Couple of you boys watch this main stairs. Couple more go back of the place and watch he don't depart thataway. Now—"

The barkeep called through the Gold Room. "He went up thisaway, gents."

The outfit swarmed into the bar and aimed for the stairs. Jim Chaffee reached Moran. "What are you cookin' up now, you blamed fool?"

"What you figger, Jim? He's goin' to swing! He ain't got a Chinaman's chance to get away with it! Don't yuh argue none with me—hell, he's red-handed—"

The foremost men of the Stirrup S outfit were preemptorily halted by a call from above.

"Stay there—don't climb another inch! You're not going to put me on the cross! First man that tries it is going to get killed! You hear that? I didn't shoot Satterlee! I swear I didn't! Don't come any farther!"

It was the gambler, out of sight on the upper landing, yet commanding them by his higher position.

"Cut this out, boys," urged Chaffee. "We ain't so sure he did it. There's others just as likely. He'll go to jail while we get some better dope."

"No, he don't go to no jail," contradicted Mack, so thoroughly enraged that not even the affection he felt for Chaffee would sway him. "Some o' you jaspers go around the front way. He ain't bluffin' me! I'm walking straight up this stair! Lemme through!"

"I'm warning you!" yelled the gambler, voice as shrill as the scrape of a file. "I won't be taken! Where's the sheriff—I want to talk to him."

"Stop this foolishness," said Chaffee. "We don't do no such lynching. We ain't sure."

The calm voice of William Wells Woolfridge came from behind. "Let me through this way, boys. I want to talk to Clyde."

They made a path for him reluctantly. Though the Stirrup S outfit detested Woolfridge for his Eastern airs, his position commanded a certain respect. Mack Moran was not above speaking plainly, however, "It won't do you no good. We're goin' to take him out and leave him cold."

"Let me talk to him," said Woolfridge, never varying the softness of his speech. At the foot of the stairs he called up. "Clyde."

"I won't be taken, Mr. Woolfridge," the gambler answered. The man had the sound of wild desperation about him. "I will not!"

"That's all right, Clyde," said Woolfridge soothingly. "I want to have a talk with you. I'm coming up."

"Come alone—nobody else!" warned the gambler.

"That's right, Clyde," reassured Woolfridge. And up the stairs he went, turned the corner, and was beyond the crowd's view. Mack Moran was utterly astonished. "I never give Woolfridge no credit for nerve like that, Jim. Say, he ain't half so bad as I figgered. But he ain't stoppin' us none."

The murmur of talk drifted down; the nervous, jerky tones of the gambler running into that softer speech of Woolfridge. Moran grew restless at the length of time, but Jim Chaffee shook his head, eyes narrowing. Maybe Woolfridge had cold nerve, and maybe it wasn't nerve so much as confidence in a man he secretly owned. Feet dug into the flooring above. The gambler's voice rose shrilly; a gun's report filled the upper recesses and rolled back. Mack Moran made a tremendous leap upward, hauling himself by the banister.

William Wells Woolfridge walked into view and stood with his gun swinging idle in one hand; he looked down, soft cheeks a little paler than usual and his chest rising to harder breathing.

"I'm sorry, boys. I've taken care of Clyde. I shall hold myself fully responsible to the sheriff. This man came here more or less at my suggestion. He went crooked and he killed my best friend. I want you to know I feel deeply about it. After all that has happened I couldn't do anything else. No man can violate my trust and get away with it. I always thought Clyde a gentleman. You'll find him lying in the hall."

He descended and passed through them. Abreast Jim Chaffee he raised his face and looked squarely into Jim's eyes. Chaffee, returning the glance, felt the full shock of a personality he had never seen before. Woolfridge went out; Stirrup S men moved to see the gambler's body. Chaffee pulled Moran into the street. "You red-headed fool, some day you'll be ashamed of this party."

"The man deserved to die. I shore have advanced my opinion of this rancher dude a heap."

"Yeah. So have I. Only not in the same way. Put this in your pipe—no more dangerous man ever walked the streets of Roaring Horse.

Now, if you've got some of your judgment back again, come along. We've got to have a look through that stable and around behind it."

William Wells Woolfridge walked the whole length of the street and toured the dark oval of the rodeo field, head dropped thoughtfully.

"I have violated the first law of my life. I never should have taken Clyde into my affairs; never should have revealed to him a single syllable of what I planned. What a man wishes well done he must do himself. I violated that rule. And I should have paid for it if I hadn't killed him. Woolfridge, don't do that again." But after a second rounding of the field he shook his head. "It is unfortunate. I will have to use other men in the future. Can't hope to get out of doing it. Craib is safe. I do not fear him. He is tied too closely with me. And Craib can never testify to a single move of mine that is not legitimate and above board. Perrine—he's a dangerous instrument. I will not use him except as a last resort. But if it comes to force he will serve—and go out of the picture." With that he started toward the hotel. "Jim Chaffee is a man I must be careful with. I may have to deal with him later. The issue is too big to let him interfere."

The stable doors were closed when Chaffee and Moran reached the place; shouldering through a side entrance they found Doc Fancher, the town marshal, and Sheriff Luis Locklear, conducting a post-mortem examination. They had put a blanket beneath old Dad Satterlee; a lantern revealed his bulldog cheeks, still somewhat florid. Moran swore bitterly. Jim Chaffee looked only once and turned aside. Sheriff Locklear stared at the pair.

"What are you two doin' in here? Don't yuh see we locked folks out? Go on—travel."

"Who are you?" grunted Chaffee. Locklear was new in the office, a stubborn, unfriendly man who enjoyed his authority; the acquisition of his star had turned his head, had made him both arbitrary and unreasonable. He never had been a friend of Chaffee's.

"You know who I am," snapped the sheriff.

"Don't bark at me, Luis," said Chaffee. "You ain't big enough around the chest. What are you piddlin' away time at this for, when all the evidence is outside?"

"I know my business. Don't try to tell me what I should do. You Stirrup S lunkheads don't own Roarin' Horse."

"Mebbe yuh think *you* do," interposed Mack Moran. "If yore so hot about the ears, why don't yuh get out there and take hold of the excitement?"

Chaffee turned to Doc Fancher. "Where

did the bullet hit him, Doc?"

"Don't tell him," commanded the sheriff. "He ain't got a right to know."

"Why hasn't he?" asked Doc Fancher mildly. "Right square in the cheek, Jim."

"Thanks." Chaffee strolled on deeper into the stable. Satterlee's calico pony was in a stall near the back end. The old man, entering the stable, had never advanced that far. If, as Fancher had said, the bullet had struck dead on, then the killer must have been stationed deep in the shadows, directly by the rear door. Satterlee had been framed in the light as he crossed the street and came to the stable. The killer had figured on that—and retreated through the corral behind the stable.

"Mack, you get another lantern out of the office."

"All right. But it ain't necessary none. We done got the gambler. The whole thing's finished."

"Maybe," was Chaffee's enigmatic answer. "Get a lantern, anyhow."

"Listen," called the sheriff, "don't go monkeyin' around. That's my business."

"When I want your advice, Luis, I'll ask for it," said Chaffee, profoundly irritated. "And that will sure be a long time from now." He thought for a moment that Locklear was going to come forward and challenge him. But the man scowled and kept his place by Doc Fancher. Mack came back with a lantern. Chaffee took it and stepped to the exit, swinging the light along the ground.

He was careful not to set foot out there. A watering trough's overflow made the whole area mucky and treacherous. The hoofs of many horses had churned it in spots to a black mud. Chaffee played the light from one side of the area to the other and presently called quite softly to Mack. "See those boot prints— creepin' along the buildin' wall? Fellow tryin' to keep out of the mud. Toes pointed this way."

"Shore, gambler fella prob'ly made 'em."

"Said person wouldn't be so careful in makin' his departure after the shot was fired," mused Chaffee. The lantern went questing again and swooped toward the deepest mud of the area. "Yeah. He went sloggin' through this to make his get-away. See?"

"It don't sound unreasonable," agreed Mack. "But what difference does it make? The gent is defunct, ain't he?"

"Do me another favor, Mack. Go down to the storeroom and get a couple of handfuls of tar. Go heat it somewhere so it'll run free and come on the gallop."

"What in the name of—"

"I'm askin' a favor."

"Well." Mack departed. Fancher and the sheriff finished their examination and went out, leaving the marshal alone with the body. A group of Stirrup S punchers threw open the big doors and went about hitching up a rig. When Mack got back with a bucket of hot tar he found Chaffee smoking a very thoughtful cigarette.

"The soft ground is full of tracks, Mack. Two-three different sets. Give me that bucket. You hold the lantern and follow close." He walked gingerly through the loose dirt and bent down before one particularly clear imprint. The tar spilled into it. Mack grumbled a question, but Chaffee emptied the bucket in two other such imprints before replying. "I'm fillin' tar into 'em. When it hardens we'll have the size of somebody's boots."

Another Stirrup S man came forward, "Listen, Jim, we're all set to take Dad back home. He's in the rig. But you better come along and break the news to Miz Satterlee. It ain't a job any of us is wishful to do."

Chaffee rolled a cigarette before replying. "She's always been good to me. Here I am bringin' back a story like this. All right, Tobe." He turned to Mack. "You've got to stay here and pick up those tar models when they get hard. And be blamed sure nobody else gets 'em."

"I'd ruther do that than face Miz Satterlee," said Mack. "But what do you figger a bunch of frozen boot prints is a-goin' to do you? We got the jasper. That's enough."

Chaffee shook his head, subduing his words. "Mack, I'm layin' all my money the gambler didn't kill Dad. Where was Theodorik Perrine all this time? Where is he now? And wouldn't it sort of mean something to you if you happened to see a man walkin' down the street with mud on his heels?"

"Plenty of mud around town besides here," objected Mack.

"Maybe so, but a careful man wouldn't be walkin' in it unless he was powerfully excited. The name of the gentleman who had said mud on his heels right after the shot was fired is—"

The rig moved out of the stable, and one of the Stirrup S crew called back: "Come on, Jim." The sheriff, Luis Locklear, walked rapidly toward the pair.

"I'll hunt through this stable," said he, "just as a matter of formality. No doubt but what Clyde killed Satterlee. Mr. Woolfridge did a fine job."

Jim Chaffee turned and got his horse, following the rig sadly back to Stirrup S. This tragedy had been so sudden, and his own search for the murderer's identification had been so engrossing, that not until now did the full sorrow of the thing fall upon him. Nowhere in the length and breadth of this country had there been a more sturdy and uprightly honest man than Dad Satterlee. His life was woven into Roaring Horse. At a dance or at a round-up—at any of those occasions where the folks of the section met—Dad Satterlee's presence had always been a certain and cheering fact. And for every dollar that Dad had in the bank, another dollar had gone into some kind of charitable help. What was he, Jim Chaffee, to tell Miz Satterlee?

When at last the solemn and silent party drew into the yard Jim Chaffee sat in the saddle and struggled with himself. A light shimmered through the house window, and while he debated the door was thrown open, Miz Satterlee standing on the threshold and peering across the shadowed porch. "All back, boys?" she asked. "Didn't Mr. Satterlee come with you?" In a moment she seemed to sense the troubled spirit of the party and her eyes made out the dim bulk of the rig. "What is it, boys?" The calm, self-contained tones shamed Jim Chaffee. He got down and came to the steps. He had figured to break the news easily, to start from afar. Now he knew there was only one thing to say.

"Ma'am—Dad is—dead."

He was to remember that choked sentence the rest of his life, and feel at each remembrance the same pinching at his heart. That night he was sending a woman down into the black pit of despair. Nor did he ever forget the manner in which she received the news. He couldn't see her resolute, motherly face in the black vault of the porch, and for that he was thankful. But he heard the rising and the settling of her breath; and then breathing seemed to cease. She seemed to grow away from them; the outline of her body became blurred in the shadows, and the long moments went by with never another sound. Every man in the party was as if cut from so much stone, and in this strange, profound lull Jim Chaffee heard the faint drip-drip of water in a remote part of the house, like a fatal pendulum accenting the swift passage of all things living. It grew unbearable; he stepped toward her to speak again.

"Bring Mr. Satterlee in the house," said she, very quietly.

The crew obeyed and passed out. The door closed; the light of the room after a short interval was snuffed. The rest of the Stirrup S men went to the bunkhouse, but Chaffee, somehow feeling his place to be on the porch, sat in the shadows and waited.

He didn't know how long it was before that

door opened. It seemed to him a matter of hours, in which he heard her rocking-chair slowly traveling back and forth, never varying the tempo, never slacking until at the end of the long vigil she called to him.

"Jim. You are a good boy. Tell me about it."

He stood on the threshold, facing the darkness of the room, and told all that he knew of the story, even to the boot prints he had filled with tar.

"You don't think Clyde—had anything to do with it, then?"

"No ma'am."

"Poor *soul*. I am sorry for him. Do you think you will find the right man, Jim?"

"I will."

"What will you do with him?"

"He'll go down," muttered Jim Chaffee.

"No," said Miz Satterlee. "We don't live according to tablets of stone, Jim. When you find the man put him in jail. Let others decide. And Jim—"

"Yes, ma'am?"

"Send the boys out to-night to notify Mr. Satterlee's friends. I want them to see him go to sleep up there where the rest of my family sleeps. Don't you go. I want you on the ranch. That's all. Don't stay up. This is—my affair."

So, in the middle of the following afternoon, surrounded by his friends, Dad Satterlee was laid beside his three children; and presently the Stirrup S was alone to itself again, save for one man who tarried. That man was William Wells Woolfridge. Jim Chaffee watched him go to the house porch and bow to Miz Satterlee. A few minutes later the mistress of Stirrup S beckoned and Jim crossed the yard, receiving an abrupt nod from Woolfridge.

Miz Satterlee was in her black silk dress; she carried herself erect, her dark eyes lifted proudly toward his visitor. "I am making it a policy, Mr. Woolfridge, to discuss all my business affairs in front of Jim Chaffee from now on. He will be interested. Go ahead."

"I mention this to-day only because I wish to bring before you without delay a matter that has long been discussed by myself and your husband," said Woolfridge, paying no attention to Jim. "Frankly, as I told him, I wanted the Stirrup S. Vanity, perhaps, but I should like to be able to say that my brand runs from the bench to the alkali wastes. I am quite able to pay for my foibles."

"What was Mr. Satterlee's reply to that?"

Woolfridge gave Chaffee a rather long and close survey. "He said it was entirely a matter of price."

"What price?" asked Miz Satterlee, never

letting her attention stray from Woolfridge's smooth cheeks.

"As a matter of fact, I had not yet gotten a price from him," admitted the man.

"I didn't think so. I have heard him speak about it."

"There is no reason why you should wish to run the place now, Mrs. Satterlee."

"There is every reason why I should. And I do not care to ever hear of an offer from you again. As long as I live this ranch is mine. When I die I shall will it to friendly hands. I want it to go on. That is absolutely final."

"You are quite sure?" asked Woolfridge, urbane and mild.

"I am. Never think you can change me."

"In that case I'll not bother you again today. I think, perhaps, it is unnecessary to remind you, Mrs. Satterlee, that I regarded your husband as my best friend. If there is ever anything you want of me please ask. And if at any time you change your mind I wish you'd let me know."

"Thanks, but I won't."

Woolfridge got on his horse and rode down the trail. Jim Chaffee turned a puzzled face to Miz Satterlee. "What did you want me for, ma'am?"

"Like I said. To keep your fingers on the

business. I am making you manager of Stirrup S to-day, Jim. I'm too old to fight. And, if I know anything about affairs, there is going to be trouble here. Act from now on as if the place belonged to you. I give you absolute charge."

CHAPTER SIX

FENCES DOWN

Midmorning of the day after Dad Satterlee's funeral Chaffee went to town. His purpose was to see Doc Fancher and ask a few questions concerning the dead gambler; also to find Mack Moran who had never returned to the ranch. Once in Roaring Horse he went directly to the Red Mill. Mack wasn't there, nor did Chaffee find him at any of the other saloons; however, the red-headed puncher had left a broad trail of ruin behind him. According to several citizens, Mack had gone moody—not an unusual thing for him when he started to think about the injustices of the world—and had indulged in several free and sanguinary battles. With this much information Chaffee wasted no more time hunting. He went to the jail; there was Mack down in the basement cell, smoking glumly.

Mack's rosy face was a little scarred; but there was relief in his eyes. "Wondered how long I'd cool here before yuh got worried. Lemme out of this stink hole."

"They's twenty dollars assessed agin him," stated the marshal. "If his carcass is worth that much to yuh on the hoof, Jim, he's yores."

"That's cheap," agreed Chaffee. "Let the catamount loose,"

"He'd ought to be put under a perpetual bond," said the marshal, jingling his keys. "When he gits sore he's a natcheral borned assassin. Mebbe yuh think he didn't plumb devastate Roarin' Horse fer about three hours. Took six of us to lug him down here. It happens once every four months, regular as a clock." He let Mack out of the cell and accepted twenty dollars from Jim. Out of his mellowed and easy-going comprehension of the range and its ways, he spoke a mild warning. "I don't mind, personal. Boys have got to blow off. But be careful from now on. Things is changin' around here. I ain't goin' to enlarge on the statement. But let it hatch in yore coco. Things is changin'."

"I will shore testify to that," grunted Mack. He shook hands with the marshal. "No hard feelin's, Will. I'll see you get a new shirt for the one I tore." The partners went out and ate a bite. Afterward they rolled along the street, smoking. "It gets me how a place can change," said Mack. "A month ago any Stirrup S man was high card around here. Our credit was good and we never got slung into the calaboose except to sober up. Now look. The talk about us boys is terrible scandalous. That's why I got started. Run into three separate gents that made tough passes about what an outfit we was."

"What was their complaint in particular?" asked Chaffee.

"I never found out," replied Mack, very casually. "They didn't wake up in time to tell me. You figger I'm goin' to stand around and fiddle my finger while they get wise? It's the same all over town. Funny how quick it's changed. Somebody's behind it. Somebody's put a bug in certain ears. And that Luis Locklear person ain't no help to Stirrup S, either. I saw him chinnin' with Callahan in the Red Mill other night. You'd 'a' thought they was twins. When a sheriff of Roarin' Horse get neighborly with Callahan it shore means somethin' poisonous."

"Where's those tar models?"

"I left 'em bundled up in the stable."

They went into the stable and away down an alley between bales of hay. Mack dug around, retrieved a gunny sack, and handed it to Jim. They went out and crossed the street to Doc Fancher's office, which was over Tilton's drygoods store. "Seen Theodorik Perrine since night before last?" asked Chaffee.

"Nope. He's skinned out." Something struck Mack suddenly. "But here's a funny thing. Last night I was in the jug. That cell's got a window flush with the back side of the buildin', you know. And I heard Luis Locklear talkin' to a gent out there among the busted wagon frames and loose balin' wire. Mebbe it's all my imagination, but it shore sounded like he was meetin' up on the quiet with Perrine. What do you figger?"

"Maybe. Listen, Mack, I'm going to be around here for an hour or better and it's a long ride home. Anyhow, Miz Satterlee wants somebody to lope over to Nickerson's. Seems like Nickerson has got some old tintypes of Dad Satterlee which he is goin' to give her. You better bust thataway. Be dark when you're home."

"All right. Now don't *you* go get in the calaboose."

They separated. Jim Chaffee climbed the stairs and let himself into a door labeled: "H. T. Fancher, M.D., County Coroner and Bone Specialist." The term "bone specialist" was not the exact technical term for that branch of medicine, but Doc Fancher was a most untechnical man. He knew his public. At present he had his feet on his desk, reading a copy of the *Breeder's Gazette;* he seemed genuinely pleased to see Chaffee.

"Doc," said Chaffee, "I'm not coming to see you in your capacity of public official. I want to chin with you, friend to friend. All this is private. What do you know about this Clyde fellow?"

"I know he was lyin' dead on the second story landing of the hotel when I found him," said Fancher. "Funny thing about that. He had two guns, a .38 and a .44. He was holdin' to the .38 as tight as a vise with his right hand. The .44 was lyin' loose, near his head. Don't often see a man packin' two different styles of weapons. No shots fired from the .38, but there was one empty cartridge in the .44. I may add, Jim, that Satterlee was killed by a .44 slug."

"What do you think about it, Doc?"

Fancher raised his shoulders. "Officially, nothing at all. As a private individual a whole lot. Let it ride like that, Jim."

Chaffee reached into his sack and took out his tar models, ranging them on the table. There were four all told, and Fancher lowered his boots to look at them with a professional eye. "I poured hot tar into a lot of tracks out beyond the livery stable the night of the shootin'," explained Chaffee. "These models are a little rough on the bottom and edges, but they'll give a pretty good idea of somebody's boots."

"Jim, you work fast," observed Fancher. "Wait a minute." He went back to a closet and drew therefrom a pair of high leather shoes. "I took all of Clyde's personal effects out of his room. Locklear didn't want to bother with that business, but I figured it might come useful. Here's some of the man's shoes. Same size and style as the ones he had on. Now let's look."

Three of the models were obviously too large; but the fourth, laid against the shoe's bottom was an approximate fit. "Looks like it might be it all right," observed Fancher.

"That's interestin'," mused Chaffee, a light sparkling in his eyes. "For those tracks were away off at one corner of the corral. Nowheres near the back door. Now, it wasn't possible for a man to shoot Satterlee unless said man stood inside the place. It was dark; Satterlee was framed in the front opening—an easy target for anybody within thirty feet. The fellow with shoes corresponding to this model never got within two hundred feet of Satterlee. Couldn't hit the old chap with a .44 at that distance. And he wasn't lined up right to even look through from back door to front door. He was clear over in a corner of the corral."

"What print was nearest the rear door?" asked Fancher.

Chaffee indicated the model. Fancher turned it over and studied it carefully. "This is not a cow country boot, Jim. Too broad and flat a heel, too wide at the arch, and also a way too blunt at the toe." He looked at the remaining two models. "This third one doesn't mean anything to me. Curious-shaped foot, though. Keeps right on widening from instep to toes. Funny. Now this last one—" and Fancher fell silent for a long while. "Regulation puncher's boots—and as big as a house. Took a heavy man to make a hole in the ground deep enough to match this model." He looked at Chaffee, seeming to hold a thought he was too cautious to express openly. Chaffee nodded. "I'm thinkin' with you on that."

"Interesting to know who wore the shoe with the flat heel and blunt toe. We might discover something of interest."

"I'll find out," Chaffee replied, grim all of a sudden. "Don't worry about that. Keep all this under your hat for the time being. And I wish you'd take charge of those models until I need 'em. They'll get battered if I pack 'em around much."

Fancher agreed. Chaffee started for the

door; Fancher stopped him on the threshold with a very casual remark. "If I were you, Jim, I wouldn't spill any of this dope to Luis Locklear."

"Not in a thousand years," said Chaffee, and descended the stairs.

His next point of call was the hotel. "Miss Thatcher here?" he asked the clerk.

That gentleman shook his head. "She went over to the Woolfridge ranch around noon."

Chaffee departed, somehow feeling cast down. All during the ride to town he had debated seeing her; and he had screwed up his courage and rehearsed what he wanted to say to her. Going toward the stable, he tried to erase the dissatisfaction from his mind. "I guess," he murmured, "I had better lay that bright dream aside. I had better forget it. Her road runs a long ways from mine. A sixty-dollar man has mighty poor sense to be thinking about her kind of a woman. My life is out here. She belongs somewhere else. Why be a kid about it and nurse ideas that won't ever work?"

He was so engrossed in his own problems that he almost ran headlong into Mark Eagle, the bank cashier. Mark's round moon face was always grave; now it seemed overcast with an unwonted solemnity. Chaffee stopped and forgot his own affairs. "You look like a heavy load of grief, Mark."

The Indian never circled a subject. He spoke directly always. "My father is very sick up in Oregon. I've got a letter from him. He ought to go to the city and see a good doctor."

"Won't he listen to anybody but the tribe medicine man, Mark?"

"No, he's civilized, Jim, like me. He'd go to a doctor. But that's a hundred mile trip and it takes money." Mark looked across the building tops, dusky eyes roaming the distant peaks. It was always this way with the man. He went quietly about his business, obeying his mind while his heart seemed to pull him away to a wilder country. "My father is not old. And he is a chief. I am not a good son to be here and unable to help him."

Jim Chaffee's hand worked on impulse, reaching down to the pocket that carried his last material wealth. "You're on the wrong track, Mark. You've got friends, lots of them. What's a friend for? Here's eighty dollars. You get that to him. Quick."

The Indian's hands were stiff at his sides, and Chaffee knowing the danger of prolonging a scene like this, tucked the bills into the other's coat. Mark Eagle's copper cheeks contracted, "You need your money, Jim. I'll be a long time paying it back."

"Who said anything about that? Get it

mailed off in a hurry."

Mark Eagle straightened. A burst of light came through the dark eyes. He placed an arm on Jim's shoulder and spoke with a sonorous dignity that somehow carried him back to his forebears. "You are my friend. You will never regret that. An Indian never forgets."

"You'll maybe be doin' me a favor some of these days," drawled Chaffee.

"Sooner than you think," said Mark Eagle. And he moved swiftly away, which was also his manner. Chaffee got his horse and swung out of town, his mind dwelling for a moment on Mark Eagle's last phrase. Few people made any pretense at understanding the Indian; nor did Chaffee try to understand him. But he liked Mark, and since he liked the man he was instantly ready to help. There was nothing complex about Jim Chaffee's nature.

Outside of town Chaffee left the main trail and quartered into the desert; this was a habit he had been trained to since boyhood. He had never forgotten the shrewd maxim laid down by his father. "The beaten trails don't teach you nothin', Jim. Ride open country with yore eyes propped apart. Yuh may never be no world beater, but if yuh learn to read the good Lord's signs yuh won't never be a fool." The early afternoon's sun came out of a cloudless sky, the breath of winter blew over the eastern peaks. Chaffee soon forgot his problems; this land had the power to completely absorb him, to mold him to its own mood. Up and down the rolling reaches he traveled, blue eyes questing the horizons or dwelling upon the minute testimony unfolding along the ground. A jack had scurried off here; a coyote's tracks zigzagged east and west aimlessly. One clear mark of a shod horse struck along the bottom of a minor draw, traveling fast. He spent more than a casual glance at this. Somebody riding from the road due east to Woolfridge's ranch. Rising over a billow of the desert, he found a rider about a quarter mile in front and going at a sedate pace. His own rate of speed soon closed the distance and presently he recognized Gay Thatcher. She turned and saw him; reined in and waited until he came abreast.

"Lost?" he asked her, raising his Stetson.

"No, I'm exploring. I started out for the Woolfridge ranch. But it is so glorious an afternoon that I just gave my pony free head and told him to go wherever he wished. I think I'm headed for Roaring Horse canyon. I want to see it. Can you make it and get to Woolfridge's by sundown?"

"I think so. That's the way I'm heading. If you don't mind company I'll trail along."

"That will be fun." They rode side by side,

silent for a spell. The girl made a wholly different picture to Chaffee. The shimmering dress and the lamplit softness of her features—these were gone. She wore a buckskin riding skirt, stitched boots, and a loose jersey that seemed to have been long used for just such excursions as these. She was still feminine, still graceful and poised; but the change of clothing at once fitted her into the country. A passer-by would have looked once and decided she had lived hereabout all her life. Jim Chaffee marked the lax sureness of her riding. That was a trick that didn't come out of an Eastern riding school.

She turned her head slightly and looked up at him, her eyes smiling beneath the brim of her hat. "What are you thinking?"

"Asking myself questions."

"So am I. If you will ask them out aloud perhaps we can get better acquainted. I'd like to—and I believe you would. Or am I taking in too much territory, Jim Chaffee?"

"You're not a pilgrim," said he.

"No, I'm not," she answered. "I was born and raised in the West. I went East to school. I came back and both of my folks died. I have been doing many things in many places since then. There. I am answering questions you didn't ask. Now it's my turn. What's ahead of you?"

"Sixty dollars a month and found, I reckon."

"You're not fair to yourself, my dear man. Nobody looking at you in the rodeo yesterday would ever think you were easily whipped. You're not either." That last sentence rang quite strongly. He turned to her a little surprised.

"Now what—"

"That's fair, isn't it?" she broke in, her cheeks pink. "We're asking questions."

A tension inside him snapped and left him smiling at the horizons. All at once he was a slim and lazy and slightly reckless figure. Fine sprays of humor wrinkled his bronzed temples. "Maybe my luck is changin', but I don't think so."

"I have often found that a person makes his own luck," said she, and gravely folded her hands on the horn. "Whose cattle off to the right?"

He studied a scattered band in the distance. "Stirrup S. Well, a man can make his luck up to a certain point, but he can't change the universe to do it. Now look at me and then look—" Right there he stopped. This was going pretty far. But the surprising and insouciant Gay Thatcher blandly finished the thought for him.

"—Then look at me. All right Jim Chaffee,

just you look at me. I don't think you have seen me yet. Oh, I know—but I mean you haven't really seen *me*. How far is it to the rim?"

"Just a little piece now. I can judge men, but not women. I reckon I'll have to pass that bet."

"They told me you were a man of courage," said the girl in a mildly plaintive voice. And as an apparent afterthought she added: "They also told me you knew something about women."

He said nothing to that, and she tucked one sure observation in the back of her head. "He is a gentleman." They worked up along a slight incline. Fence posts spread before them. The canyon's black and foreboding depths yawned abysmally beyond the wire. They got down. Chaffee helped her through the barbed strands and took her arm as they advanced to the precipice and looked below. He didn't want her to think he was assuming an undue freedom, so he explained.

"Some people get dizzy looking down there. It ain't only the distance, but when the light hits that moving water it does funny things to the eyes."

She said nothing for several minutes, but he felt her body alternately tighten and relax and sway slightly as she studied the grim, sheer walls and the remote river heaving itself turbulently onward. The immensity of the picture, the solemn and inspiring force of it seemed to grip her as it always gripped him. Steadied by his arm, she leaned a little forward, her clear face utterly absorbed, her eyes somehow puzzled. It reminded Chaffee at the moment of a child watching the heart of a fire and unconsciously captured by the eternal lure of the mystery of life. The knowledge that she, too, was affected by the elemental rawness of the canyon immeasurably warmed his heart.

She raised her face to him. "When the ground is secure under our feet we are big, important. It takes this to make us humble, Jim Chaffee."

"I don't know of any better medicine to reduce the size of a fellow's pride," said he.

"You haven't any false pride," she told him.

"I've lived too long in the open."

"Why," she asked, "do they call it Roaring Horse canyon?"

He delayed the answer for some moments. "A horse is a tough animal. It never makes much fuss. But there is one time in its life when it makes a sound that will turn a man ice cold all over. And that is when it knowingly goes to death. I have heard animals squeal; I've heard them bellow and groan and scream.

But there isn't anything so almighty heart-breaking and pitiful as to hear that half roar and half scream of a horse going down. It's pretty near human. That's why they named it Roaring Horse. Many a brute has gone over this rim. And nothing lives that goes over."

"I have heard them," she said quietly. "Where are the fords of the river?"

"Lee's Ferry is up five miles nearer the bench. It's a stiff climb down, but that's about the only accessible spot near here, and the only quiet water. Linderman's Ranch, fifteen miles below is the other. The canyon drops toward the desert level there."

"Has anybody ever navigated the gorge?"

"A fellow did it in 1892. Three different parties have tried since. All drowned. One chance in four. It can be done, but a man has to be pretty desperate to try. He's got to hit the rough water just right. The river never lets up from Lee's to Linderman's. I think we'd better start back. Getting late."

They got to their horses and turned silently south. The girl, wondered at the prolonged quietness swung to find him reading the ground; and it surprised her to see the quick change coming over his lean cheeks. His eyes were slightly narrowed and his lips were pressed tightly together. In the grip of such an expression the man's face was neither handsome nor pleasant. It was again the face of a fighter, the same face she had seen at the rodeo. Wondering, she scanned the foreground and saw nothing, save here and there a scuffed trail made either by cattle or horses. Once when the western rim began to blaze with the purple and gold of a setting sun, he slackened the pace and went to one side of his pony. And thereafter, until the outline of the Woolfridge ranch houses grew plain in the distance, he looked straight ahead of him, looked with some kind of a problem. Seeing the houses, he broke away from his preoccupation.

"There's the end of your trip. I'll leave you here."

"It has been a pleasant trip," said she, drawing rein.

Humor flickered a moment in his deep eyes. And that humor covered the profound earnestness of his words. "My luck's gone out. You will be going back to your own country in a few days. I'll not be seeing you again."

"Why not?"

The sun was down and the shadows swirling across the desert. In the dimming light they faced each other, and Jim Chaffee saw in her the vision of the woman he had always carried in his heart. She was fair and sturdy, feminine and desirable; a wisp of brown hair strayed across her cheeks and she lifted a hand to brush it back—a swift and graceful movement that brought with it a faint fragrance of perfume. Her lips were pursed, and her eyes met his glance squarely as if wishing to speak.

"I'll be riding close to my outfit the next week," said he. "Snow's falling up in the peaks. It will be here soon. And—other things are going to happen."

"Is that the only reason, Jim?"

She used his first name. So naturally did it fall into her soft and slightly wistful question that he hardly noticed it. He drew a deep breath. "No. No—it ain't. A man can make his own luck—but he can't change the universe to do it. Ma'am—"

"My name," said she, just above a whisper, "is Gay."

"I have said it many times to myself. Gay. No other name would fit you. And I will be sayin' it many more times—after you're gone. A man's got to play the cards as they fall. He can't stack the deck."

She made a small gesture with her hands. "You don't know me, Jim. You are setting me too high. Oh, see me as I am!" And after another interval she added: "Perhaps I know more about affairs in the country than you think. If I asked you to be—a little careful, would you remember?"

He shook his head. "Now you're setting me too high."

"No, I'm not!" said she, the energy of her answer raising her in the saddle. "You are honest, you are—a gentleman. What more should you be?" She took up the reins and moved away. Ten yards off she turned, and he saw the blurred white oval of her face. "I am asking you to be careful. I know many things I wish I could tell you. Perhaps I'll be here more than a week. Good-night, Jim."

"Good-bye—Gay."

"No—good-night."

She pressed her horse and raced toward the house. A glimmer of light sprang out along the desert. Chaffee watched until she had faded into the falling darkness; and then wheeled and raced northward in the direction of the canyon. The premonition of trouble filled his mind.

"Those tracks struck straight for the middle herd. What else but rustling? I ain't got time to get back home and roust out the boys. I'll have to tackle this alone."

His horse was tired, he himself was weary; yet the farther he rode the more urgent and the more alarming was the warning in his mind. A gray mound stood vaguely toward the bench. The herd was in that vicinity. On he galloped, the horse gallantly stretching out at Chaffee's impatient words. Time passed; he slackened pace and veered along a great circle. Nothing of the herd was visible in the deep darkness. Impelled by the same foreboding, he straightened out for the canyon again. Cattle didn't shift so far of their own accord in the short space of time between midafternoon and night. Reasoning along line of the most probable course of travel rustlers would take with so large a bunch of cows, it seemed to him he ought to swing at right angles and head into the undulating folds of the bench. Yet try as he would, he could not overreach the impulse to keep his present trail.

He pulled up. Away to his left and somewhat ahead he caught the vast and ominous rumbling of a herd in swift motion. Without further thought he raced off at a tangent. The rumbling grew deeper and swelled above the sound of his own progress. All of a sudden he was on the flank of the herd, seeing the dark mass stretch out in an irregular line. He dug his spurs deep into the sides of his exhausted pony and shot forward among the lead steers. As he did so he felt the pressure of another bunch of stock thundering in from his right, converging with the mass he was now abreast. He was trapped in the van of a wide-flung line of onrushing brutes, frenzied by mass fear and mass sound. He thought for a moment to make one effort to break their stride. Drawing his gun he fired pointblank into the weaving formation abreast him. A brute fell, but the bellowing and the fury seemed only to rise higher. And far back he heard what he thought to be a man's voice dimly crying a warning. The warning came to him equally soon; somewhere in the immediate foreground was the canyon. He bent low and slipped his quirt, alternately yelling into the pony's ear and flailing the buckskin thongs. With one last magnificent burst of reserve strength the horse pulled away, yard by yard; and Jim Chaffee, crying, "So long, Buck!" saw a fence post shoot up from the ground and bear abreast of him. He kicked the stirrups, flung his feet far ahead, and let go, the force of the impact rolling him head first. He waited, in that flashing fragment of time, to hear the bursting and shrill singing of barb wire as his horse struck. No such sound came. Still rolling, he caught instead a distant screaming; and then the rush of the cattle engulfed that sound. His hands touched the jagged rocks of the rim; he gripped them with the pressure of death and swung himself down into the black maw. His boots touched a flimsy ledging; he got a new grip on an outcrop just below the rim; and, braced to the shock, he hung there as the dust rolled against his face and the very pit of hell seemed to engulf him.

CHAPTER SEVEN

FANG AND PERFUME

William Wells Woolfridge called his ranch house "Wolf's Head," and there was about it a blending of Western roughness and costly splendor suggesting the dual personality of the owner. The house was a veritable mansion standing massive and solitary in the desert, designed by a famous Eastern architect who himself had overseen its erection. Lava rock and squared timbers braced it; lodge pole pines framed it all around. Massive beams supported a vaulted two-story living room, along three sides of which ascended a stairway that ran into wide galleries. After dark, when the remote corners were clouded by shadow, it suggested the spaciousness of some Gothic temple; and the same fathomless mystery. There was a fireplace wide and deep enough for a tier of four-foot logs laboriously hauled from the distant mountains. From place to place were ranged trophies gathered by Woolfridge throughout the world; and as if tiring of this stark coloring he had thrown around wall and corner all sorts of tapestries and fabrics and bits of statuary of which nobody but himself knew the full price. Into this living room, half lighted by lamp and fire, Gay Thatcher stepped.

Her immediate reaction was one of utter astonishment. She stopped and flung up her head, eyes immediately falling upon objects here and there; and catching instantly the effect of the whole arrangement. "Why, Mr. Woolfridge! I never dreamed—"

He was in evening clothes, a suave and chuby-cheeked host, groomed to precision. He bowed slightly from the hips, smiling with an urbane pride. And he raised her hand in such a manner that for a moment she thought he was about to salute it in the continental style. But, looking closely at her, he straightened and stepped back a pace. "I told you that perhaps I could offer some small diversion to the monotony of this land. After all, an exile must comfort himself. You have no luggage?"

"Just a few things in my saddlebags. I never imagined such splendor, Mr. Woolfridge, or I would have done you greater honor in clothing. In the open country I always go about ragged. And since this was but an overnight visit I didn't bother to—"

He interrupted her. "My dear, make no excuses. You are lovely, in whatever dress, wherever you are." A wiry Filipino lad darted through the door with the girl's saddlebags. Woolfridge raised his voice. "Ysabel." A Mexican woman came down the stairway and took the bags. "You will want to freshen up," said he. "Ysabel will show you to your room."

When the girl returned fifteen minutes later Woolfridge had changed back to his riding clothes and a table had been placed by the fire, silver all aflash in the light. He came toward her.

"Really," said she, "this embarrasses me. I—"

"That," said Woolfridge, tremendously earnest, "is the last thing in the world I want you to feel. I mean that as I never meant anything else. It was only a foolish fancy of mine. The pomp and circumstance of a lonely exile." He placed her in a chair and went around the table to his own seat. "I was worried about you. I should have disregarded your instructions and sent a man over to guide you here."

"I like to ride alone. I had no trouble at all. I have so little chance to go adventuring as I grow older that I always look forward to the opportunity." She lifted a salad fork and spoke as an apparent afterthought. "But I found company. Chaffee—Jim Chaffee took me to the canyon. And came nearly home with me."

"Interesting," said Woolfridge, engaged with the serving. "Would like to have seen the chap. There is a character for you. Did you say he was traveling back to Stirrup S after you left him?"

"I believe in that direction," replied the girl. She had a moment's glance at his face as it turned away; nothing but serenity dwelt upon it. "You spoke of being an exile, Mr. Woolfridge. You don't really mean that."

"Yes, very much so. Voluntary exile. What is there for a man to do in the cities? I found myself growing soft, getting old. Going around and around. There is no place in America I cannot go, my dear lady, with credentials that will admit me to the best of homes. I am in a position to do almost anything I want to do. But I relegated all that and came here. Why? Well, because—"

He leaned forward and something of the mildness vanished from his face; she thought she saw a hint of the iron in this man. "Because I'm in the wrong century. I am a good business man. But I would have made a better buccaneer one hundred years ago. I am laying myself open to you. There is that urge in me. Something pulls me off the beaten track. I built this house on the strength of that. I live here on the strength of that. It is not good for a man to live alone; neither is it good for him to stifle his impulses and tread the machine."

"And have you found what you seek?"

He turned squarely to her. She saw the will of the man very plainly then. "I am on the very edge of finding it. There—"

"Please. I didn't meant to ask into your affairs. Let us consider that unsaid."

"Why so?" he asked. "I should like you to know. I'm too cautious a business man to show my trumps before the proper time. And yet I am egotist enough to dream of power created by my own hands. I have inherited almost everything. Now I create by myself. Miss Thatcher, the time will come—and it is not far distant—when I can say that I have achieved. When I have built up a little kingdom in my own right."

"Whatever greatness there is in us," said she gravely, "comes out in the struggles we make. And whatever evil there is in us also comes out."

"Very true," agreed Woolfridge. "But few men have the courage of their convictions. I mean the smashing desire to take everything before them and see the end. You may not think it, but I have that desire. As for evil—it is a word too much used. Tell me, what is evil, except a label arbitrarily applied by society to this case and that case as society wills? There is much injustice done in the name of that word."

"I am not a philosopher," said Gay, and smiled.

Immediately he lost his seriousness and became the affable host. They finished the meal and lounged in front of the fire, talking of idle and inconsequential things. Presently he showed her his collection of fabrics. Midway in this a horse pounded up to the front door and a rider struck the ground heavily. Woolfridge paid no attention to the distraction until the Filipino lad came soundlessly in and ducked his head. Woolfridge excused himself and went out. The girl heard the rider's voice come strongly through the door, and almost instantly was hushed and trailed down the yard. She stood with her back to the fire, very thoughtful. Beside Woolfridge in town, she had judged him from surface appearances; and, since she was a wise young lady, she had added something to those appearances and given him credit for being more than he seemed to be. Yet she was not prepared for the hints of character thrown off this evening. She felt somehow on insecure ground. Almost as if she were on unsafe ground.

He came back at the end of ten minutes; and, though he smiled easily and resumed the tour of inspection, there was about him a subtle change. He lost a little of the urbane courtesy; he made no particular attempt to carry on small talk. The girl all of a sudden decided she was weary and said as much.

"It has been a long day. I believe I had better go up."

"I'm sorry. There are a number of things yet to be discussed."

"For instance?" she suggested, standing at the bottom of the stairs.

"My dear girl, you are a complete mystery to me—and to others. Don't you think it fair to let some of us in on what you have done all these years?"

She rose three steps and poised again. "What does it matter? I am only Gay Thatcher. I have seen some of the world—and I hope to see more. I love adventure—almost as much as you do, Mr. Woolfridge. But I rather think I disagree with you about the relative qualities of evil. You see, I was brought up strictly orthodox. And the training still endures."

"I am interested to hear you say it. You show me a great many different small peepholes of yourself—all very attractive, but none of them more than a hint. What of the future?"

"The future," replied Gay, for once quite sober, "is as much a mystery to me as to you. I content myself with doing what I must do. And that is, making a living."

He bowed. "I bid you good-night. Ysabel has lighted the fire in your room. We have many things to talk about in the future."

She looked down with that quizzical, half-humorous glance so much a part of her. "My dear sir, how long do you think I am staying here?"

"I wish and I hope," said William Wells Woolfridge with extraordinary fervency, "that it be forever."

She went on up and into her room without answer. Woolfridge kept his eyes on the landing for a few moments, then turned to a desk in one corner of the vast room. He took a cigar and shuffled before him three different sheets of paper. Each of these bore the same letterhead—that of the power company down-territory. Each was brief, each doubtful and suggesting complications. Woolfridge reread them, agile mind building up meanings between the words. And at last he rose and warmed himself by the fire, rocking to and fro on his heels.

"It will go through," said he. "I will put it through, one means or another. I am not to be stopped. Not by anything, legal or illegal.

What is legality, anyhow? I am committed to this thing. I will not go back."

In her room Gay turned out the light and from her pillow watched the cheerful running of the fireplace flames. Drowsiness immediately overtook her. "I think," she told herself, "that William Wells Woolfridge is one of the most dangerous men I have yet met. And the danger of him is that he conceals himself so well. I wonder if he stops short of any of the commandments? Gay, my dear, you wiggle out of this quickly. Wolf's Head is a poor place for you." She dropped asleep, thinking not of Woolfridge but of Jim Chaffee.

CHAPTER EIGHT

THE TIDE GOES OUT

Wedged there between shoulders of rock that permitted his body to sink slightly inside the steep face of the canyon wall, and with a ledge no more than four inches wide holding him against a sheer drop to death, Jim Chaffee passed through those thundering, crashing moments of ordeal and torture. He was surrounded all at once by the crush and the bellow of a herd going to its doom. This mass swept out of the darkness to right and left of him. The brutes shot directly over the top of his head, pitching far into the maw of the gorge. Nothing could stop the force of that flight; nothing could divert it now. Sprays of sand and rock skimmed his back, and all that protected him from being struck and torn loose by those scudding, flailing hoofs was the insecure outcrop of lava substance above him. Even so, a breaking away of that outcrop by the tremendous pressure exerted upon it might happen at any instant; a chance hoof might plunge down and knock his feet clear of the ledge. He faced eternity while the roar and the confusion swelled to an indescribable pitch and his brain grew giddy from the strain of it.

Far down he heard the wailing of animate flesh; he had the sensation of a vast waterfall rushing over the rim. All muscles were growing numb from the pressure he placed upon them. Where was the barb wire that had been on the fence posts earlier in the afternoon? At this very spot he had spread the strands apart to let himself and Gay Thatcher through. Cattle stench was in his throat, and a stumbling brute fell so close to him that he got the impact of wind breaking against the carcass. He no longer was able to command his fingers, no longer able to feel the strain of them against the rock. In that second of black despair when he was about ready to give up, the last member of the herd capsized and hurtled down with a grunt and full-throated bawling. And then it was over, and a queer, oppressed silence settled along the dusty earth. He started to haul himself out and was arrested by voices."

"Got 'em all?"

"Yeah. Every last pound o' flesh."

Riders were moving within ten feet of Chaffee. He heard the rasp of leather and the jingle of chains. A match broke the darkness, but he was in too cramped a position to be able to look above the outcrop.

"Cut that out! Pinch the match, yuh fool!"

"What's the difference? Shucks—"

"Which one o' you addle-brains fired that shot?"

Jim heard denial come from a number of throats. There could be no mistaking the voice of the questioner. That rumbling tone could come only from the immense barrel of Theodorik Perrine.

"Well, by Jupiter, somebody fired it!"

"Reckon Chaffee come back from Woolfridge's in time to get mixed up with the herd?"

"I shore would like to think he was takin' his last drink o' water now," growled Perrine.

"But we ain't gettin' rid o' Chaffee that easy. Some o' you dudes is lyin' to me. When I find out who it is I'll strip said party and cut my mark. Didn't I say no shootin'? We ain't advertisin' this."

"Nobody in this outfit fired a shot." That, Chaffee decided, was Sleepy Slade. Sleepy was the only man in Perrine's gang able to talk back. "Let's sift around and see if we can corral Chaffee."

"We're goin' to get out of here," said Perrine. "It's work aplenty for one night. I got orders to be humble about it. I got orders not to get in a personal fight with Chaffee, and I don't want none of you gents to kill him afore I get directions to do it myself."

"I'll bet plenty pesos he ain't far off," grumbled Sleepy Slade. "Let's look, anyhow."

"Shut up, Sleepy. I'm runnin' this gang. I'm obeyin' instructions until I get a good crack at him when nobody's lookin'. Come on. Back to home. Stretch out."

They galloped away. Chaffee raised one half-paralyzed arm and hooked it over the rim. Then he raised the other. And there he hung for a long, doubtful moment until the cramp wore out of his hands. He pulled himself upward and back to safety, and fell flat as his muscles and nerves, stretched to the point of breaking, began to jangle and shake as they had never done in twenty-seven years.

It would have broken a lesser man—broken him for all time. But at the end of five minutes Jim Chaffee sat up and rolled himself a cigarette, shielding the flare of the match in his palms. The light wavered a little, which made him swear softly. "I never thought anything could do that. But I'm here to tell the universe and every part and parcel thereof I ain't ashamed of these shakes. Don't know when just bein' alive felt so all-fired good."

He relished the smoke as he never had relished another. The cold, sharp night fog penetrated his clothes and quickly chilled him. Still he kept his place on the hard ground, lungs reaching out for the pungent air, looking up to the unfathomed sky. "I ought to be plumb glad I'm in a shape to feel cold. So Theodorik's got orders not to kill me unless it's done private and secret. Huh. Wonder who he's takin' orders from? There's another item that comes under the head of useful information. I might make a guess. If I did I might be wrong. But sure as the Lord made little green apples there's one man or one outfit that's tryin' to get a corner on Roarin' Horse real estate. And usin' Theodorik to hurry up the process. What happened to the barb wire around here?"

He spoke mildly, as if he discussed a subject of no great interest. The manner was only a cloak. Deep within Jim Chaffee the fires were burning brighter and hotter. There was being developed a tremendously harsh anger in the man—an explosive, savage temper that ripped at the barriers he placed against it. Chaffee knew this state of heart and mind. Once or twice before he had struggled with it, half ashamed and half afraid of the consequences ensuing from it. Reason and discretion alike abandoned him when that temper gripped him, and he was apt to do things of which he was not proud. He hated to lose control of his actions, no matter how just those acts might be. So he asked himself soft and serene questions. And in the end rose to inspect the fence.

There was no fence. Not even posts for a hundred yards along the rim; the resistless sweep of the doomed cattle had carried all things away. But progressing another hundred yards he found posts intact, with the strands of wire clipped off them. And apparently thrown into the canyon, for he could find no trace of the wire. This cutting had gone on for almost a quarter mile either way from his point of investigation. Theodorik Perrine's gang had done it thoroughly and swiftly sometime beyond midafternoon.

"They must've been cached in a gulley around here, watching Gay and me," opined Chaffee. "Must've kept pretty close tab on all my meanderin' back and forth. I'll give Theodorik ample credit. And he will pay interest on that credit, likewise." He let himself go, then and there. "That damned bull-necked mountain of low-down crookedness! Nobody but a man with the butcherin', slashin' instincts of a murderer would throw all them cows over the brink. He's been growin' ugly five years, just waitin' for somebody to tip him on over into bloodlettin'. Theodorik, if you don't die sudden I'll have to brace you."

He steadied himself. Yet when he remembered that his horse and outfit had also gone into the chasm he saw red again. The Stirrup S home quarters lay five miles distant and thither he turned. An hour and ten minutes later he reached the ranch porch to find Miz Satterlee quite alone. The weary tramp had not improved his state of mind; rather it had served to enrage him the more and to crystallize his determination to close with Theodorik and settled the account.

"Where's the boys?"

"Mack heard a rumor about rustlers bein' down in the alkali flats," said Miz Satterlee. "So he took the crowd and went over there."

"Yeah, that's another angle Theodorik doped out to make himself safe," grunted Chaffee. He moved along the steps and Miz Satterlee had a moment's view of his face as it met the outthrust light.

"Jim Chaffee—what on earth—!"

"Accident," said Jim, reaching for his brown papers. "Theodorik Perrine cut a lot of wire off our canyon fence and run all the lower bench stuff into the brink. Ma'am—I hate to tell you that."

Miz Satterlee said nothing for many long moments. Chaffee expected to hear a vigorous and bitter appraisal of Perrine. He was mistaken.

"I knew this was coming soon enough," said the mistress of Stirrup S very gently. "I'm sorry about the cattle—but I'm a great deal more sorry to think what it means to you and the outfit, Jim. There will be bloodshed. I hate to think of that. I believe I'd rather sell out than have any of my boys brought home injured. Jim, where are you going?"

Her question stopped him a yard or so removed from the porch. "I'm going to get a fresh horse and saddle, ma'am."

"To do what at this hour of the night?"

"To hunt Theodorik Perrine, ma'am," said he, rage shaking the words in his throat. "To find Theodorik Perrine and Sleepy Slade and the seven other prowlin', slinkin' yella dogs that run in his pack!"

"What will you do when you find them, Jim?" She was still speaking in the same quiet, sad manner; and she seemed to be trying to bring him out of the fury that clouded the cool and shrewd judgment of the man.

"I don't know—yet," he muttered.

"I know," said Miz Satterlee, talking with more energy. "You will be killed. Jim, you're outside of yourself. Stay here until you cool off. What can you do alone against them? I depend on you—don't go back on me. I know—I know how you feel. But I will not allow you to be killed. What will happen to Stirrup S then? There is no other man I can trust—nobody else big enough to hold it for me. Jim—"

"Yeah. Wait until I cool off. Wait until Perrine is out of reach. Let him think he's gettin' away with this. Let whoever's payin' him to rustle and kill think *he's* gettin' away with it. No. They've got to be smashed! They've got to be hit sudden and hit hard! Supposin' we let 'em alone until to-morrow. Then you'll say to let 'em alone until the day after. All the while they're gettin' bolder and bolder. And some night our barns go up in smoke, and they rake the place with lead. The rest of our stock is rustled. No, ma'am. I'm goin' now, and I'm goin' to do *somethin'!*"

"Jim, you can't—"

"Miz Satterlee, I never have gone against your husband's word, nor your word. But I've got to do it now. Sure, I plenty understand it's all against reason to trail out alone. But Theodorik's got to have the fear of God planted in him. And I want him to know I ain't afraid. I'll bend that gent's neck and make him humble. If I don't nobody in Roarin' Horse is safe. Remember that."

He hurried away. She called again to him. He didn't answer. Out in the corral he roped one of his string, a fresh, tough paint pony, and he got a spare saddle and bridle from the bunkhouse. He was up and spurring away, hearing Miz Satterlee send a last call after him.

South and west he traveled, as fast as the paint horse would take him; and along down the dark vault of the desert the chill wind cleared his head to give him a clearer sight of what he was about to do. Perhaps he had no business setting out alone. Perhaps he should have waited for the Stirrup S men to return from their wild goose chase. But that would not be until morning—they'd range the flat land until dawn came—and morning was too late. Theodorik Perrine would be watching morning then. Or else the gang would be scattered. If Perrine was to be hit the hitting must be done immediately; the renegade had to be taught that there was an instant rebound to an affair like this. Once let Perrine see the range sleeping and debating over such wanton aggression and the range was lost to all security.

Such was Jim Chaffee's reasoning as he galloped arrow-straight for the southwest lava flow country where Perrine hid. Yet that was not all. There was something beyond reason that urged Chaffee headlong into certain trouble. The same unseen power that had killed Dad Satterlee also had driven the herd into the deep chasm of the Roaring Horse. Whatever different instruments might have been used for each deed, the power behind was the same. He was sure of it. Here was a chance to show resistance to that power, to break the machine-like sureness of it. And here was a chance to accept Theodorik Perrine's challenge of long standing. There would never come a better time.

"Theodorik dead will mean a whole lot to this country right now," muttered Jim Chaffee. "Me bein' dead won't make much difference."

Jim Chaffee in his normal workaday senses would never have crossed that first lava scarp and pressed along the tortuous path leading still lower into the labyrinth of pockets and pinnacles. He would have used entirely different methods. On this night Chaffee was another man. Anger tightened his nerves and muscles. His natural kindliness, his buoyant and easygoing spirit, his law-respecting judgment—all these were wiped out for the time. To-night he was a stalking savage. So at last he turned a bend of the narrow path, passed between sentinel mounds, and commanded a view of Theodorik Perrine's hut one hundred yards farther on. Dismounting, he led the pony a little off the trail and behind one of those mounds, let the reins fall, and stepped forward with both guns drawn.

Once upon a time that had been the home of an early settler; inevitably the settler starved and moved away and Theodorik had assumed tenancy. Nothing could grow within a mile of the hut, but it occupied an admirably strategic location. There was only the one trail leading in through the lava, easily commanded by day, easily guarded at night. So jagged and crater-like was the land to either side of the trail that no horse could travel there, and for a man to attempt approach or departure across the needlelike surface of the lava was to invite torn flesh and clothing. The trail was the only safe way of entering. There was a rumor abroad that Perrine knew of another route behind the hut leading deeper into the volcanic wastes westward. If such a route existed he alone knew it. Very few people cared to explore the useless and forbidding section.

A light glimmered through the hut windows, and the sparks of a fire shot up from the chimney. Chaffee crept forward foot by foot, sweeping the shadows for a possible sentry along the path. After to-night's affair Perrine would not leave himself unguarded. Yet Chaffee found nobody opposing his approach. Arriving near the house he paused, dissatisfied. He couldn't start a play unless he was certain nobody flanked him in the rimming darkness; so, turning, he began a tedious exploration of the bowl. He skirted a corral, seeing the vague bulk of the horses inside; and he dropped to his haunches, listening. In a few minutes he pressed on to the ramshackle barn and there waited until the very silence of the place oppressed him. Still not sure, he completed a second circle and at last closed on the hut. Uneasiness rode his shoulders. Why wasn't a sentry somewhere around?

He slid to a side window of the hut and lifted his head until he commanded a partial view of the interior. Theodorik Perrine and Sleepy Slade were bent over a table, playing cards. Three of the gang sat around the stove.

That made five. One man oiled his revolver in a corner. Six. Leaving three to be accounted for, and he couldn't see those corners of the place in which the bunks were built. Ducking, he passed to the other side of the window and looked again. Two men were rolled in their blankets and he thought he saw the ninth and last of that party lying in a dim corner. But, though he tried to penetrate the dark angle of the place, he slid away, still uncertain. It might be the ninth man rolled in for the night, or it might only be a pile of blankets heaped up on the bunk.

He came quietly to the door and set the muzzle of one gun under the latch; before lifting the latch and throwing the barrier wide he debated with his better judgment and again set aside the small voice of caution. If ever he was to put the fear of the Lord into the heart of Theodorik Perrine it must be now, when the man, fresh from wanton destruction, sat relaxed and confident over the card game. The gun muzzle rose with the latch, the door flew open, and he threw both guns down upon the assembled renegades. They couldn't see him as he stood outside the place and to one side of the opening, but they heard plain enough the brittle snap of his command.

"Hit for the ceilin'—you! Up! Throw 'em high in a hustle! Sleepy—don't move out of that chair or I'll spill you all over the place! That's right—now you buzzards roll off them bunks and move back. What're you stallin' for, Red? I'm not goin' to do any countin'. Get back there, you hairless Mexican pup! Keep your elbows away from that lamp, Sleepy! It won't hurt me none to send some of you lousy, putty-livered coyotes to hell and gone down the chute!"

Nobody could miss the restless, jammed-up temper of Jim Chaffee at that moment. It crackled and smashed around their heads like the popping of a bull whip; it beat upon them stronger and harsher with each word until it seemed he was on the very point of ripping the hut wide with bullets. All hands rose; those in the bunks dropped to the floor and marched back to the stove. Sleepy Slade and Theodorik Perrine never moved from the table. Sleepy's gaunt and saturnine face was an evil thing to see in the lamplight; Perrine's back was turned to the door and the lifted fists were doubled tight.

Eight men in the hut, no more. Chaffee kicked the door wider and saw only a huddle of blankets on that shadow cloaked bunk. Either the ninth man was out in the bowl or he had split off from the gang earlier. It was a gamble, and he had to move fast. "One at a time—drop your belts. One at a time—

startin' from the corner!"

Belts fell. Theodorik Perrine, staring at the opposite wall, threw a question over his giant shoulders. "What kind of a play do yuh think to make, Chaffee? Yore on trembly ground. I'm sayin' it. You ain't got no backin' in this county. Not any more. Yuh can't make the bluff good."

"Stand up, Theodorik, and slip your belt. Now sit down. Sleepy, do the same. Don't try to stall on me. It's just as easy to leave a few of you cattle butchers on the floor. Sit down, Sleepy! Theodorik, take off your boots and throw 'em back here."

"What's the need o'—"

The first shock of surprise having passed, they sparred for time. Chaffee knew by the way Perrine bent and hauled at his boots that the renegade expected a turn of the tide. That ninth man must be in the neighborhood. Chaffee pulled himself a little more to one side of the door's opening. "Theodorik, if that boot seems tight I'll help it with a little lead. Throw it back. Other one, too." They came sailing through the door. Chaffee took one of them and slid it beneath his belt. "Rest of you imitation bad men do the same. Throw 'em this way."

Perrine turned in the chair, big face grinning malevolently. "I'm plumb interested.

Yuh can't make the bluff good. The jail won't hold none of us. Politics have changed, Chaffee. What else do yuh aim to try? Stirrup S is on the slide. It don't count no more."

Boots came flying out. Chaffee kicked them on into the yard. Eight men stood in their socks, glowering. "What I aim to do, Theodorik, is to string all you jack rabbits on one rope and walk you barefoot across the lava and back to the ranch. By the time you get that far you'll be halter broke. Then—" He stopped, thinking he heard a remote sound beyond the yard.

"You can't do it!" roared Theodorik Perrine. "You can't make the bluff good!"

"Barefoot," replied Chaffee grimly. "And if a jail won't hold you, then Stirrup S will. We'll break your back, Theodorik. That's the beginning. Stand up. Sleepy, get that rope and put a hitch around your neck. You boys won't be doin' any more dirty chores for a while. Neither will your boss when we find out who he is."

"You'll last about as long as a snowball in—" began Perrine. The rest of it was cut off by a grumbling, half-awake question from the barn. "What's all that racket over there, huh?"

Theodorik Perrine's face turned thunder black. "He went asleep again! It's the last time for him!"

"What's the racket?" repeated the voice, coming nearer. Chaffee crouched as far in the shadows as he dared. Perrine began to shift weight and grumble. The whole crowd inside the hut started moving. Chaffee warned them with a sibilant whisper. Perrine laughed. Of a sudden the ninth man out in the yard yelled. His gun smashed the silence, bullets ripped the ground by the door and Perrine shouted a warning. Chaffee fired at the ninth man point-blank. The hut trembled, the light went out and confusion turned the place upside down. Another shot plunged past Chaffee; and he, marking the source by the mushrooming purple point of light, matched it. He heard the man fall.

There was no time left now. Window glass broke. Perrine bellowed his wrath through the openings. Chaffee ran five yards from the house, commanding a dim view of the door and the near window. They began to find their guns and rake the doorway from the inside. Chaffee lifted his voice. "Better light the lamp and cave in. I've got this dump covered."

"Yuh ain't broad enough to cover it!" roared Perrine. They placed him from his voice, and in a moment he heard them crawling through the window on the far side. One man raced headlong around the corner, flinging lead at each step. Chaffee dropped him. But the tide was setting out; they had gotten beyond his control and in another moment they would have him trapped in this bowl. So, with Theodorik Perrine's boot still tucked under his belt—a valuable trophy in itself—and knowing that he had in a measure shaken the gang, he raced along the path, got his horse, and threaded the lava to open country. He pointed the pony toward Roaring Horse town, dropping the spurs. He heard Theodorik Perrine following, and he knew that before the night had run its course he would collide with the giant again.

"Bad odds from now on," he murmured to himself. "If I ducked back to Stirrup S I might find the gang home. And we'd take Theodorik into camp. But if the outfit ain't back then I'm only invitin' a wholesale bonfire. That's what Theodorik would do. If I hit into the open country and try to outrun those boys I ain't doing a thing but admit I'm licked. And then I ain't of any use. I'm out. Same as havin' a price on my head. No, sir, I'll track into town and see what this boot tells me. They'll follow. But I don't believe they've got nerve enough to try a wholesale battle with everybody lookin' on. Theodorik will brace me alone. If he ain't able to do it he'll shunt another of the bunch on me. I don't mind that kind of a scrap. And I can do a lot of duckin' around the buildings in case it gets too hot."

He lost sound of the pursuing party. Halfway to Roaring Horse he stopped to listen. Presently he heard the drum of pursuit swelling through the soft shadows; so he raced on, came into the main street of the town, and left his horse down a convenient back alley. It was late, yet the saloons were still open, a few nighthawks loitered along the building porches, and Doc Fanchers' light beckoned through a window above Tilton's. Jim Chaffee climbed the stairs.

Hardly had he disappeared from sight when Theodorik Perrine and the rest of the renegades slipped quietly around the rodeo field and dismounted. There in the darkness they debated.

"Don't see his horse," said Sleepy Slade.

"He's here," grunted Perrine. "Runnin' for a hole. Hidin' out somewhere. Red, skin down to the other end of the street and block it. Duck, you stay here with me. Sleepy, wait near the Gusher. Rest scatter along the alleys. He don't get away, see? He's makin' a payment on the damage he did back at the hut." The man's tremendous body seemed to swell. "Jupiter, but I hate to let him alone! But I got orders to keep away personal. I ain't in no shape to disobey, either. So, whichever you boys see him—he's yore game. Get that?"

"Some town dudes roamin' up the street," murmured Slade.

"Never mind 'em," replied Perrine. "They don't make no difference. What they see don't count. We're protected. Listen to me. Chaffee's in this town. He don't ever leave it alive. Take no chances when yuh see him. Don't give him a break. Start reachin' before he gets a chance. They ain't nobody in this outfit except me that's as fast as he is. So keep out o' the light and let him have it. Shoot him in the back if yuh can. Now get goin'."

They spread apart, slouching down the dark lanes, closing quietly upon their designated stations. Both ends of town were closed, the alleys were covered; and one of the gang, stumbling upon Chaffee's hidden horse, led it away. So silently and discreetly was the maneuver accomplished that not a single one of the loitering townsmen knew what had occurred. Roaring Horse was blockaded; and Sleepy Slade stood in a black corner of the hotel porch, facing that stairway up which Jim Chaffee had a moment ago climbed. And down which Jim Chaffee would presently come.

CHAPTER NINE

DISASTER

Fancher was reading; he looked up to Jim Chaffee and lowered his feet to the floor, somewhat astonished. "Where in thunder have you been?"

"It wouldn't sound right if I told you," answered Chaffee. "I don't even sound right when I tell myself. It's been sort of an active evening. Here's a little trophy I took into camp. Bring out that biggest tar model and let's see what we can see."

He laid the captured boot on Fancher's table. The latter studied it with professional interest for some moments, then turned to his cabinet and drew out one of the models. Capsizing the boot, he fitted the model to the sole of it. Chaffee rolled a cigarette, his eyes half closed against the light.

"What would you think a jury might say to that, Doc?"

"A coroner's jury could easy hold a man over on that similarity," decided Fancher. "Whether a trial jury would convict on that much evidence, I ain't saying. The heels of the boot are some run over on the outer edges. Seems to show something like that in the model, doesn't it?"

"Now you're talkin' like an officer of the county, Doc. Get out and walk among humble citizens awhile. What's in the back of your head?"

"Boot and model—they fit. Of course it might be some other big man left the same kind of tracks, Jim."

"Yeah. How many fellows in Roarin' Horse with that size footgear?"

"I'm thinkin' of only one in particular."

Chaffee blew smoke to the ceiling. He seemed drawn and strangely hard-faced to Fancher. Nothing easy going, nothing humorous. "Well, Doc, the man you're thinking about is Theodorik Perrine. And that's Theodorik boot. Put it away with the rest of our relics. "I'm satisfied those were the big man's hoofprints. Ain't interested in what a jury would say. This won't get to a jury, Fancher."

"How'd you discover that boot, anyhow?"

"Took it away from Theodorik," said Chaffee, showing the first trace of amusement. It was a grim amusement, marked by a sudden flaring of the still aroused fighting temper. "At the point of a gun."

Fancher was visibly worried. "Jim, that's

bad. He won't let you get away with it. You're in a hole. And I'm blamed if I see just how you figure to whistle out of it!"

"He's in town with his playmates right now," was Chaffee's laconic announcement.

"Damnation, why didn't you say that in the beginning! Foolin' away all this time. My boy, it's high time to do some figurin'. Any Stirrup S men around here yet?"

"All gone home."

"Any of your particular friends on hand?"

"None that I know about."

Fancher swore. "You'd better begin to get worried. Luis Locklear won't lift his little finger to stop a bust of gun play. He ain't that kind of a sheriff. He's feedin' out of a different trough. Understand what I mean? And half of the town men are swappin' politics. I know that blamed well. Something's changing things in Roarin' Horse. Rest of the storekeepers and so forth won't dare give you a boost. Ain't you got any ace in the hole, Jim?"

"None."

Fancher studied Jim Chaffee. He had been in the country many years and he had seen good men and bad men take their turn on the stage and depart. Sometimes the good men won out, and sometimes they lost. He had seen them step out to fight; he had pronounced a medical verdict over them after they had gone down in the dust. He knew the meaning of the narrow, fixed expression on Chaffee's lean cheeks. Once a man reached that state of mind he never backed out. Sighing a little, Fancher turned to the wall and reached for his gun belt. He buckled it around him. "All right, Jim. Let's go."

"Did I ask you for help?" snapped Chaffee, suddenly harsh and somber.

"I didn't hear as how you had a monopoly on trouble. Shut up. Come on."

Chaffee shook his head. "It's my fight, Doc. I'm obliged for the offer. But I started this thing solo and I'll finish solo."

"You're the biggest damn' fool I ever knew, Chaffee."

"Maybe. A man likes to rope his own horse. You know what I mean, but you're just tryin' to help. Stay up here. Somebody's got to stick in the background and pull strings. That's your job."

He turned to the door. Fancher raised his shoulders and grumbled; "All right, but I sure would hate to dig bullets out of you."

"What we want to find out now," said Chaffee, "is who owns those other boot prints. What we also want to know is the name of the man behind all this excitement. I could guess, but I might be wrong. He'll overplay his hand pretty soon. So long."

He closed the door and walked slowly down the dark stairs. One step short of the street he paused, resting in the blackness and scanning the opposite walk thoughtfully. A stray puncher passed him at arm's length, cigarette brightly glowing, spurs dragging along the loose boards. Chaffee advanced to the mouth of the stairway and looked right and left. He felt a threat, yet he had no means of placing the origin of that threat. Here and there a townsman moved. Even as he watched the lights of the Red Mill went out at the far end of the town and everything down there was obscured. Somebody talked drowsily and Chaffee heard a phrase: "Well, Billy the Kid had a warp in his system. Any man that shoots a-grinnin'—" The threat was clear, distinct. He could not remain forever in the protection of the stairway. They were waiting somewhere. His hands touched the gun butts; he moved to the sidewalk and started west toward the restaurant.

In the moments of waiting he had watched the porch of the Gusher. Instinct had drawn his attention there. Yet the profound shadows had told him nothing. Now, in motion, he saw a figure coming away from the porch, walking with so slow and swinging a gait that he turned and came to a halt. The other likewise halted, sending on a challenge.

"I want to see you, Chaffee."

He knew then who it was. "Here I am, Sleepy. Ain't you kind of slow on the trigger?"

The crisscross of words floated softly outward. Chairs slammed on another porch. The underground telegraph woke and warned Roaring Horse.

"I could of knocked yuh over by them stairs," admitted Sleepy Slade. "It was orders. But it ain't my style. I figger to be as good on the jump as you are. Any old time. Nobody's ever goin' to say Sleepy Slade had to take the long end o' the teeter to win an argument. Not with you, leastwise."

"Charitable sentiments," drawled Chaffee. He felt the gathering of men along the shadowed building sides. "But maybe you also figured sixty feet was too much distance to take a chance. Better come closer, Sleepy. You know I sort of specialize on long distance."

"I ain't arguin'," droned Slade. His body swayed slightly; he advanced half across the dusty thoroughfare and stood again. "Yuh drilled Ben Gluger. Yuh did same to Jap Ruggles. If yuh ain't cut them notches yet it's too late now."

"Ain't afraid I'll get away and try it again, Sleepy?"

"Yore corralled."

"Thanks for the information. Why don't

Theodorik do his own chores?"

"I ain't arguin'," repeated Slade, the words grating more noticeably.

"Take a try," murmured Chaffee. "You're beginnin' to shake a little."

That touched off the powder. Slade yelled: "Like—" and the rest was lost in the roar that shot upward and outward and seemed to suck the echoes into small whirlpools around Chaffee's head. Slade weaved. In the velvet grayness Chaffee saw the man's feet spread wide and his arms stretched ahead as if he groped for his target. Roar ran into roar. Chaffee turned half around. A woman screamed, lights flashed on, a lantern made a series of hurdles against the night's background. "Try again," murmured Chaffee. But there were no more shots. Slade was sprawled grotesquely in the street, his gaunt and saturnine features marked by death. Luis Locklear held the lantern.

At once the street was alive with spectators. Jim Chaffee stuck fast to his place, watching the sheriff, watching the crowd. Theodorik Perrine kept clear of all this, nor did the rest of the giant's gang come into the light. They were still waiting out beyond the furor and babble, waiting for a second chance with a patience that somehow took away all the reassurance of the fight he had won. Luis

Locklear turned. "Chaffee, I'll have yore guns."

"What for?"

Locklear's stubborn, bigoted countenance could not hold back the triumph that was his. "Stirrup S don't run the town no more. Pass the guns."

"Your manners are poor," drawled Chaffee. "Likewise your memory. Don't you know what happens when another fellow draws first?"

"How could he draw first and be dead?" scoffed Locklear. "You ain't no Annie Oakley. Yuh was pleased to shoot yore face the other night in the stable. Mebbe Stirrup S had a mortgage on the county one time. Not now. I'm goin' to learn yuh some manners down at my padlocked schoolhouse. Pass the guns."

"I believe I'll keep my guns," decided Chaffee. "Now whose bluff is the best?"

He felt solid metal press into his ribs from behind. "Yores ain't," said some unknown gentleman, briefly. Locklear grinned, sour satisfaction shining out of his red-rimmed eyes. He advanced and jerked Chaffee's revolvers clear. "Now, damn yore soul, I'll do the talkin' for a spell. Promiscuous shootin' ain't stylish here no more. Neither is Stirrup S. Yore goin' to stand trial for the killin'. I lay ten dollars yuh get roped for it. Ain't very scared of losin' that money, either. Mush toward the jail."

More lanterns danced along the walks. The lights of the Red Mill burst through the windows again, and Jim Chaffee, walking silently ahead of the sheriff, wondered if that temporary darkness had been arranged for. Here and there he saw faces that not so long ago had been friendly and now were noncommittal or openly hostile. It still was puzzling to him to understand how men could change opinions so quickly when Locklear pushed him down into the basement cell of the county jail, locked the door, and walked away with a sullen oath trailing behind. What power could shift public opinion, or a good part of public opinion at least, so effectively and with so little outward display?

Men were gathering in the sheriff's office overhead. He heard the shuffle of their boots and the mutter of their conversation and the booming of a voice he knew very well. Theodorik Perrine had at last come out of the darkness.

CHAPTER TEN

VOICE OF THE PACK

Not until he rolled into the jail bunk did Jim Chaffee feel the effects of the long day's strain. Building himself a cigarette in the darkness, it came over him suddenly—a cold and cramping reaction that set his muscles to aching. The vitality and buoyancy of man sinks low during those hours around midnight; it is then that uncertainty and doubt and discouragement come like black ravens to perch on weary shoulders. There was no solace in the cigarette; nothing in the dismal, chilly cell to relieve the depressing tedium of his thoughts. He had made a fight, he had won. What of it? Jail held him in spite of that, and the fortunes of the Stirrup S seemed to be settling into obscurity. With the death of Dad Satterlee the tide had gone out. The more Chaffee thought about it, the more certain it was to him that the old man's death had been planned to accomplish just that end. Living, Satterlee was a power not to be challenged. He represented the older settlers; he represented that stiff and rugged frame of mind natural to the land owner and cattle owner, large or small. He stood for rough and swift justice; he stood for a code in which a man's oral promise was as good as a written mortgage. They had killed him, and Roaring Horse began to change from the moment of his death. Who was behind it?"

The cigarette fell from Chaffee's fingers. He slept long and soundly. And while he was thus lost to all things the outer world moved forward, the news of his capture was relayed to certain corners of the range, and certain men came quietly into Roaring Horse. The light in Luis Locklear's office never went out; the back door of the sheriff's office opened and closed many times. When, at ten o'clock of the following morning, Jim Chaffee woke, he became the central actor in a series of events over which he had no control. Unknown to him, his fate had been decided upon during those conferences; and this was the beginning of a day long memorable in the country, the beginning of a day marked by a bitterness and an uncertainty and a tension that men never thereafter forgot.

Chaffee pulled himself from the bunk, stiff in every muscle. And as his eyes roamed the barren walls, the sunlight coming through the window was shut off by a crouching figure. Looking up, he found Mark Eagle's round and solemn cheeks just beyond the grating.

"You must've been pretty tired," said Mark. "I been here an hour, waiting."

"Why didn't you give me a shout?"

"When a man sleeps that solid," replied Mark, "he needs it. I'm in no hurry."

"Come around down the stairs and let's hold a little talk session."

The Indian bank cashier shook his head. "I tried that. Luis Locklear ain't letting anybody in."

Chaffee digested the information meditatively. "Pretty careful, ain't he? Too careful. I'll be out sunnin' my heels in three-four hours. Luis Locklear ain't learned a lot about public opinion concernin' self-defense in this county."

"You won't be out," contradicted Mark Eagle. "A coroner's jury named you at eight this mornin'. Doc Fancher couldn't stand against the pressure. Nobody listened to him. Grand jury met at nine and bound you over. You're to be tried in the mornin'."

"Why the big hurry with the first two juries, and then a delay on the trial?" asked Chaffee. "If they're doin' some railroadin' it seems to me they lost a bet by not passin' sentence an' hangin' me in time for supper."

Mark Eagle moved his hands. Only an Indian could convey meaning so clearly with those swift, silent gestures. "Many things can happen between now and morning, Jim. They got a coroner's verdict for a purpose. It's a nickel's worth of dog meat for the pack. Maybe there won't be no trial in the mornin'. Town's full of gents."

Chaffee shook his head. "Don't believe sentiment in Roarin' Horse runs that way, Mark."

"I do," was the Indian's blunt answer. He looked behind him, lowered his voice. "I know. I have heard. You are too dangerous. You die. I have heard."

Still Jim Chaffee was not convinced. He walked around the cell and came to the window. "Blamed if I read the cards that way, Mark. Shucks, I've lived among these people all my life. They ain't that kind of folks."

The Indian only lifted his shoulders. Presently he switched the subject. "One of those tar boot tracks in Fancher's office is mine, Jim. The broad-toed one is mine."

"Well, I'll—" muttered Chaffee, profoundly astonished. "What do you know about that stuff?"

"The broad-toed one is mine," repeated Mark Eagle with stoic gravity. "I was behind the stable when the shot was fired. I saw you take the tar impressions. You are my friend and I tell you. I did not kill Satterlee, for he was my friend, too. But you poured tar into the tracks of the man who did kill him. Do you know?"

"One set I ain't identified yet," murmured Chaffee, studying the Indian's enigmatic features. He tried to read through and beyond the broad and flattened copper mask. Nothing was revealed to him. The dusky eyes were shuttered, without depth. He wanted to question Eagle, yet he knew that until the red man voluntarily chose to speak, such a course was futile.

"You will find out sometime," said Eagle. "If you do not I will tell you." Boots scraped along the back area. The Indian looked over his shoulder, murmuring: "I am going to Stirrup S and warn your friends."

A lank gentleman dressed like a scarecrow closed in and challenged Eagle with a surly, half-savage authority. "I been watchin' yuh plenty long. And I'm tired of lookin' at yuh. Skin outen here, yuh no-count Pi-ute Git."

Mark Eagle rose and squared himself. "I am an American, the same as you," said he solemnly.

"Don't gimme no sass. American—like fun. Yore a darn worthless Injun. The kind my pap used to skelp for bounty. Git yore greasy mug outen my sight."

Mark Eagle never stirred. Chaffee saw his

chest swell and his chin lift proudly. "I am a Umatilla, the son of a chief who was the son of a chief. We were chiefs when your people bowed humbly to a noble master. We have never bowed. I am your equal."

"Why, gol darn yore cussed hide!" shouted the stranger. "My ekal! Dum it, git!" His fist shot out and knocked the Indian from sight. Chaffee gripped the iron bars and tried to see around the corner of the window. The stranger retreated, gun drawn. "Mosey, and don't come back."

Chaffee stared at the stranger. "What makes you so proud? Where'd you come from?"

"Who wants to know?" grunted the stranger, plainly contemptuous. He took a chew of tobacco and kicked a spray of dust through the window. "What business o' yores is it?"

"Like to know where your kind of trash grows," drawled Chaffee, holding down his wrath. "Seems to be a lot of it driftin' in. Your old man must sure be proud of you, providin' you ever had an old man."

The last phrase sank in. The stranger's malarial features took a red tint. "I've heard ki-otes howl before, Mister Chaffee. So I won't pay no heed to yore remarks."

"I wouldn't figger shoe polish tasted like

much," went on Chaffee. "Never had an appetite for it myself."

"What's that mean?"

"You're a boot licker. Whose boots?"

The stranger whirled and tramped away, swearing fluently. "I'll see yore boots from the bottom soon enough! Git that? I'll see 'em swingin' in the breeze. That's what we're here for."

Chaffee roamed the cell restlessly. "He sort of let the feline out of the bag. Maybe Mark Eagle's right. That gent with the fever and ague map looks like a hired gun artist. Another mark of somebody's thoughtful plannin'. A whistle and a jerk—and a bunch of tough eggs come out of the woods on the lope. Planted there a long time and waitin'."

Noon arrived, and a tray from the restaurant, packed in by yet another stranger. Luis Locklear came along as an extra precaution and stood back while the tray went through the door.

"Who's all these flunkies you got, Luis?" Chaffee wanted to know.

The sheriff's red eyes slanted across Chaffee. "I ain't answerin' questions to-day. Eat that fodder or I'll take it back. No time to waste on you."

Chaffee put a cheerful face on the situation and tackled the food. "Luis, a kind word is like a lightnin' rod. It averts much trouble. You don't appreciate that right now, but you will when the weight of the star begins to sag heavy on your vest."

"You ain't scarin' me none whatsoever."

"All right," agreed Chaffee. "But just remember I warned you against playin' with fire. Small boys and damn' fools should never do it."

"Take his grub away," snapped Locklear. The helper obeyed, grinning at this petty punishment. The sheriff's caviling, ignorant face peered between the bars. "Chaffee, I wish I could use a rawhide on yore frame. It's a regret to me them days have passed. I mean it. They's no way to break a man's stubbornness or humble his pride like a whip or a screw. You're just downright poison to me. Allus have been, and I'd appreciate the satisfaction o' payin' off. But I will content myself with knowin' what I know. And that is ample."

They climbed the stairs and left Chaffee alone. Beyond the barred window the shadows marched farther into the strewn back area and out along the dessert. Above him was a ceaseless tramping of feet and a ceaseless murmur of talk. During the morning a guard had been posted beyond Chaffee's view. Now a pair of them, neither of whom Chaffee had ever seen before, stood in front of the window with shotguns. He could tell that the town's traffic grew heavier as the afternoon passed, for he could hear the echo of feet on the sidewalk and the passing of horses. Something of the rising nervous tension was likewise communicated to him in the abruptness of the talk that drifted down, and in the increasing watchfulness of the two guards. Around three or four the whole jail trembled to the furious passage of a cavalcade. One shot broke the air and boots pounded up the courthouse steps, crossing swiftly into Locklear's office. Chaffee heard the talk swell angrily. Three more guards came running toward the cell window, muttering some sort of news. The cavalcade whirled away. Another shot was fired.

Chaffee was in the process of rolling a cigarette. He threw it to the floor. "That's Stirrup S. They wouldn't let Mack come in. By Jupiter, have I got to pull this place apart?" Discouragement rode him. For a moment he felt like a rat cornered in a hole. "Maybe I made a mistake comin' into town last night. But I don't think so. I left a mark on that bunch, and they're callin' my bet. If I'm forcin' an issue I guess that's better than hidin' out." What hurt him was to feel so absolutely helpless.

Mark Eagle made a quick trip toward the Stirrup S after leaving Chaffee. Halfway to the ranch he ran into Mack Moran leading twenty riders in the direction of the lava country, loaded down with ammunition. He gave them the news and swept away. Mack swore, setting in his spurs; and it was Mack's party Chaffee later heard thundering through Roaring Horse. It was Mack's impatient tread that sounded across the floor of the sheriff's office. Locklear, surrounded by six or seven full-jowled strangers, refused Mack entrance to the cell.

"The patient," he explained with a malicious pleasantry, "ain't in no shape to see company."

"Since when," challenged Mack, ready to do battle, "has this country started keepin' folks in solitary?"

"Since I took office!" snapped Luis Locklear. "Somethin' else has happened likewise. Stirrup S ain't welcome around here. Go on, get out!"

"Ask me what reminds me of a peanut," said Mack. "I'll answer it myself. You remind me of a peanut. I been hearin' a lot of smart remarks about Stirrup S lately. I'd think you started 'em, except yore brain ain't big enough to start anything. Yuh ain't been on the job but a couple weeks and yore hands are all callused from pattin' yoreself on the back."

"Get out of here!" yelled Locklear, rising

from his chair. "I'll throw you in the cooler, too!"

"Yeah?" drawled Mack sweetly. "Go bareheaded, Luis. Yore, conk is swellin' so fast no hat would fit it. If yore goin' to pull some dirty work on Jim, Stirrup S is goin' to show you a good time."

"Try it—I wish you'd try it!" yelled Locklear. "Go out on the street and see how you stand! Yore day is done hereabouts! Kick up a battle and you'll get singed. Go and try it!"

"Peanut," snorted Mack and stalked away. He led the Stirrup S party slowly down the street to the rodeo field and dismounted in the shade. "Boy's, this is sure a jam. That fella means business. Notice all the tough-lookin' pilgrims loafin' by the courthouse? Where'd they come from? I feel creepy. I dunno just what to do, but we got to look alive or we're plumb foundered."

He heard his name called. Swinging, he saw Mark Eagle standing behind the fence of the rodeo field, sheltered from curious eyes. The Indian motioned him to come near.

"Mack, it is your play."

"Yeah," agreed the red-headed cowpuncher.

"I know blamed well it is. But what's the play?"

The Indian's round face was tremendously

solemn. "You get Jim clear of that cell right after dark. They aim to take him out and ride him off a horse."

"Why the low-down bunch of pig stickers! Who aims to do it—how do you know?"

"I know," said Mark Eagle. "It's up to you to figure a way. Keep your men in a bunch while it's daylight. And however you break that jail, do it quick and quiet. They're watching. They'll expect trouble."

"Yeh, but say—"

The Indian shook his head and turned away, losing himself behind the wings of the fence. Mack Moran went back to the group and passed on the warning. They held a long powwow, arriving at no satisfactory solution. One plan after another was brought up and discarded. "Trouble is, that jail is built like a doggone castle," grumbled Mack. "Too much on top of it. Can't get down to it from the front except by goin' through a flock of doors. Only direct entrance is by that rear window— and they'll be every son-of-a-gun in the county back there watchin' it."

The oldest puncher of the Stirrup S, one Gil Daugherty, reached into his memory and unearthed a long forgotten episode. "I remember a jail in Arizona like that," said he. "Basement cell, one window even with the ground. Shucks, it's been twenty-seven, no twenty-eight, years ago. Was a fellow in it. We got him out. Same layout about as this heap."

"How?" chorused the assembled Stirrup S crew.

Daugherty scratched his head to bring back the details. "Well, it was a plumb dark night. Musta been four fellas guardin' that winda. We boys couldn't nowise get near it. So, final', one of us clumb the roof of a house farther down, haulin' a couple ropes along. Meanwhile before, we'd tied said ropes with other ropes till each length was blamed near two hundred feet long. Fella clumb from one roof acrost to the roof of the jail, two stories high it was. Pays these ropes down quiet like until they swung right in front of the winda. Gent in the jug grabs 'em, makes a tie around a couple of the bars and gives a tug to let us know he'd went and done it. We boys git back offen the roof to where the main party was awaitin' in the dark, yonder of the jail winda some distance. Dallies the free end o' each rope around a horn and pulls like hell. She come—she shore did come free like a loose tooth. Afore we started the play we put couple of the fellows off acrost from us fifty yards to break a little dust and sorter attract the guards." There the old man stopped, eyes glistening with the ancient scene.

"Well," grunted Mack, "did it work?"

"Worked swell," said Daugherty. "Jes' worked slick. We got him out. They wasn't but one hangup in the whole proceedin's. The gent cleared the jail when the bars went bust but he didn't duck low enough. Met a bullet, which we never did know if it was one of ours or the guards'. But we got him out of the jail, anyhow, even if he was killed before we could git him away."

A stifled groan rose from the listeners.

"Ain't that a cheerful idee? Operation shore was successful but the damn' fool patient died."

"It won't work."

Mack checked the talk. "It's a good idea, boys. They ain't any other plan that we can lay a finger to. I believe, by gum, we'll just set our loops in that direction. The big point is to get word to Jim somehow what he's to do. We got to let him know we'll be danglin' a rope down from the buildin' top after dark."

"It ain't so easy," objected another. "Yuh can't git within forty yards of that dump."

"Got to," was Mack's succinct answer. "We'll figger a way."

"Ahuh. Who is goin' to be the gent that skins across the buildin' tops and lowers the ropes?"

Mack ducked his head at the veteran, Gil Daugherty. "He did it before. He can do it again. Yeah, that's a good idea. Now, Gil, you just amble around the back end of town and have a good look at the rear side of the courthouse. Line up the cell window with the top of the roof so's you'll know where to climb when it's dark. Meanwhile, I want Rube and Chitty and Tex to split and sa'nter about the joint. See can you pass the word to Jim. I'll be dopin' out some other scheme to get a message to him likewise. Fluke, you take what's left of the bunch and mosey t'ords the front door o' the courthouse. Don't start anything, but look like yuh meant to go plumb through the place. That'll draw some o' them guards away from the back. Vamoose."

The bulk of the crew ambled into the street, drawing immediate attention by the compactness of their ranks, as well as by the reputation that hovered over them. Stirrup S always had been a fighting outfit, a young and recklessly exuberant outfit. This late afternoon they made a striking picture as they slowly split into smaller groups and drifted casually onward—tall, rangy fellows for the most part, with the air of competence about them; a lazy-moving, slim-hipped clan looking somberly to the front as if nothing existed save the far horizon on which they seemed to be speculating. Even Mack Moran, dropping back, was proud of them.

There could be no mistake as to the meaning of their presence. A current seemed to sweep outward and run along through the bystanders and back through the stores and houses. Folks came to the front and watched them pass, and retreated into the depths again, feeling the impact of the threat. Roaring Horse once had been a town entirely sympathetic to Stirrup S. And Roaring Horse knew every man of the group. Yet times had changed and there were many on that street who stood aside, tight lipped and unfriendly. These were the strangers who had arrived out of the desert and seemed to be waiting only for a signal.

Mack Moran cruised idly from one saloon to another, and from one store to another. He talked little, but he listened carefully, and presently he found himself abreast the Gusher, scowling at the westering sun.

"It looks dubious," he murmured. "I dunno where all them gents come from, but they's shore a raft of unbranded critters floatin' around. It don't look prosperous a-tall. Even the counter jumpers in this layout are crawlin' into their shells. Scared stiff. Ain't I seen some o' Theodorik Perrine's gang among those present? Yeah."

He was, all of a sudden, knocked back. A young woman with rosebud cheeks and alert eyes had collided with him. She stepped aside, half confused, half-laughing. "I beg your pardon, Mr. Moran."

His hat came off instantly, and he suffered the agonies of embarrassment. "Why, say, I'd ought to be shot fer blockin' the way. Ma'am, you'll excuse me."

"Really," said the young lady, still smiling, "it was my fault." And, looking straight into his eyes, she added a low and swift command. "Come up to my room, eighteen, right away." With that Gay Thatcher passed into the hotel.

Mack Moran replaced his hat and surveyed the landscape with a bland, indifferent air. He rolled a cigarette, stopped a passing acquaintance, and talked a few moments. He rocked on his heels, looked at his watch, and rubbed the face of it with a scrupulous concern. Then, having sufficiently established an apparent idleness, he ambled down the street. Abreast the bar's entrance to the Gusher, he paused and admirably portrayed the state of mind of a gentleman debating over the desirability of going in for a drink. Temptation, resistance, and surrender passed plainly across his shrewd, fighter's face. He walked in, lifted a symbolic finger to the barkeep, and imbibed. Paying for the potion, he seemed to be hit hard by a novel idea.

"Say, is that jewelry salesman still around?"

"Yeah," replied the barkeep.

"I want to see him," muttered Mack. "Figger to have an elk tush mounted." Obeying the idea, he marched up the back stairs of the Gusher and down to the room numbered eighteen. He started to knock, but was forestalled by the sight of Gay Thatcher on the threshold, beckoning him in. The door closed quickly.

CHAPTER ELEVEN

THE ATTACK ON THE JAIL

Mack Moran was a plain unadorned product of the range. He walked and he rode with his head up, asking concessions of nobody, claiming the freedom to do as he pleased and go where he pleased. He had nerve enough to pass that popular and mythical test of spitting in a grizzly's face; and Roaring Horse, in furtherance of the idea, allowed that Mack was perfectly willing to let the grizzly have first spit. He was a small man, but he never allowed that to handicap him; and his conversation was open, unhemstitched, and sometimes slightly scurrillous.

Such was the reputation of the gentleman as

he stepped inside Gay Thatcher's room. Yet the moment the door closed behind him and he found himself closeted alone for the first time with a young woman of recognized standing and undeniable pulchritude a sort of panic struck him, unnerved him, paralyzed him. He was at the moment as nearly petrified as it is possible for a human to become and yet draw breath. He grew as rosy as a Kentucky belle at her first ball. With his hat removed and the weight of his body canted over on one foot he looked exactly like a man who had been caught stealing sheep; or, what was worse, eating sheep. And he mumbled incoherently: "Yes'm."

The worry on Gay Thatcher's forehead relaxed an instant. She smiled. "I am perfectly harmless, Mr. Moran. Your reputation is perfectly safe. Perhaps if you rolled a smoke you'd feel more at ease."

Mack sought for something to say and found it. "Ladies and hosses—yuh never know just what they'll do." That was out and it sounded funny. He was immediately sorry.

"Many a man has gone through life not recognizing that," said Gay. "It isn't complimentary, but it is almost true." The smile departed. She bent forward, her clear eyes searching Mack. "I have heard about Jim Chaffee. Tell me—there isn't anything serious about it? He'll be out of jail soon, won't he?"

Turned to a familiar topic, Mack lost his embarrassment. "Two weeks ago I'd of said yes. Slade drew first. A bunch of men have told me. The town was full of Theodorik's gents, all layin' for Jim. Shucks, any other time, Jim couldn't of been jugged. It's an iron-clad rule hereabouts, and always has been, that the fellow which pulls first is just out of luck if he stops a bullet. Only exception is when some hire gun artist does the job. Such a gent is apt to win a fight and still lose his neck. Accordin' to sentiment." He stopped, not sure what he wanted to say.

"Well?" prompted Gay.

"Jim's in a heap of trouble. Country's changed a lot since Satterlee died. They's a raft of strange dudes roamin' the streets. I've had a bug put in my ear. They aim to haul Jim out after dark. That's what the schedule calls for."

He thought the information would shock her. It usually shocked people who were not accustomed to range tactics. But he was mistaken. She didn't flinch, she didn't break out with a lot of comments about injustice. All she did was ask a quiet question. "Will the sheriff permit that?"

"I bet a hat this sheriff will," said Mack

vehemently. "It's a crooked game all the way through. "If they thought they could get a packed jury they'd let him stand trial. But they ain't that sure of themselves. Apt to be a kick back. So it's the easy way out they're takin'."

"Who is behind this?"

Mack pondered. His training was all against naming names. And he had heard since time immemorial that women couldn't keep secrets. "I ain't sure," said he evasively. "Might make a bum guess."

"But you think you know?" she persisted.

"You bet."

He was immensely relieved to find she didn't press the question. She walked around the room, her oval face drawn sharply. Mack was no hand at judging women, but he was struck by the thought that she didn't seem like a stranger in the land. Didn't act like one. And she was pretty.

She turned back to him. "Is there anything I can do?"

It was on the tip of his tongue to say no. Then it occurred to him that here was a possible solution to his main problem. "They got Jim in solitary. I ain't able to get within shoutin' distance of him. Mebbe you could."

"I think so. What do you want me to tell him?"

That took Mack off his feet. He was dumfounded and he showed it. The girl shook her head, almost impatiently. "You are mistaken about me, Mr. Moran. Which is not unusual. Most men are. What you have told me is just what I have heard myself. Perhaps I know a little something about conditions here. If there is no other way—then we have to fight fire with fire."

"Ma'am, yore dippin' yore clean fingers into skulduggery."

"What do you want me to tell him?"

He rehearsed the situation in his own mind before answering. "Tell him to watch that window about eight o'clock tonight. Gil Daugherty will try to make the courthouse roof and lower a couple of ropes without the guards' catchin' on. Jim'll get the rest of it."

"All right." And she further astonished him by the activeness of her thoughts. "Now supposing there is trouble and you miss connections with him after he gets free? Where is his horse to be—where will you be?"

"Son-of-a-gun," breathed Mack. "Where have you been all these years? I will remove my hat to yuh. The hoss will be in the alley between the restaurant and Tilton's. If he can't make that, tell him to hit for the rodeo field. Be another there. Me, I got to make connections. I'm ridin' wherever he rides.

The rest of the boys'll block off trouble for a little while."

"I'll go down now," said Gay.

That was all. Mack wanted to express the proper sentiments, but didn't know how. So he bowed himself out and left the hotel by the same way he had entered. A little later, loitering by the stable, he saw her walking toward the courthouse. And, free from the disturbing effects of her immediate presence, he caught the lithe grace of her body. She was more than pretty; nor was he the only man on the street to come to that conclusion.

Gay went directly to Luis Locklear's office. There wasn't even an argument. She smiled at the man and said she wanted to visit Jim Chaffee. That was all, and it was very simple. Yet Gay Thatcher was a shrewd judge of men, and before Luis Locklear could reply yes or no she added that she had heard pleasant things of him from the sheriff down in Bones County. Locklear swelled visibly and reached for his keys; and he looked around at the other men loitering in the room, his glance seeming to say: "Ain't I a hell on women?" Unlocking the upper stairs door he motioned her ahead.

"I will not presume to listen in on a lady's conversation. Take all the time yuh want." Gay nodded and descended the stairs. Locklear left the door ajar and turned quickly to one of his followers. "Go tell those boys at the window to see she don't pass him no gun."

The cell was at the far end of a dark, chilly corridor. A patch of light crossed the cell from the windows and broke the grating, making a grim pattern on the corridor wall. Chaffee had heard her footsteps and was in the middle of the cell. She had seen him always before as a clean-shaven man with cheerfulness lurking around the corners of his eyes; therefore she was not prepared for this Jim Chaffee. The stubble of his beard added a hardness to his features, brought out the high cheek bones, and accented the hollows of his jaw. His clothes were dirty and ripped in places. One fist seemed swollen to her. That physical injury drew her attention instantly.

"What happened to your hand?"

The light of pleasure flashed down in his eyes. He came forward, first looking across his shoulder to find the guards squatting outside the window in a position to command all that happened. "It's been a slow day," said he, "up till now. How ever did you get Luis to let you in?"

"I bribed him with a smile," answered the girl. "But your hand?"

"Rock cut it some," was his explanation. "So Luis is human, after all? That's a discovery. Now you oughtn't come around a filthy place like this."

Locklear was already impatient, perhaps sorry of his bargain. She couldn't see the man, but she heard his boots advance and retreat at the top of the stairs. "Do you know what is happening?"

"I can guess," said Chaffee, somber again. "Those boys are down to trumps. Aim to play the high one to-night."

There was little time to delay. Locklear would be down in a moment to reassure himself. Yet, apropos of nothing at all, she said:

"Jim, I think I have more faith in you than any other man I have ever known."

Chaffee took hold of the bars. "Thanks, Gay."

"I wish," she went on, quite subdued, "you felt that way about me. Oh, now what am I saying? You are without defense against me. So I pick on you. Cross that off."

"The remark goes double with me," murmured Jim.

She was smiling. "Which remark—first or second?" But she knew what he meant. "Jim—you honestly do? Knowing nothing at all about me—even knowing I have gone to a man's house who—"

"Cross *that* off," said Chaffee. "What I said stands. Who am I to be askin' questions? It's your life."

"Sometime, I wish you would ask questions—ones that hit right down to the bottom. I'd answer them." The rose color came to her cheeks. "Is it the mournfulness of a jail that makes me so frank? But sometimes I wish you would."

"Why?"

"Because," said she, taking a woman's privilege of the word. Luis Locklear had stopped at the top of the stairway, as if debating. The girl bent nearer Chaffee. "Mack Moran is in town."

"That fellow—" began Chaffee, and broke off, arguing with his feeling. "Mack Moran is a man, Gay. I wish I knew another one like him. Tryin' to see me but can't get by the bloodhounds, I reckon?"

Her voice dropped to the faintest whisper. "Eight o'clock. Watch for a rope dropped down to the window. Tie it. Horse in the alley by Tilton's. If you can't reach that go to the rodeo field." Locklear was at last on his way, moving clumsily. The girl reached through and touched his hand. "I don't know—but the Lord bless you, Jim."

Locklear was in the corridor, able to hear what they said. Jim Chaffee spoke casually. "When are you goin' back?"

"I don't know," replied Gay. "But—but not for a while."

"Through?" asked Locklear, trying to be jovial.

"Thank you, yes. I didn't want to leave Roaring Horse without seeing him. I'm sure you understand, Sheriff Locklear."

"Oh, certainly, certainly," agreed Locklear. "I will escort you to the door."

Leaving the courthouse the girl went quickly back to the Gusher. She saw Mack Moran standing by the stable and she nodded to him. Mack's wiry cheeks never changed. But he got the message she intended.

Five o'clock was dusk. And at that hour Theodorik Perrine entered the Gusher by an alley door and climbed to the suite always set aside for William Wells Woolfridge. The gentleman was there.

"All right?" asked Perrine, thrusting his head through the door.

"Come in."

"Nobody saw me," volunteered Perrine, standing in front of Woolfridge. As tough a character as he was, he never ventured to sit down in the presence of Woolfridge unless the latter asked him, which was seldom.

"I am relaxing my precautions," replied Woolfridge. "It becomes less important—secrecy. Very shortly now this country will know just exactly where I stand."

"Well, then, let me take charge of this party to-night. Yuh been holdin' me off long enough. Chaffee's my game."

"I see his friends have come to town. What for?"

"To get him out," said Theodorik Perrine, his great jowls snapping. "But we got 'em stopped. Outnumbered. If they start a play they're sunk."

Woolfridge absorbed the news. "Any idea how they'll go about getting him free?"

"No, I ain't. But they can't make a move without exposin' themselves."

"Then," said Woolfridge, biting into the words, "why not let them try?"

"Never thought about it."

"I have." Woolfridge rose, smoothing the lapels of his coat carefully. The chubby cheeks squared, the businesslike blandness fell away. There was a queer, shuttering light in his normally expressionless eyes. "I have thought of it a great deal. It is much better to let the gentleman break jail and be shot down than to take him out and hang him. In the former case he is legally killed. In the latter we are going pretty strong. It might trip us up later. Stirrup S is working nicely into the whole thing. Are you sure you can control the situation?"

"You bet."

"Chaffee is a dangerous man. He knows

entirely too much. More to the point, he is the kind of a free agent I don't want on my trail. He possesses more initiative and imagination than I care about. I repeat, he is dangerous, both for what he has found out and for what he will find out if he gets clear."

"He won't," said Perrine, shutting his massive jaws on the words.

"Then let them try to make the jail break. And take care of Chaffee when he shows himself outside the cell. That is all."

"Now have you birds got this all clear?"

Mack Moran and the rest of the Stirrup S crew stood in the deep darkness of the rodeo stands, rehearsing the event about to take place. Horses moved restlessly behind them, long lengths of rope lay on the ground. "We can't afford to have any mistakes. One horse here. One horse down the alley by Tilton's. Spec, you take care of that. Gil climbs the eatin' place, crosses the Red Mill room, and swarms up the courthouse turret dingbat, draggin' ropes behind. Got it all straight, Gil?"

"Yeah. Some harder to do than that time in Arizona. Roof is crooked. But I'll make it."

"All right. Lin Tavish, you follow Gil along the roofs to keep the ropes from kinkin' up.

McDermitt is on the ground, holding to the loose ends of said ropes, ready to dally 'em. I'm busy with the horses. McDermitt and me does the business of jerkin' the bars loose. Rufus, Baldy, and Ed Wing go along back there with us to do any necessary shootin' that comes to a head. Which leaves thirteen to ride hell bent down the street to the front of the courthouse when the time comes and draw everybody's attention thataway. You gents wait right here until the signal goes. Gil does his job, eases back from the roofs, and walks out to the middle of the street. And howls like he's poisoned. That's the signal for all of us. You come in, make a lot of noise, and bluff the sheriff. We do our duty at the back. Jim gets out. And him and me breaks for the brush. You boys stick around to cover us while we get a head start. There's the dope."

Somebody came into the field afoot, breathing hard. "It's Chitty," said the arrival, identifying himself.

"What'd yuh find?" asked Mack.

"Them fellows is movin' around town like they smelled a skunk," replied Chitty.

"Which is natural," observed Mack. "They know we're up to somethin'. We can't hide that. Only they don't know which way we aim to bust. What else?"

"Far as I can make out," proceeded Chitty,

"they's about four-five back there guardin' the winda. Must be a whole dozen hangin' around the courthouse steps. And about the same number just moochin' here and there. All over the premises."

Mack drew a breath, speaking quietly. "I guess we're set. Let's go."

He moved away, trailed by the six who were to do the main job in back of town. They made a wide detour of the street end, going a quarter mile into the open desert and cautiously closing in upon the south side of Roaring Horse. Past a corral, past sagging sheds and around all the junk and litter of twenty years' making. A light sprang suddenly out of a hotel window and nearly transfixed them; they fell away and skirted a mountain of dry-goods boxes. Directly against the malodorous rear porch of the restaurant they came to a halt. Mack bent. Gil Daugherty stepped on Mack's cupped hands. A small "hup" exploded from Mack, and Gil shot upward, twisted across shingled eaves, and was lost in the velvet shadows. Rope payed out with a soft snoring murmur. "Goin' back now," whispered Mack and disappeared.

He had elected to make the trip twice in order to keep in touch with both groups and see that nothing went wrong. The bulk of the Stirrup S crew waited with an increasing skittishness in the rodeo field. "I'm takin' my horse, and I want Spec's buckskin. It's the best of the lot, and Jim'll need it. Correct?"

Evidently it was correct. One of the bunch wanted to know what to do if the whole gang got split up following the fireworks. "Every man for himself," decided Mack. "But figger to meet on the road home at about Chickman's creek. And stay home. They might come there and try to burn the outfit. I'm goin'." He took the horses and followed a still wider detour around to the south side. This time he avoided the back of the hotel entirely and left the ponies standing a good fifty yards distant, himself closing on McDermitt and the others. McDermitt was softly cursing. "Damn' rope fouled once. Lin come all the way back to clear it. He's got all I can give him now." This much in a pungent, nervous whispering. Mack moved off, crawling along the end wall of the Red Mill. A hundred yards farther, cloaked in darkness and silence, were the guards. It seemed to him they were unusually silent. That worried him. He returned to McDermitt.

"Think it's done," was the latter's sibilant whisper. "Judas, I'm wringin' wet!"

Lin Tavish dropped down from the roof. Another minute and old Gil Daugherty followed, badly winded. "Fixed."

"Wait." Mack groped to the horses and brought them in. McDermitt dallied a rope end to each horn. "All right."

Mack had trouble in keeping his words muffled. "Ed, Rufe, Baldly—yore turn now. Inch around to the far side of the courthouse. When the boys larrup down the street you start shootin' high. Draw the attention of them guards offen the window. Yuh got three minutes to make it."

Those three minutes dragged interminably. The night seemed to be full of extraordinary sounds, yet nothing emerged from the area around the window. Mack sighed. McDermitt swore. Gil muttered, "Time now?"

"Yeah." More waiting while Gil threaded the alley. Yet as they swung into the saddles they heard the wild Apache yell of Gil Daugherty ringing like a trumpet over the housetops and sounding down the street. The echoes of it were still alive when the main body of Stirrup S came thundering in. Guns were out; the beat of shots surged one into another. The clamor rose; those dark shadows pulsed to shrill cries of defiance launched along with the fusillade. All this swirled and smashed along the street and back through the alleys; then gathered into a whirlpool of fury in front of the courthouse.

"Now!" breathed Mack.

"Let's go!"

The three men over at a corner of the courthouse opened fire in unison, waking an immediate and vicious response. The horses walked five yards before the rope set a tension on the horns. "Now," repeated Mack. "Into 'er!" Spurs sank. Beyond, the gun reports spat and crashed, wood popped, and Luis Locklear was shouting angrily. Behind the courthouse a pitched battle seemed to be in session.

"She's out!" muttered Mack.

"Yeh. Gosh I'm thirsty!"

"Slack off—let the ropes go! Come on—we'll get Jim or bust a laig! T'hell with them dudes!"

The two of them started side by side toward the courthouse window. Lin Tavish stumbled against them and joined the galloping advance. A back door of the Red Mill swung ajar and Mack whipped a shot directly beside it. Somebody shouted, and the door slammed hard enough to shake the rickety structure. Somewhere Gil Daugherty was still howling and the sound of it added to the weird and battering and blood-stirring pattern of violence abroad in the shuttering blackness.

"Wait a minute."

A galloping figure came toward them, beating bottles and boxes out of the path. Came recklessly. *"Quien es?"*

"Jim?"

"All right, Mack. Where's that horse? Give me a gun. I'm naked. Damn your soul, you sure can wreck a town once you get started! Come on—let's sift. Where's that horse?"

All of them racked back past the Red Mill, the restaurant, and Tilton's. Down that alley were the horses. Chaffee caught one and swung up. Mack was stabbing orders at the rest of the group. "McDermitt, ride around and holler at them boys sendin' slugs into the breeze. Say it's all over. Tell 'em to bust. Hey, Jim, where in hell yuh goin'?"

Chaffee was pushing his horse down the alley toward the street. "Come on, Mack. I've got to let these fellows out here know it's time to depart. Don't want 'em holdin' the sack till somebody gets hurt. Here we go!" He reined the pony about and clattered across the sidewalk, swirling into the middle of the street. He rose in the stirrups with the lamplight of the Gusher falling fully upon him and sent out the long, rising cry of the range. Mack shot in front of him, urging haste. Chaffee turned. And together they raced eastward and out of Roaring Horse. A hundred yards beyond the rodeo field they looked back. The street was a merry-go-round of men and beasts, and lights were springing up from building to building.

CHAPTER TWELVE

THE JAWS OF ROARING HORSE

Just beyond the rodeo field Jim Chaffee reined in. "Wait a minute, Mack. We can't go and leave the boys all bound up with trouble. Let's—"

But Mack had fought too hard to see his victory dissipated. "Hey, cut that out. Don't get no fool ideas this late at night. Yore an escaped prisoner, an' they's a bounty on yore scalp. If yuh go back there now somebody'll knock yuh down. Never mind the boys."

"I know that," muttered Chaffee. "but it don't seem right. What's the use of tradin' my scalp for some other Stirrup S man? Locklear's just the lad to take out his grudge on whoever he can."

"No chance," Mack reassured him. "We got it all figured. The whole outfit is scattered by now. And Luis is too busy lookin' for you to monkey with anybody else. Hey, they're comin' thisaway. Let's travel."

A sizeable party galloped eastward along the street, gathering recruits and speed as it traveled. Still a little reluctant, Jim Chaffee wheeled beside his partner and the two of them raced across the undulating expanse of the dark desert. "I guess—" began Chaffee, and was cut short by Mack.

"Hush, Mister Chaffee. This is my party, ain't it? You lemme do the figurin' for the next few minutes. Now spill the scandal. What happened to you last night?"

Chaffee told him in clipped sentences. Mack never said a word until Chaffee related the stampede of the herd into the canyon. At that Mack Moran began to swear passionately. "They'll pay the bill, Jim! They'll pay it if we got to start snipin' from bush to bush! Damn their measly hearts!" Then he fell grimly silent and did not speak again for a full five minutes. "Well, that shows us they's just one thing to do. Yuh got to depart the country for a spell, Jim."

"I've been arguin' that point with myself," said Chaffee. "It goes against the grain. If I do, I'm out of the fight altogether. I'm useless. I'm runnin' away. I'm a licked dog. It don't sound good. I figure I could pick up some grub along the way and hide out over in the lava country. That's close enough to the ranch to keep connections. I could duck around and lay an ear to the ground."

"Won't work," contradicted Mack. "If it was an ordinary case o' holin' up it might do.

But yore on the official records as an escaped killer. Locklear will be on yore trail from now till somethin' drops. He's got plenty of men to do it. He's got somebody's money behind him. And they'll be a few homesteaders to squawk when they ketch sight of yuh. What'll happen? They'll get yuh cornered in the lava like some mis'able Modoc. Either they starves yuh down or they run yuh into a pocket—and yore gone. No, sir. It's over the hill for Jim Chaffee."

"How long?" asked Chaffee, knowing that Mack's logic was sound. It tallied with his own belief, but he hated to admit it.

Mack was indefinite. "Oh, till things blow over."

"That don't mean anything."

"Means a whole skin," retorted the small partner. "You've had yore fun for the time bein'. Things can't get no worse. Stay awhile till the excitement dies down and folks have a chance to see what kind of a deal the county's gettin'. Locklear'll lose his support. Then come back."

They rode two or three miles in silence. "All right," agreed Chaffee with evident reluctance.

"Fine. We'll curve toward the canyon and cross above or below. Leave that to you."

"Cross below at Linderman's," decided

Chaffee. "I don't trust Lee very far."

They had outrun the pursuing posse, lost themselves deep in the thickening night. Gradually they swung around and laid a true course toward Linderman's ferry on the lower reaches of Roaring Horse canyon. Such a route brought them nearer the main road between town and Stirrup S. The bridge at Chickman's creek lay in front of them and to the left. So they went, abating the speed to save the ponies. The hours ran along smoothly, the night air turned intensely cold to the east wind whipping down from the peaks.

"It's snowin' up on Thirty-four Pass right now," reflected Chaffee. "Early winter ahead of us."

The twin pines guarding the Chickman creek bridge stood faintly against the immediate shadows. They approached at a slow walk.

"Gang was to meet here. Mebbe have met and gone home."

"Hold it, Mack!"

There was a confused, staccato murmuring down the road in the direction of town. The partners pulled up. A group of horsemen came along at a fast gait, wavered abreast the partners about a hundred yards distant, and pounded over the bridge. "Too many for Stirrup S," grumbled Mack. "Them's the bloodhounds goin' hell-bent for the ranch."

"Listen—they're leaving the road." The clatter died almost instantly, and by that Chaffee knew the party had veered from the packed dirt and taken to the loose sand.

"What's it mean?"

"Looks to me as if they had this figured out about as cute as we have," replied Chaffee. "They're takin' a short cut to Linderman's. Mack, I've got a hunch we'd better draw away and strike for Lee's. We don't want to bust into that outfit. They'll be strung all over the landscape. I don't like Lee—he's treacherous, but it seems the best way."

"Come on, then. We shore have lost a lot of time."

Once more they changed course. And since the pursuers were off at another end of the country they forbore pressing the horses. Midnight came and passed. The angling route brought them within a mile of the canyon's rim, and this they paralleled until Chaffee's former homestead broke faintly into sight. Chaffee tarried a moment. "Seems like sixty years since I lived there," he murmured. "I'll never find a better place, or one half as good, Mack."

"Let's bust."

"I hate to pull out. It don't seem right. Almost got a notion to go back to Stirrup S and fort up."

"Expected yuh'd come to that point. Now just use sense. What would happen? Locklear'd get word damn' quick yuh was in the country. It'd give him a fine chance to bust Stirrup S wide open. No, sir, yuh'd only draw fire down on Miz Satterlee's head.'

"That's right. We travel."

They proceeded and within a half mile were warned again. A murmuring rose up from the foreground and trembled back along the earth—an illusive shuffling, tapping sound that defied location. Either men were crawling slowly through the darkness close by or they were galloping rapidly in the distance. The partners fell into a deep gully—that same gully which William Wells Woolfridge meant to use for his main ditch—and stopped.

"Can't be them buzzards has got around us," said Mack Moran. "Wish I could smoke."

"Think it's another party."

"Great snakes, how many parties is out on the warpath? . . . Blockin' both ferries against yuh. Hell . . ."

The murmuring sprang to a definite rhythm of scudding hoofs. Bridle chains jingled, and the partners, warned nearly too late, pulled out of the gully. Riders went by, leaving a backwash of talk.

"A little further . . . "

"Naw, this is foolish . . . Go back to the ferry."

Mack waited a safe interval. "Don't sound like nobody I ever heard. Now, what?"

"They're strikin' all around us. We wait awhile."

Time dragged. It might have been a quarter hour or it might have been a half hour before they picked up the signal of that scout party again. It had left the gully and split into sections. One ranged over nearer the canyon. The other seemed to be wandering piecemeal southward. Once this latter section came so close that Jim Chaffee thought he and Mack were about to be run down. Then that exploring fragment drew up and retreated, making a sudden flurry elsewhere.

"Mush smell somethin'," grumbled Mack. "Else they wouldn't be so nervous. What to do?"

"Wait it out. If we go ahead we'll maybe bust right into some wandering galoot."

The search party gathered itself eastward, between the partners and the trail to Lee's ferry. It moved away and seemed to leave the neighborhood entirely. Yet there was a queer drop-off to the sound of their retreat that left Chaffee unsatisfied. Mack was restless, muttering dire things under his breath.

The shadows fell more thickly about the land, but as they waited with patience ever shortening they saw the promise of light soon to break across the peaks.

"Got to tackle it," whispered Mack. "Can't delay no longer."

"Swing wide—don't go straight ahead."

They veered, the soft abrasion of the ponies' progress running ahead and sinking into silence. They lost a mile in that detour and much good time from the slack pace. In that interval the eastern sky broke to the coming day's first thin and cheerless wedge of light. The peaks stood dim and cold. Without speaking the partners increased their speed, and in the pale dawn they came to the rim at a point where a road dived downward into the misty depths and stopped short at Lee's ferry. They saw a light glimmering through the fog. The ferry itself was just visible, resting on the far bank. A lantern sparkled over there, too. Behind them the desert broke its vigil, pale and frosty.

"Ferry's acrost. That's bad. Make us wait twenty minutes. Meanwhile we're plumb in a trap. Jim, supposin' some o' them suckers is below waitin' for us?"

"I'm thinkin' about that item," replied Chaffee.

"Doggone, it's cold. What to do? It looks

spooky to me."

"I guess we'd better brace it," decided Chaffee. "Can't turn back now." The horses, single file, walked stiff-legged down the grade as the barren wall threw its shadow over them. Halfway, they halted and studied the house, the yard, and the surrounding buildings. Nothing but the light indicated people up and about. If any of the pursuing men were below they could only be hiding in the flimsy barn.

"It's doggone ticklish," averred Mack. "Why don't that ferry start back?"

They finally came out upon the narrow beach—the only foothold of any kind for fifteen miles along the river—and advanced to the door, still in the saddle. The door came open and a woman, old and suspicious, peered out. "What you want?"

"Ferry across."

"Ferry was stoved again' the far bank yestiday," said the woman. "Old man's over tryin' to cork up the hole now. You'll have to wait till noon, mebbe more."

This was disaster. Mack's weary face settled. Chaffee never had seen his partner take any piece of news so hard. As for himself, he was very tired, and the swift shuttling of fortune and misfortune during the last forty-eight hours left him somewhat hardened to a bad break such as this.

"Well, you've got a rowboat, haven't you?"

"Can't take horses over in a rowboat, mister," said the woman. She looked closely at the pair. "You must want to git away powerful bad. We've had lots of 'em like that. What's your name?"

"Look up!" cried Mack.

Chaffee tilted his chin. A line of horsemen tipped over the rim and started downward, headlong and reckless. A shot broke the cold air and rocketed between the towering banks, sounding strange above the unchanging surge of the river. Mack drew his gun and at sight of it the woman screamed and slammed the door. Both partners were out of the saddle and racing toward the rowboat drawn half from the water. "Boost that brute!" snapped Mack. "We'll get acrost, which is plumb more'n they'll do!"

The rowboat slid into the stream, both men scrambling aboard. Chaffee seated the oars in the rowlocks and pushed the skiff away from the shallow gravel. The swift current gripped the boat in a vise and shot it downward; Chaffee threw his weight full against the oars; they quartered across the grass-green surface.

The posse was almost down; guns began to wake the echoes. Across on the ferry side old man Lee straightened and ran momentarily out of sight. When he reappeared there was a short barreled shotgun in his fists. He peered through the thin fog, raising the gun uncertainly, not knowing what to expect. Mack Moran yelled at him, but the sound of the water only blurred Mack's meaning. The posse raced to the river's edge and laid a line of fire against the boat, all shots falling short. The woman screamed again and it may have been that Xavier Francois Lonestar Lee heard that scream, though the noise of the canyon might have absorbed so shrill a sound before it reached the man's ears. But at any rate he saw the posse through the fog and he heard them shooting; and he obeyed a natural, primitive impulse. Raising the shotgun he fired point-blank at the nearing boat. The fine shot sang and snapped in the water. Mack yelled again and ducked. "Let 'er go! The crazy loon's reachin' for more shells!"

The second blast came sleeting across the interval, indescribably vicious as it sheered and spat in the current and whined against the boat's side. Jim Chaffee felt a thin, sharp pain slicing into his shoulder; turning, he saw that Lee was making ready for another aim, and he understood then how impossible the situation had of a sudden become. Buckshot was deadly; he dared not attempt to bluff through it. So he reversed the impulse of the oars and the boat, urged onward by the added force, raced into the dim, droning depths of the canyon.

Mack Moran's immediate reaction was one of absurd, hilarious satisfaction. "Doggone that Lee person. He'll never get this boat back again. Serves him right." Then he noticed Chaffee's wrist muscles snapping hard against the oars and at that point the full realization of the approaching ordeal smote him squarely in the middle of his shoulder blades. His leathery cheeks tightened; through the gray gloom his face seemed to pucker owlishly, and there appeared to be a withdrawal of blood from his compressed lips. "Man, let's you and me hit for the shore sudden."

"What shore?"

"Huh?" Mack looked around, startled. The lower end of that gravel strip upon which Lee's house precariously perched was sliding past them, narrowing swiftly to nothing more than a ledge. Even as he looked that ledge fell away into the river and was absorbed by the sheer face of the canyon wall and there was nothing left but a stubborn, black expanse of pitted rock rising and vanishing beyond the curling mists. The booming fury of water struggling through the farther recesses grew perceptibly louder. Chaffee threw his weight against the oars and the skiff, traveling stern foremost, shot along like a thing alive. Mack protested. "Say, we're goin' thirty miles an hour, or I'm an Australian boomerang thrower. What's the need of all this hustle? Let's slow down some and consider the matter in detail. Me, I don't like to rush."

"Ain't going as fast as we seem," said Chaffee. "But we might just as well get this over with. It don't do any good to think about Devil's Boil too long. Wonder if that posse is racin' along the rim to reach Linderman's ahead of us?"

Sight of Lee's ferry long ago had been shut off by the fog wreath. "Last I saw," said Mack, "they was all lined up on the shore, gawpin' at us. Didn't seem to be in no hurry."

"Reasonable for them to look at it that way," was Chaffee's grim observation. "Better take off your boots and shirt."

"No, sir, I hate to get my feet wet."

"Well, here's where we start. Lay down on the bottom, Mack, so I can see the rocks comin' up."

Mack obeyed. The boat began to pitch, stern rising and slapping into the rollers. Up from the throat of the gorge came the sound as of a high wind beating through a forest, of water pouring mightily over a cliff. Chaffee lifted his oars and let the craft drift of its own momentum. Ahead, the river seemed to slant at an increased angle—another piece of deception moving water holds up to man—and from wall to wall there was nothing but white spearheads flashing dully in the half light. The boat leaped onward and began to turn. Chaffee dipped an oar, almost losing it. He dug in, pulled the boat square with the current, and rested again. The black jaws of a rock yawned beside him, spray lashed out and spattered the prone Mack.

"Sunk?" yelled Mack, half rising.

The boat rose and dropped with a force that knocked the puncher flat on his face. They were gripped by warring eddies, pulled and battered and rocked. Chaffee lowered both oars and braked the boat's speed, body weaving, muscles and joints crackling with the immense pressure. Mack lifted his head again and found himself canted against one side, staring into a hollow that appeared to be carved from green glass. The boat sprang back; all this was behind them, smooth water lapped against the boards. Chaffee sagged and wiped sweat and spray from his face.

Mack crawled to the stern seat and rolled a cigarette, trying to speak casually. "Well, guess that was the worst of it, uh?"

"You know better. We ain't been nowhere yet."

Our sunny, light-hearted friend speakin'.

Never thought I'd ever get seasick out in the middle of the desert. But I shore squirmed back yonder. Say—look—there's a place we could step ashore. See that shelf?"

"Yeah. And see what's back of it. A wall, straight up. Would it buy us anything to land? Can't fly out of this hole. And nobody's goin' to row down after us."

"If I ever get ashore once—" muttered Mack.

"Do you hear somethin'?"

The canyon trembled with it—a faint, pulsating snore that sounded like the guttering of some primeval monster; yet the tempo remained constant, never varying, never dying out. The farther they floated the deeper and more thunderous was the reverberation thrown across the towering walls. And somehow, for all the advancing light of day, the gorge was plunged in a more profound twilight. It began to narrow, and Chaffee discovered a point jutting out in front of them. The smoothness of the stream face was broken into warning ridges. White water beckoned. Around that approaching point began the Long Slide, terminating in the Devil's Boil. Of the four men who had started from Lee's in the past thirty years, three had lost their lives in the Boil; and to that mad, tortured area with its great vaults battered by dynamic hydraulic attacks and its tempestuous suction Mack Moran and Jim Chaffee were now rapidly approaching.

"Yuh, I hear it," grumbled Mack. He looked longingly to the faint strip of shelving on the south side. "I bet a man could cut some sort of a stone ladder up there, Jim."

"What with?"

"There yuh go again. Well, call me for breakfast, Mister Chaffee. If I hear a trumpet or a harp I'll know it won't be beans and bacon. Go to it, kid."

The rough water took them, the boat shot around the jutting point of the south wall. The incline of the river's bed seemed far greater than at any previous stage of the trip. As they straightened into the Long Slide a vast roar battered either precipice and they were actually dizzied by the impact of a vibrating, stuttering conflict of force against force just beyond sight. In another moment a charging white wall of water broke through the fog; spray covered them. Chaffee, dog tired, pulled in the oars.

"What's the use of dippin' a toothpick in Niagara?" The torrent of sound tore the words out of his mouth. Mack looked backward. Chaffee leaned down. "One man made it! Hang on to your pants! Here we go!"

Mack's face was blurred in the mist, but he

winked and clamped both arms around the stern seat. Chaffee jammed his feet between boat bottom and the middle seat. The skiff swayed and lurched into a trough; at that moment Chaffee had a clear view of the Devil's Boil—nothing but cascading fury to one side and a slick, uprearing wall of water that seemed to defy the law of gravity on the other. Seeing it, he pushed the oars under him, pulled himself as low as he could, and tightened all muscles.

There is in water a power that nothing else under the blue canopy of heaven possesses. Man may dam it, yet the slowly impounding force laps away at the barrier, constantly making sallies and thrusts and forever threatening to break free; man may ride upon it, but never with a sure sense of safety, for it is a thing alive, ceaseless and destructive. It wears away all before it; it moves onward, nor can anything check its final victory. So, as Chaffee rode into the mists of fury, he resigned himself to death as others had done, even though in the dim recesses of his being the unquenchable flame of life desire still burned. One man had made it, and therefore some alley existed through the wild and charging torrent. Thus, with hope and despair alternating, he saw himself being drawn into the terrific maw of the Boil. The boat was past anyone's power to check, racing along the slide with a speed that taxed his senses. He felt a suction pulling it lower in the water. Whether or not it was true, he did see that the surface of the stream sliced nearer the gunwales, accompanied by a sound that was something like the frying of bacon in a pan. The mists turned by degrees from a damp blanket to an actual downpour; moment by moment the canyon walls became dimmer and his ears were drummed with an intensity of attack he had never yet experienced. From the heights of the canyon he often had heard the drone of this cataclysmic force; down here, caught in its grip, the sound was more like a mingled screaming and exploding of the elements.

The boat was filling with water. So far the speed or the suction had kept it from pitching much, but as the last sight of the walls obscured and died, and even the bulk of the craft itself was barely visible, the suction appeared to let go; instantly it began a crazy, side for side and end to end careening. The water gushed around Chaffee's feet. Great cascades drenched him, strangled him; and all the while he was alone, one tiny cell of living life surrounded by destruction. In a moment of clearheadedness he wondered if Mack was still in the boat. He didn't know, couldn't hear his partner even if Mack shouted at the top of his lungs, and couldn't see him. More things were happening in those few seconds than he could grasp. But he did feel a slacking off of the punishment, and then the suction took hold again and the boat began to travel in a vast circle, impelled to a greater speed, thrown higher at each revolution until it seemed certain that in time it would reach some top-heavy angle and turn over. Nothing, he knew, kept the boat from being beaten into fragments but the steady rhythm of the whirlpool they were in. And he lost count entirely of the time.

But it seemed forever. It seemed like days since he and Mack had embarked from Lee's ferry. So much for the illusion of time. The mighty reverberation played tricks with him; seemed first behind him, then in front of him. And actually appeared to sink below. Then—and it was like being released alive from a burial vault—he caught a faint sight of the sky, and he saw one rim of the canyon perched at some crazy angle. They were traveling upward, no doubt of it. The sensation was too acute to be mistaken; and in another moment he had a small view of Mack, all in a knot. They were traveling again at great speed—and straight ahead. The sky became clearer, and for an interval the drenching sprays diminished; Chaffee even wondered if he might try the oars. It was an idle thought at the moment, for the boat was checked, smashed by some reverse current; and then they fell dizzily, the pit of Chaffee's stomach rising and his feet pushing harder and harder against the floor boards to avert what must be the fatal crash.

The crash never came. It was as if they were hooked to a great cradle, swinging from side to side. Then, in one more flashing interval of time, that was all changed. The boat leaped high, swung around, poised and turned over, with both of them struggling beneath it. Chaffee, trying to keep some order in his head, unlocked his body, pulled himself to the surface and looked around. Mack was perched on the upturned bow, and ahead of them lay the finest sight, the most beautiful stretch of nature Chaffee thought he had ever laid eyes upon—calm water.

The Boil was behind, and somehow the sound of it was no longer sinister. Actually it looked like a pretty fine spectacle. So they went rocking precariously through the lee riffles and struck a sluggish eddy.

"G-got a cigareet?" said Mack in a voice that was but a thin shadow of itself.

"What makes you stutter?" questioned Chaffee, nor could he understand the reedy little noise in his throat.

"Got a bit cold," explained Mack, and then began to swear. "Y'don't look so light hearted yoreself, by—"

Chaffee studied the receding Boil. "Mack, have you got any mortal idea how we squeezed through that cataract? Hell, it's a mile high and forty feet thick."

"No, and I ain't aimin' to go back to find out, either. Man, I died so many times in the last few minutes I got no fear of the grave left. I bet St. Peter is hangin' up a set of wings right now which he was aimin' to try on me."

"Well, it's over. Oars gone, boat leakin', everything ready to fall apart, includin' the contents. Let's try to push this thing ashore and empty it out. Then proceed with due leisure to Linderman's."

Hank Linderman at sunup of that morning was skinning hides on the north side of the river where Roaring Horse made a slack eddy. The bluffs here were sloping and not very tall. His house stood on top of the bluffs, and his ferry swayed against its cable, also on the north shore. The day was young and promised to be fresh and cold, but down in the eddy was a vast stench where the Stirrup S cattle had lodged after being driven over by Theodorik Perrine. And he was skinning hides when something attracted his attention up the river. Rising, he saw a boat floating toward him, oars gone, and two men sprawled against the seats in postures of infinite, mortal weariness. Knowing as much as he did about this river, Linderman was so completely astonished that he dropped his knife and walked three feet into the water.

"Great jumpin' Judas—where yuh been?"

Chaffee shunted the boat inward by sculling with his palms. Mack Moran was smoking a cigarette that had miraculously escaped the deluge, and he didn't seem to hear Linderman. Later, when they were nearer shore, he began talking to himself. "We made history. Yessir, we shore made a lot of history in damn' little time. Them pearly gates opened, and I heard distinct a gent callin' the roll. Got to my name and began lookin' around. 'What, not here?' thunders Peter. 'Nossir,' says a guardeen angel. 'He's late—got hung up down yonder.' 'Put back that pair o' number four wings, then,' yells Peter, 'and let him be deprived of everlastin' joy fer another few years.' Then them doors closed, and I shore did hear the lock click. We made history, you bet."

The boat touched land and both men crawled stiffly out.

"From Lee's?" asked Linderman, knowing it could be from nowhere else, yet still unbelieving.

"Yeah," said Chaffee. "Seen anything of a posse on the south bank lately?"

"And he passes it off like that," mourned Mack Moran, having trouble with his legs.

"So that's it?" grunted Linderman. "That's why they was fellas foolin' acrost the river all night long. I ain't seen none this mornin' yet. Who would it be, Jim?"

"Perrine—et al. Not here recently, huh?" Chaffee looked to Mack. "I guess they didn't think it worth while to ride along the rim."

"Goram my soul," breathed Linderman. "Down the river from Lee's! Just you let me tell this, by the shades! Down the river from Lee's! I will be everlastingly condemned!"

"Got a couple of horses and saddles, Hank?" asked Chaffee. "Trouble over in Roarin' Horse. New deal, and it ain't exactly on the level. I've got to pull freight for a while. Mack's goin' back after he's got his bearings."

"No deal is straight with Perrine in it," reflected Linderman. "Yeah, I got a couple of horses. But, boys, I don't want Perrine on my head. Don't want him to think I willingly helped folks against him. And, still, I wouldn't like to lie about it."

"A light dawns," murmured Moran. He drew his gun and waved it in Linderman's direction. "Fella, you see the business end of a forced request."

"That's better," grinned Linderman. "I'm bein' urged at the point of a gun. No lie to that. Now put your hand artillery away and climb up the slope." They followed him along the trail. On the way he spoke about the hides. "You fellows know an awful lot of your cattle went over the rim? I'm skinnin' hides. Your fences must be out of commission."

"Wire cut," was Chaffee's brief reply.

They reached the top of the bluff. Passing the house, Linderman raised his voice. "Mamma, git a snack on the table in a hurry for a couple of outlaws.

Mrs. Linderman peered through the door, smiled, and disappeared. Linderman took the partners to the barn and indicated a pair of ponies. "Both stout. Both a little wild. But they'll do. Bring 'em back in your own good time. Now let's go get that snack."

Ten minutes later Chaffee and Moran were in the saddle.

"Well, kid," said Mack, "be good. Where yuh goin'?"

"Think I'll cross Thirty-four Pass into Miles Valley. Won't be gone long. I hate to run away."

"Nothin' else to do," replied Mack. "We got that all figgered. They got you on a nail, for the time bein'. Best to clear out so's we boys won't be all complicated. That gang ain't got nothin' but a little general hell raisin' against us. Won't dare get too hostile about it. Locklear can't force his hand that strong. But they'll go the limit to get you. So beat it, and don't worry. We're all safe. Stay away till the fire burns down and Luis stubs his toe."

"It ain't Luis altogether," said Chaffee, wistfully studying the horizons. "It's somebody else. Woolfridge, I'm pretty sure, though I don't get all his ideas. And maybe it won't blow over so soon. Well, I'll drift across the pass and write a letter from Bannock City. You keep me posted. I ain't going to stay away forever. May be back in a week or so. Meanwhile, you watch out."

"They ain't got nothin' on me," reassured Mack. "I'm hittin' home. We'll take care of Stirrup S."

"I hate to go," repeated Jim Chaffee.

"Yeah, I know."

"Well—so long, kid. Take care of yourself."

"So long, Jim. Be good."

Chaffee turned and galloped eastward. Some yards along he turned and Mack raised his hand, shouting: "We shore made history." Then Chaffee was beyond earshot, and Mack swung down the bluff and crossed to the south bank on the ferry. Hank Linderman returned to his hides, still marveling. Sometime later he heard a faint gunshot report come over the south bluff, but he thought nothing about it. "All the way from Lee's," he muttered. "Goram my soul!"

Chaffee went arrow straight for the bench. The sentinel peaks glittered brightly in the morning light, and snow covered the slopes well below the timber line. Storm caps hovered along the summits. Veering away from the canyon, he reached Gorman's Lodge at a thousand feet above the desert's level early in the afternoon. He bought a couple days' supplies and pushed upward. The trail stiffened, the first trace of snow appeared on the ground, and the wind grew shriller. The pass, he knew, would be deeply banked, but he had made this trip previously as late as Christmas and he never doubted his ability to reach the summit by night and sleep in the cabin there. From the summit it was another day's ride into Bannock City.

The sap was drained out of him. For three days he had been fighting and riding continually; twice in that time he had seen his very existence trembling in the balance. The stampede was bad enough, but the ride through Devil's Boil had scattered his nerves beyond belief. So he rode the trail slackly. The snow grew heavier; the wind grew whiter with the thickening flakes. His horse shied at something and Chaffee fought the animal back to the path. Dusk found them a steep and rugged mile short of the cabin, breasting the powdered drifts. And of a sudden, from the distance, there floated a weird call, borne abreast the rising gale. The pony, just recovered from one spell of skittishness, leaped aside. Chaffee was sitting loose and the unexpected maneuver threw him clear of the saddle. He struck half on one arm and half on his heels, the weight of his body checked by a boulder rising above the snow crust. The pony wheeled and galloped down the trail, soon lost in the shadows.

Chaffee's first thought was to rise and follow back. Pushing himself upright, he braced his body by the rock; as the pressure shifted to his feet a stab of pain ran him through. He fell to the ground, realizing one ankle was either broken or so badly twisted that walking was beyond question. The rising wind in that short time had molded fine drifts of snow on his shoulders and in the wrinkles of his coat.

CHAPTER THIRTEEN

SURRENDER

Miz Satterlee sat at one end of the table, pushing the contract of sale, the deed, and the conveyance of all Stirrup S brands and marks down to William Wells Woolfridge, who sat at the other end. Josiah Craib from his place at the side took the legal instruments and scanned them with a severe glance. He signed as witness, and Mark Eagle likewise affixed his signature. Then Eagle retired from Craib's office, and Woolfridge accepted the papers, in turn passing a check to Miz Satterlee. And by that gesture all the wide-flung range land that was the dream and the pride of old Dad Satterlee passed out of the name and into alien hands. Persistence had finally won—persistence and subterfuge and pressure; the property now belonged to Woolfridge.

Miz Satterlee accepted the check, hardly looking at it. She sat very straight in the chair. Her mouth was tightly pursed, and her eyes, still the vigorous and expressive eyes of her youth, fell squarely upon Woolfridge.

"I have given in, sir."

Woolfridge bowed. "In my life, Mrs. Satterlee, I have found that everybody has a price. It is only a matter of finding that price. You must admit, madam that in this case I have not tried to haggle. You must admit I have paid a just sum."

"I never argue," replied Miz Satterlee, and for once the weariness showed through. Yet she was too proud to reveal the resentment. "I only say that I sell to you in order to avoid further shedding of blood. I will not stand by and see my boys killed and driven away and ambushed. Nothing is worth that."

"Surely, Mrs. Satterlee, you are not laying all that to my door—"

"I detest a liar. Do you deny driving Jim Chaffee out of the country?"

Woolfridge's chubby cheeks flushed until the freckles were buried in color. The formal politeness congealed. "The man was a murderer. He was escaping from justice—"

"Do you deny having Mack Moran shot down in the road and nearly killed?"

"I regret that. I had nothing to do with it. You must realize that he was instrumental in Chaffee's escape and that the posse, disappointed in not bagging him, might have gone beyond reason in shooting Moran. And Moran was really an accessory."

"Do you deny ordering my cattle stampeded over the bluffs?"

Woolfridge raised his hand. And at once his face hardened; the autocratic and arbitrary mandarin spirit slanted out beneath his slightly drooping lids. "I owe you all respect, madam, but in fairness—"

"Fairness, Mr. Woolfridge? I detest a hypocrite. You have won. Why not be proud of your weapons, since you do so well with them?"

"I have never denied that I wanted Stirrup S badly, Mrs. Satterlee," was Woolfridge's sharp rejoinder. "Nor have I ever hesitated about the price to be paid. If you desire honesty, I will add that the price includes other items besides that check I have handed you. Now if I can be of any assistance in helping you move—"

"I require no help. I will remain in the hotel."

Woolfridge permitted himself a thin smile. "I do not wish to take any further advantage. Knowing that you certainly would not wish to remain under my hospitality I might say that I own the hotel."

Miz Satterlee rose. "I am glad to know it. In that case I will look for a house."

"You may probably find that I own a great many of the houses as well," added Woolfridge. He was enjoying this; such courteously spoken phrases with a barbed tip to them were much to his taste now that he was in a position to reveal the extent of his power.

"Do you own all of Roaring Horse, Mr. Woolfridge?" demanded Miz Satterlee, losing a little of her self-control. "Are you trying to drive me from this county?"

"I own a great deal of the county—all that I need. No, madam, I am not trying to drive you away. Why should I? But it would perhaps be far better for your own happiness if you did go."

Josiah Craib broke his long silence. He, too, rose and his bony head bobbed at Woolfridge. "That will be enough. Ma'am, let me escort you to the door." The two of them crossed the bank room. At the door Craib spoke earnestly. "Miz Satterlee, whatever has happened, I wish you could still regard me as a personal friend."

The woman turned and looked into his sparse, raw-boned face. "Craib," said she with more of sadness and emotion than at any other time during the interview, "I wish I knew you."

He was about to answer that. Yet he never did. Instead he bowed an awkward, craning motion of his gaunt neck and turned back. Woolfridge was smoking, and Woolfridge studied the banker coldly.

"My friend, I do not relish orders, nor suggestions."

"The remark stands," replied Craib without a particle of emotion. "I will not have Miz Satterlee badgered."

Woolfridge studied Craib, and a gleam of cold amusement became visible. "You have a stiffer backbone than I figured." Then he was blunt and peremptory. "Go get these instruments recorded. Then lock them in your safe. Keep your mouth closed as to all that has transpired between us. What is to be revealed I will reveal."

"Yes," said Craib.

Woolfridge left the bank. In passing the teller's cage he discovered Mark Eagle's following glance, and it seemed to irritate him. He paused. "My friend, I do not require my help to be friendly. I do not wish friendliness. But I do expect both politeness and respect. Think about that."

Eagle's round cheeks never moved. Woolfridge frowned and appeared to debate another idea. Whatever it was, he suppressed it for the time and went along the street to the hotel. In his suite of rooms he relaxed. There was a map on his desk. To that map he directed his attention, erasing certain boundary lines and inserting others. And when, later that afternoon, the stage dropped a passenger from down-territory, he was still studying the map. In that posture the newcomer found him.

"You are late," said Woolfridge, neither civil nor uncivil.

"Very sorry sir. I couldn't get away from the capital a moment earlier. There has been so much ado—"

"Well?" interrupted Woolfridge. "What do I care about all that chatter? Come to the point."

The newcomer looked at a vacant chair. Since no invitation to rest was forthcoming he remained on his feet. "I am afraid I have no good news. That is what delayed me. The governor has been on the warpath. The legislature is about to convene, and there have been many radical bills proposed. Also, nobody understands just how, there was a repercussion in Washington. On top of that the irrigation commissioner has become unfriendly. In short, T. Q. Bangor has instructed me to say to you that his company can no longer be interested in the proposed dam up here. That is quite final."

He was somewhat nervous, having once delivered the news, and he looked apprehensively at Woolfridge. Yet if he expected an explosion of wrathful disappointment he was to be disappointed. All that marked Woolfridge's state of mind was a sardonic gleam.

"So Bangor got cold feet and threw me down?"

"No, sir, that is not the impression he wants me to convey—"

"It amounts to just that," snapped Woolfridge. "He's got the courage of a jellyfish. All of those fools down below are the same. If I had stayed there I'd be the same way. Thank God, I got out of it. Now I suppose Bangor expects I'll come weeping on his shoulders. I suppose you think I mean to discard all the plans I had you draw up. Well, I do not intend any such thing. We are going ahead."

"I don't see—" began the newcomer.

"Of course not. If you did see you'd have an imagination. If you had an imagination I wouldn't be hiring you. Sit down."

The newcomer sat down, uncertain, puzzled, and distraught. He had worked for Woolfridge many years, and he thought he understood his employer. Yet here was a man he didn't know at all. Woolfridge was changing; he was hardening to internal pressures. There was a squareness to the chubby face and a cast to the lips; a suggestion of saturnine confidence that never before had been visible. The newcomer never had known what went on in Woolfridge's mind, but hitherto he always had felt more or less secure of a certain routine. He didn't feel it now. Woolfridge looked at him in a way that made him wish there were others in the room. In fact the newcomer was somehow afraid.

"All our plans were based on the fact that the dam was coming in," stated Woolfridge. "We were to sell land on that basis. We will still sell land, but on a different basis. You go back. Revise your advertisements. State in them that here is a land that will grow anything with water. Dwell upon the irrigation possibilities of the canyon. Do not promise that a dam is to be built, but convey by every clever word you have that a dam is sure to go in. Don't promise—hint. Hit 'em on the head with that hint. By Saturday—two days from now—I want a copy of that advertisement on the way to all the country newspapers in the surrounding states."

"But Bangor positively states the dam isn't going in."

"What do we care? You do as I tell you. That hint will draw a class of men who are always ready to drop what they've got and rush to some other place on a shoestring prospect. The world is full of such. They will buy my land, pay something down, and wait for water to come."

"Then what?" queried the newcomer.

"Then—what do you want to know for?" Woolfridge was about to say that then he would have their money and they would go broke. In the end they would leave and he would still have the land. "Go back and get at it. Tell them that dry farming can pay them while they are waiting." Once more the newcomer saw a touch of that cynical, sardonic amusement. He rose, fumbling with his hat.

"Very well. I will take care of it. There is no stage out of here until to-morrow."

"I said you didn't have any imagination," murmured Woolfridge. "There is a livery stable here that will rent you a rig and driver. Eat a bite and get out."

The man departed, glad to be clear of Woolfridge's presence. A stouter fellow would have resigned. This man was not of that caliber. Woolfridge had known as much at the time of hiring.

For perhaps an hour after Woolfridge had gone from the bank Mark Eagle tended to business. At the end of this time he very quietly laid down his pen, removed his light coat, and slid into his heavier one. He left the cage, closed the door, and went to Craib's office. Craib was busy, so Mark Eagle waited in entire patience until the older man pulled free from a ledger.

"I'd like my money," said Eagle.

Craib solemnly figured the days and dug into his own pocket for the cash. "Your dad pretty sick?"

"Yes," replied Mark. "Thank you." It was still before closing time, yet the Indian left the bank and walked to his room in a private house over near the rodeo field. A little later he reappeared on the street again with a paper bundle beneath his arm, going directly to the stable. Will Leaver, the spare stable hand, saw Mark enter and spoke casually. "How's tricks, old-timer?"

"Fair enough, Will. It is getting colder. Winter early this year."

The stable hand nodded. Mark Eagle walked to the rear of the place and slipped into a little alley made by the high stacks of baled hay. He was gone for quite a while and the stable hand, thinking it somewhat curious, at last rose and started out the back. Midway, he was stopped dead and struck speechless. Mark Eagle stepped out from the alley.

When Eagle entered that alley he was much like any other man in Roaring Horse — dressed in the same conventional clothes, using the same speech and owning the same manners. Possibly he was more reserved and possibly he carried himself a little straighter, for he was proud of his education and proud of his place in a white man's society. Nothing about Mark Eagle, save the color of his skin, set him apart from the average run of townsmen, and even that was overlooked through many years of close contact. Roaring Horse spoke of him as a good man, nothing more and nothing less. Yet, as he stood now before Will Leaver, all the trappings of civilization had been flung aside. The woolen suit was gone, the derby hat and the leather shoes were cast aside. Mark Eagle was stripped to the waist; he wore a pair of leather breeches and a set of moccasins. His jet black hair stood upright, heavy with grease, and twin blotches of red paint emblazoned his cheek bones. Poising there in the half light of the stable's vault he stared at Will Leaver out of burning, haughty eyes, and the perfect picture of some wild savage emerged from the past.

Will Leaver started to speak. Mark Eagle raised a hand, around the wrist of which dangled a beaded quirt. And he muttered: "Ha—me red! I go!" His body bent, he slipped around Leaver at a dog trot. Down the driveway to the door and into the street. There he halted, copper body shining in the cold sunlight, crimson paint creating a weird and repulsive mask of his face.

Leaver woke from his wonder and ran after

Eagle, shouting: "Hey, Mark, yuh can't do that! Yuh'll get pinched. Come back here, yuh damndarn fool, before folks see yuh!"

Mark Eagle threw up his hands. A wild, exultant cry went ringing down along the building walls of Roaring Horse, waking barbaric echoes, shocking all hearers out of the afternoon drowse. Then he whirled. When Will Leaver reached the door he saw Mark Eagle leaping into the saddle of a tethered pony. Leaver yelled again, men came up on the run. But Mark Eagle, full blood, was on his way with the winds, out into the open desert, bound for the high and distant ridges he had looked at so long from the imprisoning streets of the white man's town.

CHAPTER FOURTEEN

THE BEGINNING OF A TRAGEDY

Within three days Roaring Horse was visibly notified of the changing times, distinctly warned that control had passed to other hands. The notification came swiftly and almost arrogantly, as if to strike a hard lesson home to those unreformed men who had fought against change. First—and this happened the night following Miz Satterlee's surrender—was William Wells Woolfridge's public avowal of ownership. Roaring Horse woke one morning to find his name emblazoned below the sign of the land office; found it proclaimed on the panels of the Gusher Hotel, on Ellsberg's Mercantile House, above the arch of the livery stable, and as far down the street as the lumber yard.

Woolfridge was shrewd enough to know that this wide-flung display would create resentment and bitterness among the discontented; Roaring Horse was not wholly won to his side. Yet he rode his high horse with a purpose. If it created anger he also believed it would create discouragement. He had established the fact of his ruthless ability to plow ahead; he hoped that the remaining dissenters would lose heart and leave the country.

The town of a sudden came a beehive of activity. Freighters rolled in, heavy laden with lumber for the yard, against the future needs of the settlers. New lodgepole corrals rose behind the stable, and a bronc peeler from Woolfridge's outfit drove in a bunch of half-wild saddle stock and took up the business of gentling them out on the rodeo field. A man slipped off the stage and joined the clerk at the land office. Maps burgeoned forth upon the walls of that office. Small piles of the desert's soil appeared in the window with a written analysis behind each. And there was an artist's picture of what Roaring Horse would look like five years hence—a town of brick buildings surrounded by a country of square, green farms in which great barns and fine houses and tall poplar trees stood in shapely arrangement. A crew of men began to dig out the foundations for some unknown structure beyond the rodeo field.

It all went to create a picture of optimism and growth, yet Roaring Horse looked on, half believing, half disbelieving. Even Woolfridge's flaring ad in the weekly paper failed to convince the skeptics. Roaring Horse had been exclusively a cattle country for some generations. It would remain so, believed these skeptics, after Woolfridge was dead and gone. But when on the fourth day a line of wagons drew into town and stopped abreast the land office the skeptics were silenced and an electric thrill of surprise woke the citizens from their doubt.

It was the vanguard of the homesteaders, the first answer to Woolfridge's broadcast invitation. Gay Thatcher, looking down from the window of her hotel room, saw the wagons, their occupants and contents, and marveled. Somehow the spectacle was so full of pathos that it almost made her cry. On these long and clumsy vehicles was packed the assorted gathering of a lifetime—plows, stoves, kitchen cabinets, barrels of dishes, bedding rolls. The household articles overflowed and hung outward from every possible angle of suspension. The men—she counted five—were middle aged and weather beaten; the women sat silently, bonnets pulled down and hands folded. Children and dogs swarmed to the ground the very instant this queer caravan halted. Presently Woolfridge came out of the land office and shook hands with the arrivals. And the men descended and slouched back with him. These were not the prosperous farmers from which a successful project was made; they were the type who had left one hopeless stretch of land and always were ready to travel on the hint of something better.

"It is criminal!" exclaimed Gay. "Nothing less than criminal! All the money they have will go into this desert and—why, those poor women!"

They looked cold and very weary. Probably they were hungry as well. A baby cried somewhere in the clutter; the men returned, all smiling broadly, and swung up to the wagon seats. As the caravan proceeded down the street and turned into the livery stable Gay Thatcher saw that the women were smiling, too. Hope had met them. The girl turned away from the window, passionately angry. "It isn't fair!"

Probably Gay Thatcher would have thought it less fair had she overheard what Woolfridge told the men.

"You are the first to enter the project," said that gentleman, pointing to the counter map. "Therefore, you have unlimited choice. Area One, as you see it here, includes the lands nearest the main canal. Area Two is that part of the project somewhat more removed. I want to impress on you, however, that the soil in Area Two is as good as any. And since you probably are not prepared to invest a great sum of money, you will find exactly what you want there. Run your wagons into the stable, settle your families, and come back. I'll have a man with horses to take you on an inspection trip."

He was in the street later to see the prospective settlers off to the desert with their guide. And he added: 'I want you to understand, gentlemen, that a part of my fortune is invested here. All of my fortune is back of it. I expect to make money—plenty of it." Smiling quite genially he returned to his office. Inside, the smile evaporated. He sent one of the clerks down the street and told the other to take a walk. Presently Luis Locklear came in, dour and stiff necked even in front of the man he knew to be his master.

"Have you done what I told you to do, Locklear?"

"Which?" grumbled the sheriff. "Yuh been tellin' me plenty, last couple days."

Woolfridge evidenced an impatient disgust. "You're too slow on your feet. You are, moreover, rather stupid. The combination bores me. I use unimaginative men by preference, but I expect them to act fast and I don't expect them to assume an importance they haven't got. I hope that is plain enough to you."

"Now look here, Woolfridge—"

" 'Mr. Woolfridge' if you please, Locklear. I don't care for familiarity. I'm getting a little weary of that. Usually I don't have to warn my men more than once. Now what have you done about those fellows I brought in for you to use a few days back?"

Locklear's scowling, stubborn face was pulled around slantwise. He looked like a balky horse fighting the halter. This man knew very well he was kept and paid for; he knew exactly where he stood. Yet the authority of the star had inflamed his pride; the cantankerous, caviling spirit in him would not be still. He started to protest again. Woolfridge never turned a muscle, but the veil rose above his eyes a moment and Locklear, dull and self-wrapped man that he was, received a sharp, distinct warning to be on his guard. It shocked him—just as it would have shocked him to have looked down some hitherto empty hall and found a gun pointed at his chest. He had always credited Woolfridge with certain powers, but never for what appeared at that moment to lay half awake, half crouched beneath the freckled chubby cheeks.

"I did what you said," grumbled Locklear finally. "Sent all but three away."

"That is good," replied Woolfridge. "We've got no further use for them. Such machinery is best taken apart before it turns to do us damage. Don't catch that, eh? I am sorry I can't use simpler similes. We have no opposition to worry about now. If any develops I can call the boys from the ranch. I've got them weeded out. All remaining are very loyal. When you have nothing better to do, Locklear, ponder on that word—loyalty. It will solve much for you. Now, from this point on you are to play a small part. A humble part. Above all, a silent part."

"I'm sheriff of Roarin' Horse," muttered Locklear.

"Very true. Yet sheriffs are not immortal. Nor perpetual. Keep your mouth shut, Locklear. That's all." Woolfridge saw the vast frame of Theodorik Perrine ambling in the front door, and thus he closed the interview. Locklear scowled and went out. Perrine, in passing, grinned at the official, but Locklear only grunted and kept going. Perrine cruised toward Woolfridge's desk, the grin soon dying.

"No news."

"That is your bad luck, Perrine."

"Like sin it is," rumbled the big man. The reassurance fell away from him. It always did in the presence of Woolfridge. "I ain't through huntin' yet. I'll find him."

Woolfridge tapped his desk. "You had better find him. It's your only chance of salvation, my friend."

"What's that?"

Woolfridge had a certain sparse, tight-lipped smile for situations of this sort. He used it, whereat Perrine shifted his weight; sharp creases sprang along the giant's forehead. "Mack Moran knows; but, by Jupiter, I can't get near him unless I take the bunch an' shoot my way into Melotte's house. Melotte's crew and half o' Stirrup S crew are strung around the place 's if Moran amounted to somethin'."

"Then leave him alone," snapped Woolfridge. "I don't authorize you to carry on a war with Melotte. I only fight when I find it important. You run down Chaffee another way."

"He got a horse at Linderman's. He went t'ord Thirty-four Pass. But that's only a dodge. Don't figger he hit into the pass when it was snowin' so hard. Figger he kep' goin' due north. Yeah—only where could he go north?"

"Don't ask me questions. By the way, have you heard the rumor that Chaffee took tar impressions of the boot prints back of the stable on the night Satterlee was killed?"

Perrine nodded. "I'd shore like to get my fingers on 'em!"

"Worried, I suppose?"

"Me?" was Perrine's defensive grunt. "Why should I be? I didn't kill Satterlee."

"Ah." Woolfridge bent forward, bland as a summer tourist. "And who did kill the old gentleman, Perrine?"

Theodorik took one comprehensive glance at Woolfridge's eyes and hurriedly averted his own. "I dunno. Mebbe shot himself. It ain't none of my business and I dunno. I got plenty trouble with Chaffee as it is."

"You'll have a great many more unless you bag that gentleman," Woolfridge assured him. "Get out on the trail where you properly belong. Don't swagger around town. Keep away from the settlers. Put a seal on your tongue. The day of your swashbuckling around here is done. Next time I see you I will expect better news."

"Mebbe," said Theodorik, cruising out, "he went up Thirty-four Pass, after all. I'll have a look."

Woolfridge took his hat and casually followed Perrine to the street. He was of a mind to go to the bank, but he saw Gay Thatcher leave the hotel and cross to the livery stable. Immediately he followed and met the girl as she rode out; his hat came off, he smiled pleasantly, and took hold of the bridle. "Here you are, away for an afternoon's ride. Here I am, with nothing to do and badly wanting a talk with you. Well?"

The girl studied him soberly. "I think you would find me distinctly uninteresting this day."

"Never," Woolfridge assured her, and managed to put a quantity of bold gallantry into the statement. "Not if I talked with you all the rest of my days. That, by the way, is a pleasure I may beg for rather soon."

"You are a very certain man, Mr. Woolfridge. Beginning another campaign already?"

"I believe in going forward," said he. "I surely believe in trying my luck."

"And finding other people's prices," she reminded him. "What do you think my price would be, Mr. Woolfridge?"

The humor left him; he became imperceptibly agitated. "Isn't that unkind, Miss Thatcher? I think I have always acted the proper part toward you, have always observed the punctilios. You have distinctly changed. You sound unfriendly to me. Am I to infer that you are warning me there is no chance of my winning?"

"Supposing I did tell you that?"

He stood straight beside the horse, a suave and well-groomed gentleman with the hint of sleeked-down physical comfort about him. Yet for all his efforts to maintain the even and urbane courtesy, he could not suppress the hardening of his freckled jowls nor the metal edge of his reply. "I would not accept the answer as definite," said he. The words were quite flat; they had a peculiar snap to them.

The girl watched the blending of emotions on his face with a somber interest. "Why not, Mr. Woolfridge? Don't you credit me with knowing my own mind?"

He shook his head. "Not that. But you don't see me yet quite as you should. When you do, perhaps you will change your opinion. I am sure of it."

"In other words," she answered him, "I do have a price, after all, and you are going to be very patient—and very relentless—until you find it. I have watched your business methods.

You have a set type of finesse which seems to be very successful. But in applying the same methods to a woman I think you are in error. Oh, very much so. I gave you credit for being a little more versatile."

"What have you against me?" he demanded with an abrupt, rising impatience.

"I would hate to offend your pride," said she, "but perhaps it is not so much a definite objection as a plain lack of interest."

He did change color at that. And he was stung far more than she realized he could be. "No, Miss Thatcher. I flatter myself that either I make a friend or an enemy. I am not so colorless as to be merely endured. You have real reasons. You have heard things. I should like to know what they are—and to correct the error of them."

"Remember, Mr. Woolfridge, it is a woman's privilege not to be cross-examined."

He hardly bothered to conceal the irritation. "You are pleased to be mysterious again. And elusive. I once opened to you the doors of myself. Does that not imply the return courtesy? Miss Thatcher, you must give me some opportunity. I have that right. Really, I have."

"I doubt it. I never asked for your confidences. As for myself, I have never yet found the man in whom I cared to place my confessions. It is getting late—and I have a trip to make down to Melotte's."

It was somehow an omen to the girl that Woolfridge, through all the interview, held a tight grip to the bridle. He was that sure of his own strength and his own right. He had not begged her to stop; he had simply checked her from going by the grip he had of the bridle. Nor did he immediately withdraw it; rather he took his time, studying the girl's clear dark eyes at some length. He did not carry himself with the same arrogant command that he used toward his subordinates, but the self-contained confidence had quite the same effect on her.

"You have better access to Melotte's than I have, evidently," said he. "I wish you luck. Perhaps you may find the answer to a question that greatly interests me—the whereabouts of Jim Chaffee."

She betrayed herself then; all of a sudden her eyes were flashing and anger was in her throat. "If I find out, Mr. Woolfridge, you can be sure I will never tell you."

He released his grip on the bridle and stepped back a pace, once more in full command of himself; he smiled—a smile that outraged her. "I understand quite completely," said he, bowing his head. "Now I have something to argue against. When you return I want to show you my side of the case. I am sure I will convince you."

She galloped down the street, not replying. Yet he caught the state of mind she was in—angry at herself and at him, a little confused and much disturbed, and perhaps touched by a minute fear. He watched her go until the pony carried her around the curve of the trail. Then he closed both hands, snapping them like the blades of a jackknife, and walked back to the land office. "She will find I am not a man to be disregarded, nor lightly placed aside. She must listen to me. She must see all that I am, and all that I will be. I can convince her. Why not? I have made myself a power. Is a woman any more stubborn than a county full of men? What I have deliberately started and deliberately carried on I have never yet failed in. I won't with her. It may take time, but she will accept me by and by."

In the office he wrote a brief note to his man at the capital—that man in whom he had placed the business of getting out the advertisements.

HUNNEWELL:

Find out all that you can about the past life and history of Gay Thatcher. She comes from your city. Find out also what her connections are and why she is down here. This is to be your first and immediate business. Get at it and secure the facts.

—W. W. WOOLFRIDGE

A man in love with a woman would never have written such an amazing order, never would have allowed it in his head for a moment. But William Wells Woolfridge, tremendously drawn to Gay Thatcher by her clear eyes and the fine carriage of her body as well as by the maturity of her mind, was not in love with her. He was in love with an obsession—the obsession of personal conquest, the exhilaration of scaling forbidding peaks and knocking over open resistance. Gay Thatcher, whatever else she meant to him, meant more than anything a beautiful acquisition to his gallery of rare objects at Wolf's Head.

Gay Thatcher rode rapidly toward Melotte's on the broad trail bearing the imprint of the recent stirring events. And as she traveled she grew more and more angry at having shown weakness before Woolfridge. For it was weakness to defy him. He was the kind of a man who seized upon such lapses of judgment and made weapons of them. She had given him a point of attack, just as others by some small slip of tongue or some still smaller act had played into his hands. It seemed to her he had the skill the patience of an Oriental, to which was added the Oriental's disposition to finally end some long drawn situation by a single stroke of the blade. It was incredible that so strong a man as Dad Satterlee could have crumbled overnight when faced against Woolfridge; and it was equally incredible that at the turn of an hour a whole county should somehow pass into the man's control. It amounted to that. Gay, rehearsing all that she had learned, felt the warning of fear. She could not dismiss Woolfridge. He wouldn't be dismissed.

So thinking, she came to Melotte's and rode down the yard—a yard resembling an armed camp by the number of Flying M and ex-Stirrup S men loitering about. Going into the house she went to the room where Mack Moran lay. Mack had been in pretty bad shape from a bullet through the shoulder, it had pulled the solid flesh off him and whitened his naturally ruddy cheeks. But he was past danger now and he smiled cheerfully up to the girl as she sat down beside the bed.

"Able to sit up and take nourishment yet?" she asked him, smiling back.

"This family will shore make a hawg out o' me, ma'am. Imagine chicken with dumplin's —corn bread with pear preserves. Gosh, I wish I'd been shot a couple years ago. They certainly is somethin' crooked about a universe which lays a man flat on his back before he discovers the institution of home cookin'."

"If you were married that is the way you'd eat every day," she said. "Something good has to be saved for the fellow who throws away his freedom, you know."

"Yeah," agreed Mack, and pondered over the matter with a scandalously matter-of-fact air. "All three of Melotte's girls are shore fine. One brings breakfast, one spells out with dinner, and the third sits in for supper. How's a man to decide which he ought to propose to? I'm plumb willin', but I can't nowise seem to decide."

"Possibly they may decide among themselves for you," she replied, trying to keep a straight face.

To Mack Moran that had all the earmarks of a splendid idea. "Now there's the whole thing boiled down. Wouldn't that be simple? Gosh, I even get chocolate to drink before I fall off to sleep. The oldest one—the one with the pritty hair—always fixes that for me. Chocolate—can yuh tie that, now?"

"Perhaps it has already been decided," said she, and then hoped he hadn't understood.

He muttered "yeah," staring out of the

window. His mind was on other things. "Jussasame, I'd like to be on a horse. Ain't had a letter from Jim yet, and he said he'd drop a line right off."

"Mack," said she, the words tumbling headlong out of her mouth, "which way did he go, was he hurt, did—did he tell you anything I might like to know?"

Mack reached for his tobacco and answered the last question first. "He ain't a man to spread himself out loud, ma'am. Not even to me, which is his best friend. Way back—shore seems like ten years—when he saw yuh a-passin' on the street he said to me, 'Mack, I've got to meet that girl.' I reckon yuh'd like to know it. An' when Jim said that he meant a whole lot."

"Thank you," murmured Gay, and looked down to her lap. "I—I am glad to hear that."

"As for bein' hurt—you bet. Lee put some buckshot in his shoulder. That's been a-worryin' me ever since. And he was awful tired. Dunno as I ever saw him look more tired. Goin' down the canyon is a year's work piled up into a few blamed excitin' minutes. I ain't anxious to try again. Not me. But we shore made history. And he hated to leave. Felt like he was runnin' away. I had the daggondest time arguin' with him. The fool woulda rammed his head plumb into a loop.

But I ain't had a letter—"

"Where did he go?"

"He aimed for the pass. Meant to cross over and into Bannock City. It snowin' heavy up thataway. I can see it from the winda here. When it white clear down to Sawyer Rock it means the pass is fifteen feet deep in drifts. Daggone."

"What would happen—what possibly might happen to him, Mack?" asked the girl, anxiety showing through.

"Nothin', as long as he's got two feet an' two hands. That boy can take care uh himself. But some o' that gang might 'a' winged him. And that buckshot could cause an awful lot of trouble. Son-of-a-gun, I wish I was able to ride a horse!"

She got up and went around the bed to look out of the window. "Yes, it's snowing hard up there. But it packs down in the pass, Mack. It always does. He'd have a good firm underfooting. And there's the cabin in case of trouble."

Moran was surprised. "How come you know all about those things? That's old-timer's talk."

She was apparently so engrossed in her own thoughts that she didn't hear Mack's question. "And he was supposed to have written you? Four days ago, from Baddock City? No, two days ago, leaving time for him to cross. Well, if he crossed he would certainly go to Bannock City—no other town in the valley. And the letter, if he wrote one on arriving, ought to be here now. Do you think he might delay writing, Mack?"

"No siree bob. He knows I'm on pins an' needles. He'd drop a line right off. He's punctual thataway."

She turned from the window with a strange and abrupt lift of her sturdy little shoulders. Mack, watching her, got the impression she had made up her mind about something at that instant. "I'm going back to town. Do you mind if I ask for your mail at the post office? If he has written a letter I'll bring it—tonight. If not—"

"Yeah, then what?"

She smiled at him and touched his sunburned fist. "Be good, cowboy. Eat all the chicken and pear preserves you can hold. If I don't see you again, Mack, say a prayer for me once." She was light hearted about it, but a small kink of wistfulness lay around her lips.

"Ma'am, who'm I to be sayin' prayers for you? If an old dawg like me got to mentionin' yore name to the Lord it shore wouldn't he'p yore reputation none in heaven."

"Reputation?" murmured the girl. The

smile slowly left her. "I have heard the word before, always unpleasantly. Mack, do you know what I'd do if I were you? I believe I'd propose to the Melotte girl—the one who always brings you chocolate at night. So long." She was gone from the room, leaving Moran somehow dissatisfied with her departure. The touch of her hand had been cool, reassuring, with a brisk friendliness to it. Mack had never known a woman, who without trying to play the part of a good fellow among men, was as little self-conscious of her sex. She made a brave, contained figure; with always a reserve in her eyes that held others away. Only once had that reserve dropped to give another some sight of the wistful and lonely hunger of her heart.

She returned to town and stopped a moment at the stable. A little later she came out of the hotel with her traveling bag and stepped into a waiting rig. The driver whipped away through the graying afternoon. Fifteen miles to the south she got off at a lonely flag stop surrounded by the immensity of the desert night and spoke to the agent drowsing over his keys. Perhaps an hour later the agent built a bonfire of paper in the middle of the track and stopped an east-bound train. The girl got aboard and sat very quietly in one end of a day coach while the wheels made their swift tat-a-tat-tat rhythm along the rails. Presently they were climbing through a gorge with the trucks howling to the curves; and around midnight or a little later she left the train at another junction point, beyond the lowering outline of the Roaring Horse range. A six-horse stage waited beside the tracks with some long-faced gilded lettering hinting at the name of a hostelry. She was the only passenger, and the driver, peering through the gloom saw nothing but the blur of her face.

"It's Gay Thatcher, John," said she, closing the coach door.

"Howdy, ma'am! Lordamighty, glad to see yuh again! Say, it's cold. You better take my laprobe."

"No thanks."

The coach rolled off, team stretching to an even gait. She drowsed and woke, and drowsed again while the clumsy vehicle pitched along the uneven road. And always there was in her mind the memory of something fine and pleasant; once she repeated a name very softly to herself. "Jim Chaffee." And added: "Gentleman." Before dawn the coach brought her down the main street of Bannock City. She ate breakfast by the smoky kerosene lamp of an all-night restaurant and went directly to the stable. It was a misty daylight before she left town, bundled up in another rig. In the interval she talked to the clerk of the hotel and to the night marshal, asking only one question of each. And then she was away, leaving behind her the news of her passage. The men who had seen her said nothing at all. But there was one woman in the hotel—the wife of the clerk—who had risen early and who had caught a moment's glimpse of the girl. And this woman spoke with a bitter acid in her words.

"So that Thatcher girl is back again. But she ain't got courage enough to wait until folks can see her brazen face by plain day."

The clerk was sleepy and therefore he made a tactical error. "Oh, she's all right."

"You hush! She always could pull the wool over the eyes of menfolk. Don't start that argument again. It's been dead five years. It's better left that way. She ought to have the decency to keep wide of this valley."

CHAPTER FIFTEEN

TURBULENCE

Thirty-Four Pass lay hard locked in the grip of the storm. For almost a week daylight had been little more than a gray and weaving half light. Sight of the distant valley was blotted out; even the timber line was lost somewhere down the driving mists. Twenty feet below the drifts lay the trial, and the wind, booming across these drifts, ripped high sprays of snow upward and sent them sheeting against the summit cabin, like tall waves smashing across a stormy sea. A bitter and bleak world it was, with the peaks obscured and enshrouded, and sending earthward the errie scream of the gale as it sheered the sharp points; a world of torturing cold and uneasy loneliness. Even the cabin, perched on a ledge above the trail, was banked to the eaves. Inside, a fire burned, and the heat formed layers of thawed ice against the panes, adding to the interior darkness. Water dripped through the roof; wind and snow sifted between every minute interstice. Jim Chaffee sat hugging the stove and studied the dwindling pile of wood.

"I always figured Purgatory was a hot place," he muttered. "But I reckon I must have been mistaken. If this ain't hell's back door then I'm a monkey's lineal cousin."

One foot was bare and soaking in a pan of hot snow water. He lifted the member with patient care and ran a thumb around a swollen ankle bone. "No use tryin' to walk on that for another week. It won't hold me up none before. Then what? In a week I won't have energy enough to open that door. Fact is, I'm awful gant right now. Chaffee, old horse, if you got a brain, now is the time to use it. If I stay I starve. If I try to crawl out I freeze. From these simple facts let us proceed somewhere."

A fat and sedentary man could have lived on the strength stored in his surplus tissues these five monotonous days. Jim Chaffee was not fat, nor never had been anything else than muscularly thin. And he always had lived the kind of a life that absorbed the energy of each meal and left none for storing away. He was feeding on his life's vitality, slowly breaking down the fine machinery of his body. After the horse had thrown him he had crawled better than one mile along the gathering darkness to the cabin. The place was just as some itinerant trapper had left it—a pile of wood by the stove, a half-dozen battered utensils hung along the wall. But excepting a rind of bacon as hard as a rock and an empty flour sack there was nothing left to eat in the cupboard. During the first two days he considered himself absolutely destitute of food. After that an empty stomach jogged his wits and he experimented. He filled a lard pail with water. Turning the flour sack inside out he took his pocket knife and scraped away the gray film of flour left in the seams. This went into the pail of water. After it went the bacon rind. He stoked the stove and let the mixture boil of an hour.

The lard can smelled bad to begin with, the bacon rind was not easy to look at. "However, it's nourishment, ain't it?" he consoled himself, and poured out a small portion of the brew. He had always heard that a starving man could eat anything and say that it was as good as a king's dish. The first drink of this rancid, anemic soup convinced him that was gross error. Nothing in all his mature experience tasted half as horrible. He choked down the revolt of his stomach and optimistically took his pulse. Maybe it was the last jog of nourishment in the bacon rind and flour that made him feel a kind of glow. Maybe it was just the hot water, maybe it was only the excitement of hope. All in all, it was a poor experiment. In fact, it seemed to make matters worse, for the hot water further aggravated the sensation of being as hollow as a drum. He drank a little more on the third day. But on the fourth day disgust took him and he threw can and contents across the room. "I'd as lief eat dead rats."

Meanwhile, the snowdrift piled higher around the cabin, and he knew that unless he kept some sort of an alley cleared from the door the time would come when he couldn't get out, as weak as he was becoming. On hands and knees he crawled across the room and opened the door, to face a solid wall of snow. Very patiently he burrowed a tunnel upward through it, working in the manner of a mole. He reached daylight and looked into a dim, bleak world blasted by the bitter wind; he heard the shrill and weird wailing of the peaks lost above the pall. A minute or two of this was ample. He slid back into the cabin and built a stronger fire to thaw the frozen marrow of his bones.

By the fifth day he had used all of the wood. The next fuel was the bunk. The posts and the lodgepole stringers went into the stove. All that was then left was the cupboard, and he was afraid that once the cupboard came down more rifts of the cabin wall would be uncovered there. Debating over this, the fire died and the snow water in the pan cooled. He pulled on his sock and shoe and rose to his one good foot.

"Got to keep the fire burnin'," said he with a spry cheerfulness. "While I'm warm I might as well be good an' warm. When I'm cold it won't make no difference, anyhow. Mister Cupboard, come to your uncle."

The cupboard was only a dry-goods box nailed to the wall. He hopped over to it and gripped the edges, hauling downward with his weight. The cupboard gave slightly and resisted. Jim Chaffee let his arm fall; and an expression of shocked surprise flickered across his slim face. Two ten penny nails — nothing more — anchored that box. And he couldn't pull it down. This was bold handwriting on the cabin wall. He became aware than that he was weaker than he figured and he made no further attempt at getting firewood. Instead, he hopped back to the stove and plunged into an involved train of thoughts.

"Now this ain't really so bad. I'm alive, ain't I? I'm not hangin' by mere perspiration to the edge of the canyon. And I'm not dodgin' any bullets. Nobody can poison my soup, because there ain't any soup to poison. It bein' cold, I don't need to worry about bein' bit by a hydrophobia dog. Shucks, there's lots of things that can't happen to me. The point is, I wonder what Mack's up to?"

He had promised to drop a line from Bannock City. Mack would worry about not getting a letter. Mack would begin to look ahead and count over possibilities. Knowing his partner very well, Jim understood that after a certain length of time had elapsed without word Mack Moran would not sit idle. The battling puncher would get aboard a horse and investigate. Right there was a definite hope.

"Question becomes, how long will he wait?" pondered Jim Chaffee. "If everything had gone according to schedule I'd have written three days ago, and he'd have said letter by now. He'll be wonderin' right now. But he'll wait another twenty-four hours, anyhow. Then he'll start up this way. If I can hold out till Tuesday—"

Tuesday seemed remote. In fact the longer he studied his position the more impossibly distant Tuesday became. He took himself to account. "Listen, Chaffee, what's the idea of expectin' somebody else to hoist you out of this pickle? It ain't your style. You're twenty-one, free, white, and hungry. You got into this jackpot. Now it's up to you and nobody else. Do somethin'."

A gunny sack lay over in one corner of the room. He boosted himself across the floor and got it. Taking his knife he cut a hole in the sewed end and shook out the dirt. Then he measured himself against it and slit an aperture on either side. Throwing the sack over his head he found he had a smock which, though quite dusty and smelling very evil, gave him so much extra protection. Thus far he had no idea at all of what he meant to do. The next logical thing seemed to be an inspection of his gun, and following that he moved toward the door.

"It's a long way back to Gorman's lodge," he muttered. "Too far to crawl. But do somethin' anyhow. You can't expect a break unless you go out there and make one. Stick here much longer and you'll be pickin' bananas off the wall. It's serious when a man begins talkin' to himself unless he's a sheep herder. Just amble out and have a look."

He opened the door and found the tunnel half filled in. So he took up the bitter work of clearing another alley to the surface. Once again the knife edge of the slashing wind bit into his bones, and once again he heard the shrill wailing of the peaks above him. According to his judgment it was around noon, but he had no way of exactly determining. There was no hint of sun in the cheerless snow mist, no hint of time's passage at all except the waxing and waning of the thin, bleak light. He was isolated, cut off from human kind in this high, storm battered world.

The rounding alley of the pass beckoned either way. West was back to timber line, back to Gorman's. East was into the adjacent valley. All landmarks were buried, and the weaving, driving snow choked out everything but the immediate foreground. Rising to one knee he studied this desolation neither hopefully nor otherwise. He could fight, and he was so prepared to fight—the last great fight for simple existence; yet at the same time he was a gambler at heart and, being a gambler, studied his chances with a critical eye. Not for a moment did he allow himself the folly of optimism. He knew very well that the elements had him hamstrung, that they were pulling him down to a soundless and not unpleasant death. So much he admitted.

"Why lay down and quit in that cabin? I might make it to Gorman's. I *might*. Wind's behind me and it's down grade. Well, if there's any other chances I'd better think of 'em right now before I start."

He was conscious all of a sudden that the intense cold didn't bite him as it should. He wasn't feeling it like he ought to feel it. "A good man can stand lots of this," said he. "But it gets a thin old wolf like me sudden, I better be movin'. I sure do wish I could eat coffee and flapjacks in that little log house of mine once more."

He crawled away from the tunnel, testing his strength against the snow. Ten yards left him doubtful. Twenty more yards and he stopped, breathing hard and feeling the quiver of his muscles. It may have been a momentary flash of despair that turned him about for a last look at the summit cabin; it may have been a recognition of defeat; or it may have been some impalpable note of warning singing along the whipping wind. But he turned at any rate; and deep in the mist, beyond the cabin, he saw a tall silhouette moving across the gray background of the storm. It woke all the hope he had left; it dredged up the last of his strength. He stood on his knees, trying to penetrate the pall; he shouted, knowing that the wind whipped his words on down the slope—the wrong way. Then the silhouette disappeared.

"Eyes goin' bad. Why don't I get sore about it? Why don't I kick up a fuss? Now what—"

The silhouette reappeared, quartered along the lifting clouds of snow, and halted. Didn't have the shape of a man. Maybe a horse. But what would a horse be doing up here? The tricks of the snow tantalized him, thinning and thickening, giving him an instant's glimpse of the moving object and then shutting it from sight. He dropped to all fours and crawled against the wind. He came abreast the cabin, toiled on, and stopped out of exhaustion. The silhouette grew plainer, broke the mists. A mule-tail buck deer stood fifty yards away, ribs sprung out against sunken flanks; the animal braced its feet wide in the snow and lowered its head.

Chaffee reached for his gun. "Mister Buck, just take your time. Don't be in any hurry. And drift this way, you son-of-a-gun!"

The deer advanced a few more yards and again took a stand. The wind was driving him onward across the pass. How he had gotten this far up Chaffee didn't understand, but he was not disposed to reflect on the vagaries of the animal kingdom at this precise moment. Flat on his stomach, he crawled ahead, wishing the day was still darker. He stopped, afraid to move into the buck's line of vision, and he made a tripod with his elbows and propped the gun between palms.

"That's all right. Take your time. You got this far, now come a little farther. No, that snow ain't fit to eat. And you can't smell me a-tall. Not a-tall, Mister Buck. Wind's the wrong way. That's right—one foot in front of the other. Same way my mamma taught me to walk. Nossir, you can't see me, either. I'm all covered with snow. It's only a log you see. Yeah."

The buck plowed ahead, directly in line with Chaffee. The man pulled back the gun's hammer and took a test sight. Right in the chest and a little to one side. But it was still too far. The buck had trouble in making traction, and three times during that long spell of waiting the beast stopped. Chaffee throttled the impulse to shoot. Another yard would make it surer. And when the deer advanced the necessary yard Chaffee argued with himself again as if he were lecturing an impatient child. Still another yard to be more sure. "Yuh look hungry. Well, they's all sorts of nice grass down beyond me. Don't take my word for it. Use your own judgment. Ain't that what you come all this way to find? Now next time you stop, turn halfway round. I'll be obliged. I'd rather aim behind a forequarter. Won't hurt you near so much."

All this was under his breath. Feeling fast fled from his arms. The muzzle of the gun had a tendency to droop. The buck halted twenty yards or more away. Chaffee sighed and squeezed the trigger. The report of that shot roared in his ears and was flung back by the wind; the buck reared, whirled about, and raced into the teeth of the driving mist. A moment later he was beyond the pall, and all of Jim Chaffee's hopes went with him. The revolver dropped to the snow, nor did the man make any effort to secure it. Very, very slowly he hauled himself toward the cabin. He was sleepy and he began to argue with himself about the blamed, well you got to exert a little more steam. Cabin ain't but a mite off. Hoopa—one more boost." His head dropped and he never knew when he went to sleep. The descent to oblivion was very easy. Gay Thatcher and Ranzo Taber, coming along less than five minutes later with Taber's huskies, almost ran over him.

His feet hurt—that woke him out of the stupor. They stung like fury. So did his hands; so did his ears. And somebody worked over him with a great deal of unnecessary roughness. He opened his eyes and saw Ranzo Taber, whom he didn't know. Beyond stood Gay Thatcher.

"I missed that doggone buck," he murmured.

"I guess you did," said Taber. "He went by us like a shot out of a gun. How do you feel?"

"All the symptoms. Yeah, I know you're pinchin' my legs. Feelin's comin' back."

"Guess you can stoke up the fire," said Taber to Gay.

The girl went over and ripped the cupboard down with one single motion. Chaffee couldn't help grinning. "I wasn't able to budge it a little while back. When I get out of here I'm goin' to hire somebody to haul six-eight cords of wood alongside this cabin. Where did you come from?"

"Have a drink first," suggested Taber. Chaffee strangled over a jolt of whisky, but the benefit derived therefrom was immediate.

"When did you eat last?" asked the girl, breaking the cupboard into the stove.

"Not since I left Linderman's."

The girl pulled a canteen from her shoulders and came over to Chaffee. "I thought something like that might have happened. This is chocolate. One big drink, Jim. No more."

Ranzo Taber started for the door. "Want to look at the dogs. We better be hittin' out of this pretty quick. Ain't long till dark."

Chaffee took a long drink of warm chocolate. Every minute brought an added sting and jab of some reviving piece of skin, but he felt in pretty good shape, almost as if he were waking from a turbulent dream. Gay Thatcher he began to study with freshening interest. In the week's interval she had changed some. Laying aside the effect of man's clothing and high boots, she appeared tired, somehow sad. Her eyes were of a deeper color; once when she caught his direct glance a tinge of crimson slowly rose to her cheeks — and went away. He remembered their meeting in the jail and he wondered what she thought about now.

"You tell your story; then I'll tell mine," said she.

He took another pull on the canteen. "Takes a woman to think of a drink like that. Wouldn't this be a haywire world without women? My story don't amount to much. I got out of the jail, ran the lines with Mack, ended up at Linderman's, borrowed a horse and hit for the pass. Was kind of tired, so the horse caught me sleepin' and threw me. Twisted my ankle. Got to the cabin. Been here ever since. Was about to depart for regions unknown when you came along. How did you figure I was here?"

"I saw Mack. He told me you hadn't written. He was worried. I got the whole story from him and put two and two together. So I circled around to Bannock City and went to Ranzo Taber's ranch. It is only ten miles east of here. Ranzo runs two or three strings of huskies every winter for sport. I knew that. You weren't in Bannock City, and I figured you must be somewhere along the trail. So we came." She fell silent. But a moment later he was startled to hear the swift vehemence of her words. "Jim, do you know how close to death you were out there in the snow!"

"I can make a guess at it," he muttered, bothered by something else. "I don't just see why you went to all this trouble."

"Don't you, Jim?"

The color came to her cheeks again; her lips were pursed tightly and she held herself very straight and still. He turned his head to the wall, stirred by strange currents. "Well—give me that canteen." He downed the last of the chocolate. Ranzo Taber came back.

"Better be going. How do you stack up, Chaffee?"

"Nothing wrong with me except a weak ankle and an empty stomach. Once I get about half a cow inside me I'll be ready to r'ar."

He sat up, feeling a little bit giddy, and drew on his socks and boots. But he wasn't ready to stand on his own strength yet, so Ranzo Taber bent a shoulder, and in this manner they left the summit cabin. Chaffee rolled into the sled; Gay Thatcher pulled the blankets around him and stepped back.

"You take 'er down, Miss Gay," said Taber. "I'll trot behind. Mush!"

So in the deepening mists and with the peaks shrilling dismally the dog team snapped into the traces, ran the sled across the level mouth of the pass and down the eastern slopes. Full dark found them inside Taber's ranch house at the foot of the bench, found Jim Chaffee sitting up to a table and eating his first good meal in five or six days.

"Once a sourdough, always a sourdough," said Taber, smiling reminiscently. "It's been ten years since I left the Klondike, but I never been without huskies in that time. Folks have always wondered why I fooled with 'em. Well, you're the fourth man I've found up around the peaks. Two of 'em came in stiff. You're lucky. Now it ain't any of my business, But I'm wonderin' what the next play is."

The girl said nothing, leaving the question for Chaffee to answer. She had slipped back to feminine clothing, and the transformation somehow bothered Chaffee. He recollected moments when she had seemed close and intimate, when she had appeared to be fashioned out of the same simple, sturdy clay that he himself was made of. Now she had withdrawn and become silent and aloof; and she added a touch of grace and beauty to the table that marked her of another world. Nothing definite. Only the lamplit casting a glow on her clear profile. The slender suppleness of her fingers twining around the water glass.

"I've got to get into Bannock City and drop Mack a note," said Chaffee. "Then I reckon I'll give my foot a week to limber up. After that I reckon I'll sort of breeze back into Roaring Horse again. Maybe—maybe not. Depends."

"Mack is laid up with a bullet in his shoulder," said the girl.

"Who did it?" demanded Chaffee with so much force that Ranzo Taber's interest switched away from his coffee cup.

The girl went through the story, her soft voice rounding out the details of Stirrup S passing into other hands, of the arrival of the first homesteaders. Chaffee's face settled. "Where's Miz Satterlee?"

"She left. I don't know where she went."

"Where's the crew?"

"Some are at Melotte's watching over Mack. Others just took the trail. Times have changed, Jim. It is Mr. Woolfridge's country now."

"I suppose," agreed Chaffee, heavy hearted. "It was a sweet little valley. Just made for a man to live out a comfortable life with good friends. Jupiter, but I hate to see that swept from under my feet."

"Aren't things always going out from under our feet?" murmured Gay. "Isn't that life—nothing sure, nothing settled?"

Ranzo Taber looked at her with a significant bobbing of his head. "Now yore talkin' from experience, Miss Gay."

"I suppose. I have never known a certain day since I was fifteen. And the older I grow the less sure I am of anything—even of myself."

"Well," went on Taber, "this is a darned good place to rest up, Chaffee. Make it two weeks. I'll teach you how to run huskies, like I taught Miss Gay when she was a youngster. Both of you stay on. Miss Gay"—and again significance dwelt in Taber's words—"you need a little rest. Won't be anybody around here to pester you. I'll see to that."

"I'm obliged, but I better get on to Bannock City and get in touch with some folks," said Chaffee. Taber's talk concerning the girl stirred his curiosity, though he tried to keep from showing it. She looked across to him in a manner that for a moment reminded him again of the scene in the jail. Wistful—asking him unvoiced questions.

"Thanks, Ranzo. You have always been kind to me. But I must get back to the capital."

Therefore the both of them were in a rig driven by Taber by starlight the following morning. They reached Bannock City an hour or less before the stage started south to the railroad. Chaffee felt a little flimsy and he allowed them to help him into the hotel and up to a second floor room, although it touched his pride to be thus nursed. He had always been self-sufficient, always had leaned confidently on his strength. Ranzo Taber shook hands and left behind him a hearty invitation. Gay walked into the hall and spoke a moment with Taber in a subdued voice; then Taber went away and the girl returned to the room to find Jim Chaffee in a chair and studying the blank walls with a set, grim gaze.

"Well, Jim."

She had meant to say good-bye then and there. But the words got turned aside, and she found herself asking questions. "What are you going to do?"

"The hardest work I ever did in my life for the next ten days," said he. "Rest. Stay off my feet. Eat. And wish to God I was on the other side of the range. Jupiter, but it is going to actually hurt."

"Then back to fight? Oh, Jim, why?"

"It's my country, ain't it?"

"Do you know, I have heard you get stubborn like this before. And somehow I always feel a bit proud of you. But I wish—Isn't there some other little creek with cottonwoods growing around it, and peace for you?"

He shook his head. She saw his rawboned hands come together and grip hard. "I reckon not. Tell me—has Locklear still got all those burglar-jawed gents around him?"

"I have heard by the grapevine route," said she, "that most of them were sent away. When I left I saw only three or four. Perrine and his men are off in the desert somewhere. Everything is on the boom for the new settlers. Mr. Woolfridge has sent his ad through half a dozen states for them to come. Promising them everything when the power company builds its dam in the Roaring Horse. And his name is on about every third building in town.

It is his town, Jim."

He absorbed the news silently. By and by he raised his head. "Yes, I'm going back there."

"I knew you would," she murmured. "Good-bye, Jim."

That roused him. He took hold of the chair arms and half rose. "Wait a minute. Now wait. When am I going to see you again—where will you be?"

"Our trails seem to keep crossing, don't they, Jim?" She had a trick of smiling to hide the elusive wistfulness of her heart. "But—it can't go on forever. I don't know when I'll see you next. I don't know where I'll be. There'll come a time, though, when you and I will be far apart. One of these days I am going to leave this country."

"Why?"

Her sturdy shoulders rose. "Isn't it human to be seeking something you haven't got?"

"What would that be?" he persisted, worry creeping along his face.

"I don't even know," said she. "The trouble with me, Jim, is that I have no roots down. They were torn out of the ground a few years ago. There is nothing to hold me steady."

"I sort of hate to hear you talk that way," he protested. "Change—why have things got to change so fast? Here's something else sliding away from me. I wish—" But he never finished the remark, falling instead into another somber study. Presently the girl prompted him with a gentle phrase: "Wish what, Jim?"

"I reckon I've got no right to wish anything at the present state of affairs. I want you to know, Gay, I'm thinkin' of what you've done for me. And I'll remember it a long, long time." His fist doubled. "I'm not sayin' what I want to say."

She came over to him as he rose and balanced on his one sound foot. She put out her hand, manlike; his big palm closed around it and he peered down into her face, sharp and questioning. "That time I first saw you passin' on the street—I never made a mistake. I wanted to meet you pretty bad."

Her smile deepened. "And I thought you would never manage it. You are a fine gentleman, Jim. I wish you all the luck in the world. And if I could only feel surer of your safety in the future—"

Her hand was warm with her quick blood; fragrance rose from her hair. She was a woman through and through, troubling his senses with her sweet desirability. Again she appeared to be asking him questions with her calm eyes, and there was a contradiction in the firm red lips. Her chin tilted to meet his glance, and somehow the soft curves of her throat sent fire through his veins. He was still weak and his will relaxed. Otherwise it never would have happened. But the next moment he had drawn her tightly against him, murmuring some choked phrase, and he had kissed her. She was as still as death. He felt both hands resting lightly on his shoulders, and the throb of her heart swelled against his chest. Then she swayed, the pressure breaking the spell. He dropped his arms, a fury of self-reproach blazing on his lean face.

"If I had a gun, Gay, I'd ask you to take a shot at me!"

Her eyes were brilliant; she had caught her upper lip between her teeth as if to suppress the tears. And she studied Jim Chaffee as no other woman had ever studied him before. "You—you have nothing to be sorry for, Jim. Nothing! That was my reward and I'll always remember it."

"I'm God's own fool."

"You are the finest gentleman I have ever known," said she. Her voice dropped almost to a whisper. "But—I wish you had asked me some questions first. Oh, Jim, I have wanted you to ask them for so long a time. Good-bye, my dear."

He held himself up to the chair, still struggling with self-condemnation. The girl said nothing more. Slipping from the room she half ran down the stairs and out to the street.

The stage was waiting in front of the hotel, and she caught up her grip and started to climb inside. A puncher idled across the street, and her attention, struck by something familiar, dwelt on him. Poised on the coach step she beckoned to him.

"Aren't you a Stirrup S man?"

"Was, ma'am. Ain't no Stirrup S any more."

"What are you doing here?"

"Jus' a-roamin'."

"Go up to room twenty-one. Jim Chaffee is there."

The puncher omitted a wild yip and plunged through the door. She heard him pounding along the stairs and she heard him yelling Chaffee's name. Then she settled inside the coach and a moment later was bound south for the railroad. There was nobody else traveling this morning; and so she could freely cry. Which she did.

Red Corcoran—that was the name of the ex-Stirrup S puncher—rolled an endless number of cigarettes and pumped Chaffee bone dry. Throughout the story he interjected amazing epithets. "Th' hell!" "Oh, the dirty Dion-eyed dawgs!" "Jim, yore a-makin' me inhuman an' impervious to charitable sentiments." "An' so the gal pulls yuh outen the hole? Say, I'd marry a woman for lessn' that."

"How about Locklear's white savages?"

"Shucks, they wasn't paid by Locklear, Jim. Ain't it clear by now? They was imported by Woolfridge. He's the main squeeze. Well, they've mostly went away. Couple-three-four left. They did the job, didn't they? Guess Woolfridge thinks so. Got a reason to think so. A flea can't even bite in Roarin' Horse 'less he gets orders from Woolfridge. Oh, it's a turrible mess. Stirrup S gone. Half dozen other outfits along the rim gone. Some old-timers left, but they ain't doin' no arguin'. Woolfridge has done put his moniker on a flock of buildin's. He did it dirty, but he did it. And what's anybody goin' to do about it? Nothin'."

"Where's Perrine?"

"Sashayin' around the country lookin' for yuh. As far as yore concerned they got the bee on yuh."

"I guess," agreed Chaffee. "But with all those hired plugs gone it wouldn't be so hard to buck Woolfridge and Locklear. Red, how many of the gang do you figger you could collect in ten days?"

The puncher brightened. "Fight? Why, I guess pretty close to twenty if I rode hard enough."

"Think they'll back me up in any play I make?"

"What yuh think we are?" was Corcoran's indignant rejoinder, "a pack uh yella pups? Shore! Miz Satterlee cried when she paid us off. Now if that ain't enough to make us fight I guess nothin' would. Gimme my travelin' orders and I'll do the trick."

"I'm goin' back," said Chaffee, "to find the man that killed Satterlee. Ten days I lay on my back right here. You collect the gang. Tell 'em to meet me the night of the eighth at the old ranch. If it's occupied by strangers, then have 'em meet me on the south bank of Linderman's. Keep it strictly under your Stetson. Tell the boys to do the same. When we get started we work under cover and we put the fear of God in somebody's black heart. Get goin', Red."

"I'm gone," said Red Corcoran, and hoisted himself toward the door. On the threshold he tarried. "Better stay under cover yoreself. Perrine or Woolfridge or Locklear might have friends here which'd squeal on yuh."

"I'm all right. You travel."

Corcoran had one more bright thought. "Say, that Gay Thatcher ain't difficult to glance upon. Not any. Ever think of—"

But Chaffee's face turned so black and unfriendly that Corcoran closed the door in haste and departed.

CHAPTER SIXTEEN

THE SHADOW OF CATASTROPHE

Gay reached the territorial capital twenty-four hours later, and after refreshing herself at the private lodging house where she maintained her fixed residence, went directly to the governor's quarters in the domed building that sat so serenely between sweeps of lawn and trees and commanded so many vistas of the town. The governor was deep in the early morning routine, but her name forwarded by a secretary instantly opened the inner door. The tall and sparse-membered gray warrior rose with a Southern courtesy and faced his fair lieutenant.

"I'd begun to worry a little about you, Miss Thatcher. Sit down. But you look fresh and competent. I would give all that I owned to have the vigor of your years once more. You've had breakfast? Well, take coffee with me. Sereno—send out to the restaurant for coffee and rolls for Miss Thatcher and myself. Now—business."

The governor of this territory was a pure and precious type of the bearded lawyer emigrant who had risen to influence through shrewd alliances and popular appeal. He was a political being down to the very roots; he fought his battles wholly on political premises. There was something of the glorified log roller about him. He knew every man, or almost every man, in the territory who could command more than a dozen followers; his mind was a card of catalogue of names and faces, and no little of his power rose out of the ability to grip the hand of some obscure citizen and say in a booming, friendly voice: "Hello, Jeb Smith. Haven't seen you for eight years. How big is that baby boy now?" Yet because he used the old commonplace methods it was no less true that the governor was a capable officer. He used whatever instruments he could to establish his purposes. And those purposes were worthy. The territory was proud of the governor; it never had a better one. He loved his friends in the good old-fashioned way, and he fought his enemies to the last bloody political ditch also in the good old-fashion way. Such was the chief to whom Gay Thatcher reported. And to him, over the hot coffee, she rendered her report. At the end of it she added an irrelevant thought. "I'm afraid I am giving you only hearsay or only what I saw. You would have been better served, perhaps, if you had sent a man."

"No such thing," was the governor's hearty denial. "Give me the privilege of knowing what I wanted done. You have done it. Admirably. A man might have cross-examined some of those folks. Might have listened at keyholes. I didn't want that. What I wanted was a bystander's report. So friend William is up to mischief? Went out to his desert tent and brooded over this fine scheme. William is a dangerous critter. I never have any doubt about a horse that lays back his ears. That's honest meanness. But I do mightily dislike the bland-eyed brute that plays possum till you're off guard. That's William."

"Governor—how did you know he was up to anything?"

The man smiled. "I have lived a long time in public life and I have acquired a little of the serpent's wisdom. In politics, my dear girl, we credit nothing to our enemies and suspect everything of them. I like to have my foes, worthy and unworthy, near at hand where I can keep an eye on them. When they travel away from me I begin to worry over their welfare." He rose from the table and walked around the room, losing the humorously cynical attitude. His cheeks began to furrow up, his chin actually appeared to jut farther out, and a chill came to his blue-gray eyes. Piece by piece, the governor was mentally climbing into his armor.

"I have known William Woolfridge a long time," he continued, almost snapping at the name. "And I never liked him. He's lean, and he doesn't sleep sound at nights. He's got an uncommon streak of genius in him, but it works the wrong direction. He always strikes me odd. A man always has a feeling when he comes into the presence of a dangerous animal or when he is faced with some mysterious element. I always have it when I get within ten yards of William."

"I have felt it," said the girl.

"I knew you would. You can't lay a finger on it. You just know. William never set up to be a friend of mine. He has aired it in certain quarters he meant to smash me one of these days. He is hooked up with interests not beneficial to the general welfare of the territory. Now he's engaged in a promotion scheme that will give us a black eye to the world and cause many poor people much misery. I always knew he'd turn rotten, but I never was able to figure just which way he'd take. Don't understand it, either. The man's got plenty of money."

"Pride of personal power," suggested the girl.

"The governor thrust a keen, penetrating look toward her. "You have discovered his secret. Ten men would not have uncovered it.

Women feel these things. Men have to learn them. Well, he is too clever. He trims too close to legality. And many poor families will suffer. We must stop it. We must smash him!"

"I have been thinking about those advertisements he issued," said the girl. "If you will give me the morning to see certain people I think I can possibly bring you something useful."

"Who?"

"Mr. Bangor and Mr. Hunnewell."

"Hunnewell's a rat," said the governor. "Be careful of him. Bangor is trying to play the diplomat with me. He is trimming to the wind. If you want him to reveal business secrets, mention my name. Uncover your connections, and I believe he'll open up. Go to it. Now, it is very cold outside. Wrap well up, Miss Thatcher." And the governor escorted her through the executive offices and stood bareheaded in the raw December wind, watching her go down the long flight of stairs. A rough, shrewd and gallant man.

Gay went directly down Capital Avenue to the Power Building. Presently she was in T. Q. Bangor's office and pleasantly chatting over this and that. Bangor knew her social standing in town, and he also remembered her presence in Roaring Horse at the time of the rodeo. Therefore he was cordial—a great deal more cordial than a few minutes later when she swept away the polite reminiscences and came to the issue.

"Have you," she asked rather bluntly, "any particular prejudices to talking shop with a woman, Mr. Bangor?"

"Not in the least," replied Bangor, puzzled.

"Are you going to build a dam in the Roaring Horse?"

"Well, now," he murmured, and raised his hands to indicate mild bewilderment. "Isn't that a leading question?"

She admitted it was. "At the same time a public utility is more or less open to leading questions. And I am not asking information for idle purposes."

"Let me ask you a leading question, then. Who is interested in this besides yourself?"

"A gentleman at the other end of Capital Avenue," replied Gay. Bangor's reaction was instant. The air of tolerant politeness went away. He studied the girl thoughtfully as if trying to reconcile her femininity to her indisputable position of trust. And he made a wry expression. "So the governor wants to know definitely? Well, he ought to know by now how the wind blows. But if he needs further assurance I wish you'd tell him we gave over the idea of building that dam almost two weeks ago. We don't want to antagonize him at this stage of the game. And our interests have switched elsewhere. Tell him just that."

"You abandoned the idea two weeks ago? May I ask at what particular date?"

Bangor didn't grow impatient, but he conveyed the air of a man not wholly satisfied. "The governor is very inquisitive, is he not? The date was—let me think—the fourteenth of last month. At a board meeting. All our applications were withdrawn then."

She studied Bangor carefully. "I want to ask you another question, but I think I had better be fair and let you know the reason for this." And in as few words as possible she outlined Woolfridge's land settlement scheme and his promise of an irrigation project to the settlers. "Perhaps you know this. If you are not building a dam you can see the hardship it is going to work on a great many people. The governor feels badly about that. He wants to stop it. Mr. Bangor, it is almost criminal. And you are being placed in a false light with these people down there. My question is, did you tell Mr. Woolfridge you were not building the dam?"

"Yes. A letter to him the evening following the meeting of the board."

"Mr. Bangor, would you care to put that information in the form of a letter to the governor?"

Bangor got up from his chair and went to a window, looking down the avenue to the stately outline of the capitol dome. He was not afraid of the governor; he was not at all doubtful of the secure position of his company. But he wanted no breach of relations between himself and the governor; no misunderstanding that might result in unfriendly legislation at the ensuing biennial assembly. At this time he was not prepared to be stiff necked. He wanted harmony. The company had enough battles to fight without adding still another. He owed Woolfridge something for past help, yet he had decided directly after the meeting with Woolfridge in Roaring Horse that here was a man who could do a great deal of harm. Woolfridge was doing some harm right now in linking the power company with his own grandiose schemes. Two weeks ago he would have been afraid to openly oppose the man; but the last board meeting had materially altered the situation.

He turned back to his desk and drew his chair before a typewriter. A little later he handed the following letter to the girl:

MY DEAR GOVERNOR:

In order to put our recent conversation on record I wish to say that this company does not contemplate building a dam on the Roaring Horse river. We did at one time investigate the possibilities of that river, but at a recent board meeting, held November 14th of this year, wholly abandoned the idea. All our applications for rights were subsequently withdrawn.

It has come to our attention that certain individuals are advertising land in that district with the assurance that we will build a dam. In this connection I wish to say that a letter was forwarded to Mr. William Wells Woolfridge on November fourteenth, by his personal agent, Mr. Alexander Hunnewell, in which we distinctly stated that no dam was to be built.

I desire to place this information before you that this company be held wholly free from any unfortunate speculation.

Very truly . . .

"Thank you," said Gay, folding the letter into her purse. "I am sure you will never regret having expressed this in written form."

T. Q. Bangor smiled, somewhat grimly. "Had I felt I might later regret it, the letter certainly wouldn't have been written. Give the governor my personal regards and tell him I hope he wins his battle. However, that's really a useless hope. He always does win. I have been charmed, Miss Thatcher—"

Gay left the Power Building and walked swiftly to a less imposing structure farther down the street. She climbed one flight of stairs and entered a door labeled: "Woolfridge Investment Co. Alex. Hunnewell, Mgr." Hunnewell was in, his feet tipped on a desk, cracking nuts between his teeth, and looking very bored. He made no effort to rise when he saw his visitor. There was, in fact, a sudden and faint insolence in his welcome. "How do. This is a pleasure. Brightens a dull day. What can I do for you?"

He was a flat, lifeless sort of a creature. In the presence of Woolfridge he trembled and was afraid of the very breath he drew. Being that type of man it was natural that he should swing to the other extreme when relieved of his superior's presence and become a petty tyrant; inevitable that he should exercise a back-biting meanness under the protection of a power that was not his own.

"My name is—"

"I know it very well," broke in Hunnewell. "Fact is, I know considerably more about you than you'd imagine."

"How interesting," murmured the girl, recognizing his quality. "I won't take up your time, then, with unnecessary information. I noticed you have been advertising for homesteaders down in Roaring Horse. Of course, I could find out by going directly to newspapers, but perhaps you'll tell me when you first issued the ads."

"Mailed out of here the sixteenth," was Hunnewell's prompt answer. He seemed to wish to emphasize his importance. "I work rapidly. But if you're interested in land don't let the date bother you. Still plenty of it open. Suggest you go to see Mr. Woolfridge."

The girl was hardly able to suppress the mingled anger and satisfaction. "In other words you got up the ads, with all the facts contained in them, two days after you were informed there was to be no dam built in the Roaring Horse."

"Cer—" began Hunnewell, and then leaped to his feet, all abluster with temper and uncertainty. "See here, what are you saying? What do you want? What right have you to come in this office with an insulting statement like that? I do not relish the remarks. Who do you represent, anyhow?"

"Whoever I represent," said Gay calmly, "be sure he is a bigger man than Mr. Woolfridge. Was my statement wrong? Did you know—"

"Never mind that!" snapped Hunnewell. "You've got no business prying into our affairs. I could have you arrested for libel." He ran his fingers through his sandy hair, the uncertainty developing into a feeling of fear. He was not the man to command a situation like this; he was only a dummy, a chore boy instructed to fetch and carry. Woolfridge, confronted with Gay Thatcher's matter-of-fact remark, would have smiled politely and never changed expression, and in good and sufficient time would have taken care of it by other means. But Hunnewell, afraid of the business from the very beginning, now saw the shadow of disaster before him. And he made a grievous error. "Who *do* you represent?"

"Was my statement correct?" insisted Gay.

"What of it!" cried Hunnewell. He came around the table and faced the girl, poking a forefinger at her. "See here, young woman, if you know what's good for you you'll drop this business and get out of the territory."

"Mr. Hunnewell, you're stepping beyond the mark," said Gay quietly.

"Am I?" snapped Hunnewell, shaking his head. "No I'm not. I've had reason to look you up. I've been digging into a little past history. What I know—and if I air what I know—will bar you from the decent folks you've been traveling with around this town. It'll drive you out. Hear me?"

The girl stepped back from him hand reaching for the door. She watched his eyes with a kind of tight despair on her own white face and her lips were pressed together until the blood ran out of them. Hunnewell thought she meant to leave and he jammed a foot against the door.

"Come around here and meddle, will you? I'll scorch you. You drop this and shut up. Five years ago you ran away from home with a man. Did, didn't you? Don't dare deny it, do you?"

She said nothing. Hunnewell grinned unpleasantly. "Lived with that man as a common-law wife in another town—"

"That's a lie!"

"So? Try to make Bannock City believe it's a lie. You can't prove you didn't. Anyhow, you went away with him. Disappeared. Where's he now? Where did you live the next three-four years? Back East, uh? Who furnished you the money? And you been traveling around mighty free ever since. Even your best friends here don't know your history. If it's a lie, why didn't you tell them? That man never went back to Bannock City to tell folks it was a lie. And I can produce a party that saw you and the fellow living in a hotel at Red Buttes a week after you skipped. A lie, uh? Why—" and Hunnewell had worked himself into such a state of mind that he almost pushed her against the wall. "You drop this and get out of town. If you don't I'll ruin you.

Good and plenty. Not a word, you understand?"

He moved away and gave her a chance to open the door. She almost fell on the stairs. Out in the street she stopped to catch hold of herself. The past had marched across the years to face her again with its grimy shadow; to leer and whisper all of that old and horrible story in her ears, to wreck the later life she had so laboriously and courageously built up. Somebody—a friend—spoke to her in passing, but she was so blinded by the struggle inside her that she never heard. She was whispering: "Oh, Jim—Jim! I'll never see you again. And you'll find it out some day—you'll hear that tale. I wish you had asked me questions. I wish you had!"

Throughout her life she had been a clear-minded girl, a rigorously self-disciplined girl. So when she came to the town's daily paper she controlled her mind and heart once more. Going in she asked the question uppermost in her head. With the information she returned to the capitol building and was admitted to the governor's office. He saw the drawn expression of her face and became immediately concerned.

"I told you to wrap well. It's cold outside. Here, sit down. Sereno—go rustle up some good hot coffee for us."

She got T. Q. Bangor's letter from her purse and handed it to the governor. He read through it.

"I knew that. What else?"

"Woolfridge sent out his advertisement for settlers two days after he knew the dam wasn't going to be built. That can be proven by the newspapers who received copies of the ad."

The governor's eyes turned chilly. His jaw seemed to shoot outward. "Used the mails to propagate that bunco game—I see. I read the ads myself. Didn't actually promise anything definite about the dam. Suggested—inferred—skipped around the edge of the crater." He rose and put a big paw on her shoulder. "You're a better man than the usual last run of shad I've got cluttering my doorstep. I'll talk to the attorney-general about this. Provable fraud—I think." He turned around the room, stopped to study a painting of his predecessor, muttered under his breath. And turned back again to her. "I'm not going to hit him yet. Not through the regular machinery. Never like to hang a man if he'll hang himself. Don't want the opposition to say I'm persecuting an enemy. Don't want to give them any ammunition right now. There is a better way. My dear girl, I must send you off to wind up this business. Willing?"

"Governor, I almost cry when I think of those wagons coming into Roaring Horse with all the women and kiddies—"

"We'll stop him. We'll let his own machinery devour him. Listen carefully. You take this letter and go back to Roaring Horse. Have the weekly paper up there print it. You won't have any trouble about that. Sam Philips owns the sheet and he's too honest to be bought. Sam knows me well and he'll take care of the story. That's the end of the Woolfridge business right there. The county will be full of it in twenty-four hours. And the news will carry on out to the rest of the territory and stop all would-be homesteaders."

Gay left. The governor roamed the vast office again and came to a stand. He was an old campaigner, a scarred veteran, and he knew humble folk inside out—their impulses, their honesty, their angers. And so, perhaps, he knew what he had done; perhaps he understood the upheaval that would follow publication of the story. Perhaps he had some dim foreknowledge of tragedy to come. At heart the governor was kindly and without malice. He played the political game according to accepted rules. Yet once his deep sense of justice was touched he was apt to revert to the laws of the Old Testament. In his earlier days he had seen men hung by vigilante rule, and there was still in him a full approval of that type of elemental justice. So he stared at the picture of his predecessor, eyes narrowing into the future and his cheeks touched by a winter bleakness. Even so, it was not given him to foresee the swift flood of passion about to flow over Roaring Horse, not to realize how many different characters were to be caught up in the smashing, overwhelming current—to be battered, sucked under, spewed aside.

Gay Thatcher arrived in Roaring Horse a day and a half later. She placed the story in the hands of the veteran newspaperman, Sam Philips, and considered her mission ended. The paper came out on a Saturday; two days removed. Not knowing what to do, and impelled by a queer restlessness, she took up her old room at the Gusher and waited.

CHAPTER SEVENTEEN

JIM CHAFFEE RIDES BACK

Jim Chaffee left Bannock City by stage early on a wind-bitten morning, caught a train across the range, and dropped off sometime after noon at the yellow station house that served the Roaring Horse country. The Roaring Horse stage was waiting; Chaffee crossed the tracks, sharply watching the driver. Sooner or later the news of his return would be abroad; he couldn't help this turn of events, but he did hope that the tidings might be delayed until he was well into the desert. But as soon as he recognized the driver he knew that little time would be lost in transmitting the fact that he had set foot upon debatable soil again—and was again fair game. That driver happened to be Jeff Ganashayd, one of those fellows who was willing to be all things to all men. There was no malice in Ganashayd; only, he had a tongue never still. And Jim Chaffee's presence, an item of importance to everybody in the county, would certainly put that tongue in motion.

Chaffee saluted the man cheerfully and climbed to the top seat. "Only passenger, Jeff. Let's go."

"Sa-ay," drawled Ganashayd, eyes growing wider, "ain't yuh kinder unexpected?" He dropped into his seat and set the team on the homeward trial. "Gosh, Jim, yuh mean to go right into town?"

Chaffee brushed that aside, having questions of his own. "What's news, Jeff?"

"Nothin' much an' a little bit of everythin'," opined the stage driver. "Course, I ain't a man to do much talkin'. Minds my own business and says little. The country is full of homesteaders. Yeah. Never saw the beat. Swarmin' in like flies. Mostly folks from the adjoinin' countries. Mack Moran was plugged but is doin' well. Miz Satterlee left the district. Injun Eagle went back to the blanket an' sure give folks a chill. But, sa-ay, the biggest item was a story printed in the paper, tellin' how they wasn't goin' to be no dam and Mr. Woolfridge knew they wasn't all the time. New settlers seems sorter riled about that. Some talk of bringin' somebody to book about it. But, pshaw, a man'll hear lots uh things foolish. That Thatcher woman drifted back. Heard a story about her—"

"Back up," said Chaffee with a flat emphasis on the words. "Turn off on this side road, Jeff. I'm goin' up to Cherry's horse ranch."

"I got to make time," objected Ganashayd.

"Only a couple of miles out of your way," was Chaffee's calm reply. "What's two miles to an empty stage with an empty driver on it? It'll give you that much more time to cook up a good stiff yarn about me. Anyhow, I ain't walkin'."

"I know when to mind my own business," stated Ganashayd earnestly. "Won't say a word to nobody."

"Bear off," insisted Chaffee. So the stage

took the side road and closed upon a clutter of ranch houses topped by a windmill tower. Presently they were at the end of the road with a pack of dogs sounding at them. Chaffee swung to the ground. "Pay you next time, Jeff. Tell everybody you saw me. Tell 'em I'm poor in the flanks and I limp on one leg. Tell 'em I look humble and act humble and feel humble—but that I'm here and I'll see everybody soon. So long, Jeff."

Jeff Ganashayd went back the side road much faster than he went up. He took the curves on two wheels and laid his long whip across the horses' hips. His glance, ever and anon, raked the reaches around Cherry's horse ranch, and when a little later he saw a horseman questing northward from the ranch his eyes turned as bright as those of some magpie who had sighted a shoestring. "Sa-ay, won't this knock somebody bow-legged? Jupiter, what a story for Roarin' Horse! I ain't told nothin' half as good since I saw the man which struck Billy Patterson. Go 'long!" The whip popped and across the desert and down the street of Roaring Horse he charged, brake blocks snarling against the wheels. And since he was a born gossip with the love of an audience he bided his time till the customary crowd had collected. Luis Locklear was just strolling up when Jeff Ganashayd launched a liquid parabola of tobacco juice across the wagon wheel and announced in a sounding voice:

"Chaffee got off the train this noon, an' I drove him to Cherry's horse ranch. He's headin' north. Saw him ride thataway later. He looked mean; he looked awful hard. Never saw a man with so much sudden death in his orbs. Toted two guns an' a rifle. Extra bandolier uh cattridges slung arount his shoulders. And he said—says he to me in a growlin', nasty way: 'Ganashayd, doom is a-comin' down on the haids o' sev'ral gents in Roarin' Horse. I'm out to kill.' S'help me, them was his literal words."

After that Ganashayd enlarged the topic. But Luis Locklear passed quietly on and into the land office. A little later there was a rider going out of Roaring Horse with quirt flailing down, bound toward the lava stretch where Theodorik Perrine's gang was quartered.

The Cherrys were old friends of Jim Chaffee's. From them he borrowed horse, gear, and a hasty snack, and headed northward with the sun falling down the sky on his left. The stage was a-whirling rapidly beyond sight, and he knew hardly another hour could pass without the tocsin being sounded. He hated to admit it, yet those ten days in Bannock City had been the same as a visit to heaven. He had worried, but he had been physically idle. And after the slogging labor of the past years, as well as the hard punishment of those few days of fighting, it had seemed to him almost a sinful pleasure to lie dormant while the daylight hours went around.

He was again full of vital energy. The country of his choice lay stretched into the misty horizons, swelling like the surface of a placid ocean. It was sage and sand, arroyo and butte —the same as the land to the other side of the range; yet somehow it was a fairer land here and he felt freer in it. The peaks were heavy with snow, the bench was lightly overlaid; down in the flat country no snow had so far touched the earth, though the air was shot with the warning of it and the sun was dim above unusual clouds. So he traveled leisurely, timing himself against the hour when he was to meet the ex-Stirrup S men at the old quarters. And around twilight of this short day, he surmounted a knoll to confront the familiar, heart-quickening sight of his old homestead. The cottonwoods marched against the deepening blue, the creek bank was heavy with shadows. And the house sat serenely in the shelter.

But only for a moment did he feel the pleasure of revisiting. The next moment he was wistfully sad and regretful. A light glimmered out of the cabin windows. Somebody else enjoyed the comfort of the structure he had created with so much sweat and pride and hope for the future. He reined in only a moment, absorbing the picture. Then he spoke quietly to the horse and circled away for Stirrup S.

"Things change," he murmured. "That's life, I reckon. And if a man doesn't move with the times the ground is cut from under his feet. I must be getting old. Seems like I'm always harpin' back to what used to be. Well, it's hard for a fellow to bury a piece of his life in one spot of the earth and then go away and forget. I'll never find another place like it."

Twilight was absorbed into darkness. A sickle moon cast a blurred reflection above the clouds, the stars were hidden. And in the desert quietness he became aware that someone followed him. Nothing of sight nor of sound came forward to tell him this; it was rather one of those impalpable warnings carrying across the air to vaguely impinge on his nerves. Some men are given the faculty of feeling such things; some men are not. It is almost an instinct and comparable to that sense in birds which turns them south and north on the approach of the seasons. Jim

Chaffee had felt such warnings before. When he obeyed them he profited; when he tried to reason out the strange fact of their existence he invariably went wrong. He traveled onward, making certain of the warning.

Presently he shifted his course to right angles and fell into a gully, waiting. "Four-five hours would give them time to get on my trail," he said to himself. "But how would they know where to look? Maybe they figure an old dog always strays home." No signals rose behind. Far off a coyote lifted its bark and wail to the profound mystery of the universe. Somewhere was a like reply, and that was all. Chaffee tarried fifteen minutes and then went on. Perhaps his senses played him false. Both uncertain and restless he pressed the horse to a faster pace. He passed a solitary pine and a hedgelike clump of juniper bushes; he struck a beaten trail and then the outline of all that had been the Stirrup S home ranch lay dark and obscure in front of him.

He stopped, oppressed by the tenancy of those chilly shadows. Once Stirrup S had been crowded with life; a light had glimmered from the big house; melody and warmth had dwelt in the crew's quarters. Fine men had walked the yard, proud of all that Stirrup S meant— its vast range; its wide-flung herds. A domain it had been, a little empire apart, a haven and refuge, a sturdy piece of the historic West. Now it was but a cheerless relic of brave dreams gone to defeat. Out beyond in the still heavier shadows Dad Satterlee lay asleep. Miz Satterlee was gone, the crew scattered; never again would the corrals echo to the same shouts, the same epithets, the same ribald jeering. This had been his home; and the thought of it renewed the feeling of homesickness in him.

"Times change. I guess we ain't got any right to stick to the old, familiar things. But it goes hard—it goes hard."

His old-time partners were not on hand, otherwise a light would be burning. Dropping from the saddle, he led the horse nearer a corral and left it. Walking alongside the bars of the corral he was more distinctly assailed by the sensation that others were abroad in the night, behind him or about him. The farther he issued into the yard the more strongly did the belief become until at last he halted, drawing his muscles together and dropping his gun arm. He stood between the crew's quarters and the big house, facing westward toward the gaunt outline of the barn. He had not been aware of a wind before, yet there appeared to be a rustling and a whispering and a soft abrasion of sounds running here and there. It seemed to him to grow louder around the crew's quarters; it seemed to him the shadows were shifting. He stepped sidewise, closing upon the porch of the big house, at the same time watching the other direction with flaring eyes.

Was it the Stirrup S bunch, waiting for him and yet wishing to keep under cover for fear of the forces leagued against them? Supposing his friends were over there? They could hear him. Why didn't somebody challenge? Did they figure it was his play and not theirs? Well, maybe it was. He debated, more and more sure of company in the yard. At that point he heard the first definite breaking of silence—a boot dragging along a board, a subdued murmur. All this by the crew's quarters. Nothing came from the big house. He got to the steps of the house porch and made his decision; he drew a breath, lifted his gun from the holster, and sent a challenge running softly across the yard.

"Who's that?"

It was as if he had opened the door to bedlam. A staccato roar rent the silence and the blackness. Flames mushroomed at widely divergent points; bullets smashed along the porch and spat at his very feet. And above this he heard the booming sledging voice of Theodorik Perrine summoning up the attack.

"Now we got him! Snap into it! Lay lead

over there—lay lead over there!"

He leaped up the steps and over the porch. The door was closed; he flung it open, slid inside, and slammed it shut. The next moment he had jumped away and down to a window. The door seemed about to be beaten off its hinges by the impact of bullets. They came onward, Perrine's mighty, sounding wrath like the break of rollers on a beach. They were up to the porch; from the window he saw their shadowed forms weaving this way and that way, and he opened on them with a brace of shots that scattered the gang and flattened them down against the porch boards. But he knew the diversion was only for the moment. He could not stop them; he could not keep them from coming through—either by the front or the back. What he could do was play a game of hide-way. Another shot humbled them for a few moments. In those moments he slipped up the stairs. On the landing he heard the front door give and go down. Only Perrine's strength could have smashed it so suddenly and completely; and they were inside, roving here and there with a singular recklessness until the giant that led them boomed again.

"You go outside, Clipper! Watch! Back door—for the love o' God, watch that back door!"

"Listen," grumbled one of the men, "this ain't no way to get him. Damn' place is full uh holes an' shadders. Le's go outside and string around it. Burn the joint. Can't miss him then."

"I want to get my hands on him," muttered Perrine.

"Use yore head—"

"Shut up! This is my party!"

The giant had gone mad. Chaffee's groping arm touched a table in the hallway. There was a piece of Indian pottery on it. Seizing the jar, he bent over the banister and dropped it down. The smash of it on the lower floor, woke their restless guns. Smoke swirled upward; hot profanity beat along the darkness. They were falling flat, overturning chairs and tables for protection.

"That corner—"

"Chaffee—yore dead now!"

Chaffee went on down the upper hall a-tiptoe. A window opened to the roof of the back porch, and he hoped to let himself down quietly and circle around to his horse. But in treading the hall his boots struck a loose board. It sent out a sharp protest, and as he reached the window there seemed to be a general break-up of Perrine's party. The renegades broke in all directions, boots drumming the lower flooring, sounding out of the doors.

He debated, trying to catch the meaning of the move. Then he heard a brace of shots cracking from the general direction of the barn. Hard after, Perrine went a-bellowing across the yard.

"He's wiggled clear! He's monkeyin' with our hosses! Clipper—Clipper, where in the name o' Judas are yuh? Nev' mind upstairs—that's just a sound!" The rest of his vast fury rolled out unprintable and blasphemous. Chaffee shook his head, not understanding. He drew the catches of the window and raised it, noise lost in the general racket going on below. He shoved himself through and worked to the edge of the porch roof. Back here was quietness; out front the guns were playing. Looking to the ground from this elevation was like staring into some black pool of water.

"Maybe it's another neat little device of Mr. Perrine's," he said to himself. "He's as crazy as a louse on a hot brick. But I can't be speculatin' all night. Here's a break. Better take it. Now, if they's a man waitin'—"

He dropped and hit the ground on all fours, feeling the impact stabbing his still insecure ankle. So far so good. No gun met him, nobody came catapulting out of the surrounding shadows. He rose and galloped away from the house, hearing the thundering voice of

Theodorik Perrine rise and fall from one raging epithet to another. He skirted a shed, reached the corral, and hurried around it. His horse still stood, though restless and circling the reins. Chaffee never gave it a thought; he sprang up and turned the pony. A voice came sibilantly from somewhere.

"Jim."

"Who's that?"

"Mark—Mark Eagle." Horse and rider closed in, came beside Jim. The Indian's arm dropped on Chaffee's shoulder. "I am you your friend."

"How in the name of—"

"Let's ride out first."

The pair spurred off, the drum of their ponies bringing Perrine's gang down the yard on the jump. But presently they had become only murmuring figures in the distance. The reports of the shooting were damped. "Better swing," said Chaffee. "They'll be on our heels pretty quick."

"No," said Mark Eagle with the quiet, expressionless manner so characteristic of him. "I drove their horses away before I fired those shots. They will hunt around some while, my friend."

"Now, listen Mark, how did you bust into this?"

"This afternoon I saw you going north. I

was hidden in a gully. I have led a solitary life recently, Jim. I have come near nobody. But I saw you and I followed. I know many things—too many things. But I was by the corral when Perrine's outfit opened up. The rest was not hard. I am glad to see you back."

"That goes double," muttered Chaffee. "I owe you somethin', Mark. Blamed if I don't. Well—let's swing around anyhow. I sent word ahead for the old outfit to meet me back there. It's plain they won't. So we'll try Linderman's, which is the alternate rendezvous."

"They will not be at Linderman's," said Mark Eagle, never altering his tones a whit. "They were at Melotte's a little before sundown—part of them. Others are scattered."

"How do you know, Mark? You were on my trail around then."

"I saw Melotte's from a distance at four o'clock. He is building a barn and they are working on it. I saw them."

"They'd still have time to reach Linderman's," insisted Chaffee. "And they wouldn't turn me down. I told Red Corcoran in Bannock City ten days ago to round 'em up."

"Red Corcoran," said Mark softly, "never reached Melotte's, Jim. He is dead—killed eight days ago—up in the bench behind Cherry's horse ranch. I found him, with a bullet in his heart. And I saw a big boot track near by, as big a boot track as you found back on the livery stable."

"Dead!" cried Chaffee, struck clean through by the news. "Red? Why—Perrine killed him?" He sat a long time, staring up to the hidden stars, sad and outraged and remembering the sturdy, reckless courage of the man. "Another fine friend gone. Why was it Jeff Ganashayd didn't mention that when I saw him to-day?"

"Nobody knows but me—and Perrine. It is way back on the bench, Jim. The story was on the ground. Corcoran coming from the low pass—coming from you. And Perrine ran into him. Wasn't it a good chance for Perrine to settle a grudge? I buried Red."

Chaffee's hand rose and fell. "Mark, I wish you'd help me. I wish you'd round up the boys and have them meet me somewhere."

"I will. And the time has come to tell you something else. Light a match."

Chaffee found and struck a match. The light flared on Mark Eagle's rounding coppered cheeks and revealed the smeared paint; revealed as well the blanket enfolding him, the fringed leggings. The Indian drew the blanket open and displayed his bare chest. Then the light went out and Mark Eagle was speaking with a rising sonorousness. "I was raised an Indian till I went to government school. A white man's ways looked good to me. I learned them; I followed them. To be like a white man was to be honorable, to keep a straight tongue. I have kept a straight tongue. But, my friend, it is hard to go against a man's own blood. My heart kept running out even while I turned the pages of the ledgers. And one day after you were gone, when I saw how evil a time had come to Roaring Horse, I went back to the blanket. And now what have I found? That I am no longer an Indian. The blanket is not for me. My heart is divided—and always will be. It is bad. Never should I have left my father for a government school."

He paused a moment, expelling a great breath; and Chaffee thought the Indian was staring at the sky. "I have kept a straight tongue. I am proud of it. But I know things that you should know. And now I will tell. I was back of the stable that night—in the darkness, thinking of my father. Men came there, each one apart. I saw them, but they didn't see me. The gambler came, breathing very hard. Perrine came, swearing to himself—but these men did not kill Satterlee even if they meant to do it. Another man came, hardly breathing at all. And he was there long before any of the others, no more than five yards away from me. He killed Satterlee, Jim. And his heart was very cold and hard when he did it. He had thought about it a long time, or he would have breathed harder. I know these things because that is my blood. I have said nothing all this while. It is not a white man's way to keep a straight tongue—and a still one. Maybe. But it is an Indian's way to help his friends. Is that not a better thing? Satterlee was my friend. So are you. I tell you—Woolfridge killed Satterlee."

After that, long moments of silence intervened. Mark Eagle had wrapped himself in his blanket again, stolid, patient. Chaffee drew a breath. The match snapped between his fingers. Out of the distant wastes rose the ancient chant of the coyote, bearing in it the impress of primeval desolation and eternal mystery; and far, far away that cry was taken up and reëchoed, indescribably mournful. Chaffee spoke quietly.

"You go round up the boys, Mark. Tell them to meet me to-morrow night behind the rodeo stands."

He might have gone by the way of Melotte's, for his destination was to town. But sure as he was of his partners' discretion he was not at all sure of Melotte's crew. And, though his presence was known by now, he could at least keep people from guessing where he meant to strike. Mark Eagle could do the chore safely, whispering his summons to one of the boys. They would say nothing. Nor did he want to meet Perrine again to-night; and Perrine would be scouring the main road. So he took a circuitous route and arrived back of Roaring Horse near twelve. There was an abandoned barn near the rodeo field; he left his horse in it, shut the door, and advanced along the deep darkness of the street.

The land office was closed. He saw that first because it was to the land office his attention immediately traveled. Looking to the Gusher he studied the corner windows on the second floor—Woolfridge's quarters. And they, too, were dark. Either the man was abed or out on his ranch. It made no particular difference to Chaffee; he was not ready to meet Woolfridge to-night. At the same time he noted certain changes about Roaring Horse. It was a fatter-looking place. A number of tents were up in the empty lots between rodeo field and the town proper. In the dwelling houses so usually tenantless he saw lights winking. The stores were open beyond their accustomed hour, and the saloons seemed to be doing considerable business. Strange faces appeared along the illuminated window fronts—appeared and slid into the shadows. He saw

Locklear come out of the Gusher and sink to rest in a shrouded corner of the porch. And, still watching, it became evident to him that men were quietly patrolling the town. Quietly idling at intervals by the hotel porch. Passing word with the sheriff.

"Expectin' me, I guess," he murmured, transferring his glance to that room above the Tilton's store where Doc Fancher kept office. Naturally the panes glowed with the reflection of Fancher's lamp. Fancher never seemed to go to bed. He debated, half of a mind to detour and visit the county coroner. Fancher was a stout friend and absolutely safe. But supposing Fancher was being watched with the knowledge he, Jim Chaffee, might make just such a visit? It was more or less known, the close regard these two had for each other. Of a sudden Chaffee chuckled softly. "Won't do that—but I'll do the next best thing."

He retreated, circled the town at a safe distance, and gained the back of Tilton's drygoods store. This was another of those buildings with a flat roof and a triangular false front rising before the roof. Chaffee chinned himself up a porch post, set foot on a window ledge, hooked his fingers across the cornice, and teetered out in space. He achieved the tar-papered roof and went tiptoeing across it. He was directly above Fancher's office; in going to the street side of the building he passed the rectangular box that capped the roof trap door. If he opened that he could look down on Fancher's very head. But he resisted the temptation and curled himself in a corner, shielded by the false front and the yard high coping that ran around the other sides. It was very cold, but he alternately dozed and woke till full daylight.

There were small ports cut through the coping and false front to let water flow off the roof top. Flat on his stomach and one cheek to the tar paper he could command a partial view westward on the street through these. And as the morning passed a great many citizens crossed his vision. Locklear, looking more taciturn and unmanageable than ever; three of the hired gunmen walking abreast—at which Chaffee murmured some mild oath; Callahan the saloon keeper, jowls looking very fat and unhealthy by day. These and others were familiar faces. But he saw a great many new faces—rawboned and sunburned men who slouched idly here and there; who fell into pairs and by degrees collected into a crowd. Then the crowd would split and move away. But it was a singular thing that this drawing together occurred many times, and each time seemed to be larger and to hold longer. Men gestured with short jabs of elbows and arms;

sometimes the parley appeared to grow heated.

Beyond noon, Perrine and his gang rode into town. Chaffee's interest sharpened. Even from the roof's eminence he made out the giant's sleepy eyes and sand-grimed cheeks. Perrine had been riding most of the night, so much was plain; and the burly one's temper lay heavily on the scowling brow. The whole party dropped reins by Callahan's saloon and went in. There happened to be a group of homesteaders—Chaffee had decided they were such—clustered by the livery stable at the time, and Chaffee noted how these men turned to watch Perrine's crew. That united scrutiny wasn't the ordinary type of interest. Something more was in the air. Then Doc Fancher marched into sight, his bowed legs stretching toward the courthouse. Immediately after, Chaffee became aware that he himself was being sought. Fancher had hardly disappeared beyond Callahan's when there was a creaking of boards below and the squealing of Fancher's office door. The rumble of talk sifted through the thin roof. They were moving about.

He felt the insecurity of his own position. It might very soon occur to them that it was but a step and a jump through the trapdoor. Turning over, he rose and with infinite care walked to the center of the roof. Even as he settled himself prone across the trapdoor he heard a chair being dragged along the office floor. Fancher's desk groaned. A man stood on it, fingers brushing the under side of the trapdoor head near enough to render audible what he said.

"—Look anyhow. Better hurry. Fancher's apt to come back any minute."

The trapdoor moved slightly, pressure coming against Chaffee's stomach.

"Nailed down. Couldn't be up there. Let's skin out."

The other seemed to be protesting; the near fellow's answer was impatient. "What would he be climbin' up from outside for? Lots of better places to hide. Let's skin away before that wildcat Fancher gets back. Me, I don't hone—"

They left. Chaffee waited a long time to make sure. In fact he held down the trapdoor the best part of an hour, hearing the traffic of the street grow heavier. It sounded as if a great many men were riding into Roaring Horse. Leaving the door he crawled to a port and studied the street. More homesteaders were assembling in groups. He also noticed Locklear, the three hired gunmen and Perrine's crew posted indolently here and yonder. Woolfridge appeared from the direction of the courthouse and walked rapidly across Chaffee's line of vision, looking neither to right nor left. The afternoon slid along, the sun's rim tipped toward the western hills, blurred by intervening clouds. Darkness threatened to arrive prematurely. And Fancher was back in his office, swearing to himself in full, irascible accents. Chaffee, cramped and cold and hungry, felt that the time for patience was at an end. He crawled to the trapdoor, listened a moment, and struck it sharply by way of warning. Fancher challenged: "Who in the name of—" and stopped. Chaffee dragged the door half away and looked down. Fancher's face was wrinkled in anger, but that shifted to concern when he found who was above him. Chaffee dropped to the desk, dragging the door back into place.

"So you was the one who moved my furniture—"

"Nope. Couple of gents investigatin' while you were gone. I heard 'em. They tried the trap but I spraddled it, belly flat."

"They done it before. Boy, I'm certainly glad to see you back and alive. But it ain't any place for a fellow with a price tag on his jeans. You're sittin' on a crater. Whoever moves first starts somethin'. But if said fellow don't move first he's apt to be blown to perdition. Jim, unless I'm as crazy as a loon that street is goin' to run red before long."

"Who's so sore as all that?"

Fancher was genuinely disturbed. He was nervous; the mark of worry lay in his eyes. He crossed to the desk and pulled up a copy of the county weekly, indicating a story spread over the center of the front sheet and surrounded by the black border of reversed column rules. "Read that."

It was the story Gay Thatcher had brought from the governor. No attempt had been made to stretch it out or to dress it up. The first paragraph began it and the second paragraph ended it, but these two paragraphs linked together made the story stark and bitter:

This newspaper, along with several other newspapers in the territory, received from the Roaring Horse Irrigation and Reclamation Corporation copy for an advertisement to be published in our columns. The substance of the advertisement, as readers will recall, was to invite settlers into this country to buy land on the implied promise that a dam was to be built. We received the copy for this advertisement on the eighteenth of November. Remember that date.

We have since been informed by the governor of the territory of a letter written to him—

and printed below—by the president of the Power Company in which that official says the Roaring Horse Irrigation and Reclamation Corporation was notified as early as the fifteenth of November that no dam was to be built. Compare that date with the one above.

Chaffee dropped the paper, turning his head from side to side. It both surprised him and confirmed a doubt. The doubt was of Woolfridge's honesty, but the surprise came of having to believe that Woolfridge would ever expose himself to such a backslap. "Doc, this is an awful strong statement. What it deliberately says is that Woolfridge knew there wasn't going to be any dam two days or three days before he sent out the ad."

"Phillips has run a newspaper all his life," countered Fancher. "And he knows what's libel and what ain't. He ain't sayin' what you claim he says. Not in so many words. He's puttin' two facts together and lettin' folks do their own guessin'. And he got them facts straight or he wouldn't of printed 'em. When the governor steps into this mess you can bet your sweet life something's rotten."

"I don't see it," confessed Chaffee. "Woolfridge is slick. He's smart. He's wealthy and he's educated."

"An' built up a fine scheme," said Doc Fancher. "A get-rich-quick scheme. But somewhere along the line he left a gate open. Left it open an' behind him, never thinkin' about it. The slick and the smart and the wealthy and the educated dudes in this world do them tricks just as often as you and me. And what's to come of it? What's going to happen in Roaring Horse? Jim, it scares me."

"You're clear," observed Chaffee. "Why worry?"

But Fancher went right on as if he hadn't heard. "This come out four-five days ago. It's traveled like the stink of a stockyard on a windy day. Everybody knows it; everybody's been talkin' about it. It's sorter snowballed up. At first it sorter seemed to miss fire. A homesteader asked Woolfridge about it. Woolfridge laughed in the man's face. Yeah. And what he said was that plenty of people would try to throw a monkey wrench in his business. Get the idea—persecution, jealousy, plain meanness. Uhuh. It seemed to satisfy these birds for a while. I give the man credit for cold, cast-iron, double-riveted nerve. But pretty soon folks got together. Talked about it, figgered it out. It's been growin' stronger every day. They was around fifteen homesteaders here when the news broke. Thirty-forty more came since—all from the adjoinin' counties. I've watched 'em gather from the window here. And I tell you the look that's settlin' in their faces makes me cold."

Chaffee was going around the edges of this business, testing it for himself. "Woolfridge could say that the power company was only denying the story about the dam because of policy. That they didn't want to commit themselves until work was actually started."

"Which he later did say," answered Fancher. "But how does that excuse stack up against the fact that the power company wrote to the governor and the governor made it his personal business to have that letter printed? Folks have been doin' some heavy thinkin'. The governor ain't goin' to mix up with the power company if it's only a bluff. Folks have decided that much. All right. And they've been lookin' back over Woolfridge's record hereabouts. Satterlee dyin' sudden. Stirrup S being froze out. Your own case. Each of them things didn't look like so much at the particular time. Put 'em all together and they seem mighty funny. It leaves a bad taste. The homesteaders are out money. They're in a state of mind. The old-timers around here recollected all the hell raisin' that went on. And they're a long ways from peaceable. It only needs one match to light up the bonfire. From what I been hearin' this afternoon I think the match is lit."

"What's that?"

"You," was Fancher's succinct answer.

"Me?" demanded Chaffee. "Shucks, those homesteaders don't know me. Never saw me."

"Yeah, but they've been hearin' a lot about you recent. That's another item to build up a feelin' against Woolfridge. Well, they've heard you're back. A mob is funny. Anythin's apt to send it on a stampede. Woolfridge has put up a bold face. He had the situation under his hand. He's powerful. But here you are back again and that takes the play out of his control. The crowd feels the change. That's all it needs."

"Here," protested Chaffee, "I'm not going to lead any lynch party."

"Don't you try to stop none, either," Fancher warned him. "Men ain't reasonable at a time like that. Your best friend is just apt to spit in your face and knock you down."

"Which I know blamed well," agreed Chaffee, remembering the time Stirrup S was set to hang the gambler Clyde. Dusk was coming unannounced through the window. Chaffee was reminded that he had set himself a chore. "I'm goin' out a minute, Doc. Stay till I come back, will you?"

"Now listen—" began Fancher. But Chaffee

shook his head, opening the door and pulling it behind him. He went down the stairway. The walk was deserted at that particular point and he swung himself into the adjoining alley and ran along to the back end of the buildings. The Gusher was beginning to show lamplight, the kitchen door stood open and a flunkey leaned in the aperture smoking a cigarette. Chaffee knew that flunkey. He also knew the Gusher cook. So he walked on and confronted the flunkey; the latter snapped his cigarette through the air, muttering: "Great guns, where you come from?"

"Who's in the kitchen, Joe?"

"Bill"—who was the cook—"and a coupla girls."

"Get the girls out of there a minute."

The flunkey disappeared. There was a short interval. He heard the flunkey say: "All right. Clear," and he slid into the kitchen quickly. The flunkey had his back to the swinging door leading into the dining room. He was grinning and seemed excited. So did the cook who winked at Chaffee. Chaffee dropped a word and turned aside to the small stairway leading up from the kitchen to that part of the second story housing the help. He went down a hall, opened another door, and arrived at the main hall. A light broke through a transom at occasional rooms, and there was a murmur of talk. He walked casually toward the hall's far end. In front of room 101 he paused. A light came over this transom, too, but he heard no conversation. Testing the knob carefully, he dropped his free hand to his gun and pushed the door before him.

Woolfridge stood by a window, looking down to the street. He turned at the sound of Chaffee's entrance, and when he saw who confronted him his face seemed in the lamp's glow to become harsh and triangular. But he said nothing, nor did he show surprise; he had trained himself too long to give way now. Instead, his arms moved together, hand gripping wrist, and he stood with the preciseness of carriage that always marked him; stood like this and somberly studied the man he had watched and harried so persistently in the last two weeks.

"Sit down," said Chaffee as if this was an everyday occurrence. "Hustle it."

Woolfridge moved to a chair and settled.

"Pull off a boot—either one."

He saw the blood spilling up into Woolfridge's neck; he saw the compression of lips and the queer, uncanny shifting of character. At once there was a different look on Woolfridge's face—the emergence of emotions long hidden, carefully suppressed. Emotions that had driven him through the course of the past few months and caused him to become in the end relentless, unscrupulous, and astonishingly reckless.

"Hurry the boot," suggested Chaffee. "Throw it over here."

Still wordless, Woolfridge obeyed. Chaffee reached for the boot and backed to the door. "That," said he with an admirable sang-froid, "will be all for a little while. If I want you later I'll drop around. If you ain't here"—and the leisurely quality of his words was broken by the snap and ring of rising anger—"I'll come and find you."

Woolfridge shrugged his shoulders and spoke for the first time. "That," said he, "will be interesting."

Chaffee let himself out of the door. A moment later he was squirming down the stairway; he crossed the kitchen, careless of the waitress watching, ran rapidly back to the alley beside Tilton's, and with one scant moment's hesitation to inspect the street ducked up to Fancher's office. Fancher had lighted the lamp and drawn the front window blind. Chaffee was somehow bothered by the drawn lines on the man's face and the sadness in the eyes. He threw the boot on Fancher's table.

"Where are those models?"

Fancher moved back to a corner of the

room. "Them blamed models have been awful strong bait. Somebody's suspected I got 'em. They've rummaged my premises two-three times lately while I was gone. I figured something like that would happen, so I moved 'em out of the cabinet." Two pair of high boots stood against the wall, each boot stuffed with a heavy stock. Fancher pulled out the socks and turned the boots over and picked out that model with the broad arch and flat heel; he laid it on the table and placed Woolfridge's boot against it, Fancher looked at the mating just once and raised his head.

"It's a fit. I always figured that flat heel must've come from a cavalry style boot. There she is. But the job ain't done yet. We still got this splay-toed model we ain't identified."

"Mark Eagle's—he told me he was there that night. Nobody but an Indian has got a fan-shaped foot. It's complete."

"So," murmured Fancher. "What of it?"

"Mark told me something else," drawled Chaffee. Excitement piled up in him, his eyes were flickering, the lean cheeks compressing. "He was back there. He saw three men come around the stable. One was the gambler, who never fired a shot. Second was Theodorik Perrine, and he didn't fire a shot. The third man killed Satterlee. The name of that man is Woolfridge."

Fancher's head bobbed up and down. "I've had the idea in my head a long time. But supposin' you're talkin' to a jury. How strong is Mark Eagle's testimony? Why couldn't he have fired that shot? I'm not accusin' him—I'm lookin' at it from the jury's point of view."

"What reason would he have?" countered Chaffee. "He was Satterlee's known friend. That's well established. Point two—Satterlee was killed with a .44 slug. I know Mark Eagle's guns. Seen 'em lots of times and so have you. He never carries anything but a .45 and a Krag rifle. Point three—his boot prints never came near the mouth of the stable's back door, nor anywheres within a direct line of fire. Neither did the gambler's, nor Perrine's. But the marks of Woolfridge's boots crept along the edge of the stable wall and were sunk deep into the ground right at the edge of the door—as if he'd crouched and set the weight of his body on his heels. Point four—Woolfridge had a good reason for killing Satterlee. He'd been dogging the old man for a long time to sell Stirrup S. Had to have the ranch for his plans. Old man wouldn't sell. So Woolfridge took the only way out. It's clear to me. It will be clear enough to a jury."

"If it gets to a jury," muttered Fancher. "I don't understand why Woolfridge would do it himself when he had so many hired gunmen."

"One time," said Chaffee, "I overheard him say that if a thing was to be well done it had to be done personally. Another mistake. Well, Fancher, I've been hustled around the country a long time. It's my turn—"

"What in God's name is going on below?" interrupted Fancher. He ran to the window and lifted the blind. The street was filling with voices and down it came a body of horsemen yelling into the dark sky. A gun exploded, rattling loose sashes. Fancher turned. "Stirrup S crew."

"I told them to meet me behind the rodeo grounds," muttered Chaffee. "They're awful public about it."

"They know—they feel the change," said Fancher, looking old and weary. "It's in the air. Jim, a mob is a terrible thing—a terrible thing."

"My turn has come," replied Chaffee. All at once the last of the tolerance and easy-going air left him. The yellow lamplight beat against his bronze cheeks, bringing into prominence the sharp angles of mouth and chin and eyelids. To-night the impulses of the killer were leaping in his veins, and Doc Fancher, seeing this, sighed and let his shoulders sag a little.

"Jim, don't get reckless. They're under the gun, but they want you pretty bad. And it only takes one shot."

"They've tried too many times," said Chaffee. "It's not in the cards now. What have they done? They've ruined a pleasant country—left scars all over it! Chased fine people away just to make way for an unscrupulous project. Shot folks down—robbed them! It's my turn now. I'm going out there and get the boys together. Woolfridge goes to jail, and if Locklear makes a move against me he goes behind the bars, too. Those imported gun artists are ridin' a long way out before daylight. And I'm goin' to see Mister Theodorik Perrine and settle an argument with him. It's a clean sweep, Fancher. Roaring Horse needs it awful bad."

"It only takes one shot," Fancher reminded him again.

Chaffee was at the door. For just a moment a tight grin flashed across his eyes. "Doc, if you'd been with me the last three weeks I think you'd figger I'm blamed near proof against disaster. Well, here's the start of somethin'."

He went down the stairs and stepped into the street, shadowed and unobserved. Over at the livery stable was a mass of men crowding together and moving with a strange restlessness. Somebody was up on a box in the very center of the crowd, talking rapidly and angrily. The Stirrup S boys were at the other end of the street; evidently they had made one trip to the rodeo grounds and, finding nothing, were bent back to sweep Roaring Horse end to end by way of diversion. Down the thoroughfare they galloped, thigh and thigh. Locklear and Perrine, with his men, were assembled on the porch of the Gusher. The imported gunmen were there as well. And, counting heads, Chaffee observed that most of Woolfridge's ranch crew stood idly at hand. The sight of them was cut off by the charging Stirrup S partisans. Chaffee stepped into the street and raised his voice.

"Pull up, you wildcats!"

The riders came to a swirling halt; they saw him. Another gun exploded and his name was sent ringing down between the building walls.

"Chaffee!"

The crowd heard it. The man on the box looked about and reëchoed the cry. "Chaffee's back!" and then confusion hit Roaring Horse as a bolt of lightning. The crowd shifted and all its black mass came spilling onward toward Chaffee and the Stirrup S riders. A rumbling roar quivered through the chill night air, a sound sinister and fear inspiring. As hardened as he was, Jim Chaffee felt a spinal thrill. He whispered to the men about him. "Spread out—block the street. That gang will tear Woolfridge and his bunch apart."

Gay Thatcher had stayed in Roaring Horse, not knowing just why she did so. In her mind was the irrevocable decision that when she left this country it was to be forever. Perhaps, therefore, her delay rose from the knowledge that she would never see Roaring Horse again, never ride its swelling leagues again, never again mark the tall and lazy figure of Jim Chaffee coming down the street. All that was memory—to be laid sadly away in her heart along with other memories. So she stayed, very close to her room all the while. She had seen Woolfridge once in the lobby, and he had spoken with a queer and formal politeness. As the days went on and the story appeared in the weekly paper she began to note from her window the gradual forming of small clusters on the street. Homesteaders coming together. It grew to be a more common sight. And to-day she had witnessed the swift rolling up of the tide. She heard Jim Chaffee's name mentioned in the lobby, whereat the color came to her cheeks and her pulse beat the faster. She walked along the street, going as far as the courthouse and back again, impressed by a feeling of currents boiling through the air. She heard Chaffee's name many more times, murmured or sibilantly whispered. It seemed to be a kind of omen or a signal.

She was an observant girl and she was quick to observe how those men were attached to Woolfridge ranged back and forward, going into this building, turning around that one, riding out to the desert and galloping back. The activity seemed to grow more pronounced as dusk threatened the world; the watchfulness on their faces deepened. When she returned to the Gusher she saw Locklear posted there with some of his men around him; and the homesteaders formed a thicker and more restless mass over by the stable. It all created a tension that played odd tricks with her nerves. She ate supper, scarcely touching the food, and sat in the lobby; even in that short interval the throaty rumbling of the mob had deepened to a pitch that sent a cold, still fright through her body. Locklear's sullen face seemed set and rather sallow, while his men were quite plainly uneasy. Perrine came in a moment later, eyes flashing strangely as the lamplight touched him. And though the girl felt a strong repulsion at the sight of him—the utter brutish and degrading qualities of the man challenging all her instincts of decency—yet she could not help acknowledging the ruthless, elemental courage he had. The others were crumbling, ready to run; he seemed scornful of the gathering power outside.

There was a short parley between them, talk shuttling back and forth in murmuring spurts. Perrine appeared to be urging some course of action that Locklear and the others disliked. The sheriff began to shake his head, whereat Perrine tilted his massive chin and spoke bluntly that a dull color came back to Locklear's cheek bones. But his only answer was to raise one hand and point outward in the direction of the mob. The girl got up, no longer able to sit so near the center of the gathering storm, and climbed the stairs. On the landing she turned to see Perrine looking up to her with a hard grin.

"You'll git yore money's worth before this sight-seein' trip is over, sister," he rumbled.

She passed along the dark hall and unlocked her door. The lamp still burned on the table as she had left it, and so she went in, a wave of relief coming over her at the knowledge she could shut herself away from the turbulence below. Pushing the door behind her, she heard a sighing sound on the carpet of the hall, the door struck resistance and flew open again. Whirling about she confronted William Wells Woolfridge. And the next moment he was in the room, closing the door and leaning against it.

"Well, my dear lady, have you been enjoying the show?"

He had changed. The smoothness was gone, the scrupulous grooming no longer showed on his clothing, and it appeared very odd to her that he should be wearing a pair of low street shoes instead of the customary boots. These, set against the bottom of his riding breeches, gave his attire a laughable incompleteness. But she was in no humor to laugh, for she knew she faced a dangerous man. There was a suppressed fury about him, an indefinable barbaric glint in his eyes that rose above his normal colorlessness. In his question was a trace of the old suavity, but only a trace.

"Mr. Woolfridge, I have not asked you to enter my room."

"No? This is not a time for ceremony. I have played your game long enough. There is always a time when rules cease to be desirable. I trust you have found the street scene as dramatic and thrilling as the customary act."

"I am not the kind to enjoy tragedy. Please go out."

"Ah. So you perceive tragedy? And perhaps feel this tragedy is a little of your own making?"

She had not thought of that. His question brought a moment's depression. Had she been the instrument by which this fury was loosened? Her clear, sound sense told her she had not been. Long before her part in the tangled affairs of Roaring Horse had been played, this dark night was in the making. Her share had been but to help reveal the inevitable result of another's wrongdoing.

"Mr. Woolfridge, look back on your own trail. Have you come to the point where you must blame others for your own scheming? You told me once of the great things you meant to do. Look out on the street! There is the result. You ought to be on your knees, praying. You are a man of education. You have money. Why should you want to bring starvation to these poor folks? You knew it wasn't right!"

He looked down at her, his face seeming to turn to stone. "You play your part well. Is it not time to drop the pretense that you love those clods out yonder? Dull kine—stupid with their lives, dumb and unthrifty. You say I should be sorry for them. I do not have so soft and civilized a conscience."

"Please go," she asked. "I don't care to argue. No—don't come any closer to me!"

She backed away, hand behind her. At the far side of the room, in a drawer of a desk, was the small pistol she always carried. She felt the need of it now. In the course of the week she had watched carefully for just such an interruption as this, knowing that Woolfridge might at some reckless hour cross the border line that divided the two sides of his dual nature. She had never left her door unlocked and never traveled alone outside the limits of town. Yet with all her watchfulness he had caught her off guard and now, step at a time, advanced as she retreated.

"I wouldn't try to attain melodrama," was Woolfridge's cool warning. "If you are trying to get a weapon stop where you are. I must have a talk with you."

"I'll ask you again to leave my room," said she.

"And don't scream," he went on as if he hadn't heard her. "I am past pretty manners right now."

She halted. Woolfridge nodded his head and likewise stopped. Though he never let his eyes stray from her, he seemed to be listening to the undertone of the mob rising up from the street and dimly sifting down the hall. His shoulders lifted. "Time changes all things. Well, I am not fool enough to play the part of King John. The waves may come. I won't try to stop them. In this world we go from one thing to another. Some people make the mistake of trying to hang on when it is too late. I never do. My dear, you are a beauty!"

"Did you come here to say that?"

He inclined his head. "To tell you that and

more. You are worth all any man might offer. You are a beauty. You have a rare intelligence, and I love the combination. I did not, of course, bargain on your past. But, after all, what's the difference? It gives you a worldliness. And that, too, I admire. I am a worldling myself and sophistication is dear to me—"

Color flooded her cheeks. "You have no right to say that! Neither you nor your spy, Hunnewell. It is false!"

His cheeks pinched up. "So Hunnewell told you? He wrote me a very hysterical letter afterward. I'd like to wring the man's skinny neck. There is one mistake I made. I meant Hunnewell as a water carrier, nothing else. The big moments are not for him. When he faced one he fell to pieces. That was just one mistake, and not the greatest. You were very clever, Miss Thatcher. You took me in completely."

"I asked nothing of you," replied Gay. "I wanted you to tell me nothing. I came here only to see and hear what Roaring Horse did. There never was a time when I asked you a question or expected you to tell me anything. Remember that."

"Nevertheless," said Woolfridge, "it was shrewd of the governor. Ah well. He is a canny man. And he has watched me closely. I knew it all the time. But my greatest mistake was in allowing Bangor into my plans. I served him well once and expected a return favor. But he was afraid of me. The higher men go in this world the more cold blooded they become. The more treacherous. I should have held the whip over his head. Whatever I wanted done through his office I ought to have done personally. There is the secret. Do things yourself. But the book is closed. I have no regrets."

"You don't mean that," replied the girl. "You can't mean it. All this will come back to haunt you. You have taken the last penny of many families. What of that?"

"Well, and what of it?" Woolfridge shook his head. "The weak perish, the fit survive. Rightly so. Those people are only pawns, sports of fate. It is in the infinite plan of things that they go down. Why be sorry about it? I do not even let myself be sorry for my failure. That intrigues you, I suppose? All that I have has been given to me. I inherited. What can a man do to satisfy the brute instincts in a case like that? Most men would accept their fortune quietly. Not I."

The last sentence rang through the room. He squared his shoulders, looking over her head as if pronouncing the pervading gospel of his existence. "I broke away. I had the courage to smash the picayune barriers. I had a dream. Of an empire in my own making. It would have been an honest one but for the turn of events. Did I halt when I knew it could not be done honestly? Most men would have halted. I did not. I built another dream and went on. And that is going to pot this night. What of it? I have made my mark on this country. I have been a pirate for a little while. To-night, a hundred men fight for me and against me. What is morally wrong about that? In another age it ~~would have~~ would have been legal, customary. I broke through, I smashed things. And I glory in it. Now I give it up. But there is always another dream to fashion, my dear girl, another empire over the hill!"

"What are you thinking about?" she whispered, appalled by the primitive emotions boiling behind his civilized trappings.

He smiled. "That is the beginning of another dream. We will go as far as we can."

"You'll be trapped before the hour is over," said she, and slowly edged toward the desk. Watching him, she wondered if he could regard the crash of his plans so lightly, or if he took his responsibilities in so indifferent a manner. He couldn't believe, surely, that he would be able to carry on. Or that life for him would be the same. Yet all of these things he appeared to believe. He was talking, talking. Poorly masking the burning fury inside of him—the checked ambition, the shattered pride. And now that he stopped speaking he betrayed himself completely. His arms were locked in front of him; his whole body had turned to steel—somber and overmastered by a savagery of desire. She saw the blood flecking his eyes, and the color go out of his freckled face. And his next words fairly exploded in the room. "I am taking you with me!"

She swung on her heels and sprang for the desk. One hand ripped open the drawer and touched the little pearl-handled gun lying there. The next moment Woolfridge pushed her away, swept her against the wall. She tried to scream and saw his hand flashing flat against her face. Quite blindly she fought back, tearing at his coat, beating at the white blur in front of her. She had no clear vision of him; somehow, his blow had clouded her eyes and made her dizzy. But she heard his breath rising and falling, and she heard him saying shameful things that made her tremble and resist the harder. A flash of pain ran the whole length of her body; all power went out of her. And then she fell to the floor unconscious.

Woolfridge stared down at her crumpled body a moment and raced to the door. There was nobody in the hall. Coming back he bent and lifted her in his arms. "She had that coming," he muttered, trying to check his breathing. "I will gentle her or I will kill her! Now—"

He carried her down the hall to the back stairway. At the bottom he stopped to listen, ear against the panel of the door leading to the kitchen. Apparently the place was empty. Pushing the door quietly in front of him, he found the place half dark and without occupants. So he carried her through, kicked open still another door leading off from the kitchen into what once had been a storeroom, and was now nothing but a barren, half-forgotten cubicle spread with cobwebs. He laid her on the floor and backed out, turning a crooked key in a rusted lock. Then he paused, with always the rising and falling echo of the mob pressing against his ears. His breathing turned normal and there, with half the men of the county lusting for his blood and all fortune swinging against him, he reverted to the habits of his softer side and methodically brushed the dust of the storeroom off his sleeves.

"She'll be unconscious for a few minutes," he reflected. "That's time enough. Now—"

He left the kitchen by the dining door and entered the lobby, at once confronting the sheriff and Theodorik Perrine. The rest of his followers were huddled by the entrance, staring upon the street.

"About time yuh showed up," growled Perrine. "No time to pick posies with all this brimstone and sulphur yonder."

Woolfridge reached for a cigar, eyes roving over the tremendous spread of Perrine's shoulders. There was something so insolently superior, so critically aloof that the latter's smashed lips began to work wrathfully. "Afraid?" murmured Woolfridge. "I have always prided myself on picking the right men for right places. Perhaps I have been mistaken in you. I never thought you'd let this rabble get under your skin—"

"Afraid?" boomed Perrine, the mighty echo rocketing along the lobby. He lifted his great arms above him, chest muscles crowding against the shirt. "I ain't afraid of any man that ever walked, ever drew breath! Bring that pack in here, and I'll wrap my arms around this shebang and bring it down on their heads! Afraid—hell! But I'm tellin' *you*, Woolfridge, that the lids goin' to blow off this town in less time than it takes to swing a cat by the tail. If yuh got anythin' to say or anythin' to do, better get started on it now."

Woolfridge rolled the cigar between his fingers until the sheriff, almost in agony from the suspense, cried out: "My God, Mr. Woolfridge, ain't you got no order to give? Ain't you got no way of settlin' this?"

Woolfridge returned the cigar to his pocket. "Crumbling—caving in—turning yellow. The whole pack of you. When a man wishes anything done in this world he alone ought to do it. How many can you get to barricade this hotel, Perrine?"

"About ten boys," grunted the big man. "But if that's all yuh got to offer I don't think much o' the idee. Yuh either got to charge that bunch and scatter 'em with lead or else yuh got to spread the soft soap and do it sudden. Once they get the bit in their jaws yore sunk."

"Let me do the arranging for my own funeral," was Woolfridge's cold retort.

Perrine, even at that moment, was under the sway of this man. There was just one thing the hulking renegade admired, just one thing he bowed to—a courage equal or superior to his own. He clucked his tonque. "Yore a cool cucumber. Well, spit it out."

"Slip out and bring a pair of horses to the back door—to the kitchen door," said Woolfridge. "Hurry it."

Perrine's jaws worked slowly. His face wreathed up in puzzlement. "Then what?"

"Then," went on Woolfridge, holding the big man's eyes, "get your men all in here, turn out the lights, and let them have it. Let—

them—have—it!"

"What's the horses for?" pressed the renegade.

"I ask questions, not answer them," snapped Woolfridge. "Didn't I tell you I'd arrange my own funeral? Go on—get about it."

Perrine never said a word for a full minute; it took that length of time for his slow brain to catch Woolfridge's real purpose. But when the realization came to him that this cold, imperturable gentleman who had always held the whip over him was about to turn and run—and while running let his followers go to their ruin—a swift and ferocious gleam leaped into his eyes. His lips splayed back, snarling. And as one crushing paw rose and fell across Woolfridge's shoulder he was incredibly like some rearing grizzly that had turned to fight. Woolfridge swayed to the force of that massive paw and spoke sharply, yet he couldn't escape it. The stubby fingers dug in; Perrine stepped closer.

"I got yore brand now, *Mister* Woolfridge. Yuh ain't any better than a yella dawg ki-yippin' down the street with his tail draggin'. I thought yuh had cold-chilled steel in yore system. Thought mebbe yuh even was as tough as me. Why—! So yuh figger to run while we boys stick here and cover yore trail! Like hell we will!"

"What are you being paid for?" challenged Woolfridge. "Did you ever have any doubts as to what I wanted you for, now or any other time? Use your senses. I hired you to destroy for me, do my chores. That is what I want you to do now. Get out there and find my horses."

"Not me," interposed the sheriff. "I won't cover anybody's trail. All I'll do is talk to them boys."

"Yuh won't even do that!" snapped Perrine. He was grinning, though nothing but malice and savage pleasure was in that constriction of lips. "He'll pull his own irons from the fire. Listen, Woolfridge! Listen out there!"

There was no mistaking the sound. Above the steady, sinister murmuring rang a man's high and passionate challenge. And no sooner was it spoken than a roar ran from wall to wall and heavy boots came running toward the hotel. Locklear shook his head and slowly retreated toward the back end of the hotel, followed by the men near the door. Perrine pushed his ugly face close to Woolfridge. "Hear that? Yore a cooked gander. Yuh've had aplenty of fun and drawn big on the bank account. Now stand here, damn yuh, and pay the bills! When I do killin' it'll be my own killin', not yores!"

Woolfridge seemed to withdraw, to pull his

senses inward and take stock. The freckled face lost color, yet other than that no change came to his features. Only, when he raised his eyes again to Perrine a fire burned brilliantly in them.

"I have never found a man who could do a thing just as I wanted it done," said he evenly. "A man ought never to depart from his beliefs. I'll do this myself. How many guns have you? Two—well, give me one of them."

Perrine took his left gun and passed it, barrel foremost, to Woolfridge. Then he drew away, keeping a close watch. "Grandstand," he jeered. "Yuh'll scuttle the minute I'm out o' yore sight. Lord help yuh. Yore a dead dawg. Me, I'm gone." He stepped beyond the swinging doors and hesitated a moment, bold eyes studying Woolfridge with something that might have been respect or puzzlement, or perhaps a little of both. Then he was gone from the lobby along with all the others, leaving Woolfridge quite alone.

The rush and clamor of the mob swirled through the street. Voices rose higher, a gun exploded, and the foremost of the homesteaders leaped up to the porch. Woolfridge, with his freckled cheeks set tightly and his gun raised to command the door, backed slowly toward the stairway.

CHAPTER EIGHTEEN

THE GODS STAND ASIDE

When Jim Chaffee stepped out of the stairway of Tilton's dry-goods store and rallied the Stirrup S men across the dim and weaving shadows of the street, the full voice of the mob struck him like a furnace blast and he realized then for the first time how inexorable and terrifying the power of massed unreason was. An individual could be persuaded or overawed; an individual had a conscience to rally him back to a sense of order and justice. But a mob had no conscience; it was a caldron of passion without anything to check the fire burning higher and higher. Chaffee had experienced a mob once before—at the time the gambler was killed—yet that was a different affair and far less sinister.

They came onward, these homesteaders, moving with a certainty and an intensity Chaffee never before had seen in men. There were thirty or forty of them; men who had labored throughout the years with their hands to accumulate that small amount of savings now in the hands of Woolfridge. Their fortunes were involved in the land that never would see water; they were impoverished. Whatever bright hopes they had nourished for the future were gone down, and they saw, each one of them, nothing but ruin. No emotion is so powerful in a human being as that which touches his home and his family; no rage is so latent with destruction as that which comes from the knowledge of a home wrecked and a family broken. It was on their faces as they marched toward Chaffee and the ex-Stirrup S crew; somber faces darkly drawn, gaunt eyes flashing as they crossed the patterns of outflung lamplight. Standing there, Chaffee thought he saw men who were a little frightened or sobered by the destructive machinery of which they were a part. But nowhere did he see the smallest spark of mercy. He felt sorry for them. Their rounding shoulders and blackened cheeks spoke of hard work; their rawboned fists and their worn clothes told of it. And yet, as they closed about him and he saw the guns in their fists and the rifles cradled on their arms, he had a moment of pity for Woolfridge and all who were connected with the man.

They surged against the line of horses; they engulfed Chaffee. Out of the group stepped the individual who earlier had exhorted them from the soap box. He was barehead; he threw up a sorrel mane, and a zealot's light poured from his hazel eyes. When he spoke it was the voice of the mob.

"Well, come on. What yuh standin' here for? Let's go get 'em."

Chaffee mustered all the lazy casualness he could find. "What's your name, friend?"

"Alki Stryker, boy. And I'll carve it on that damn' monster's hide! Come on, we're just wastin' time. We're leavin' the gate open."

"They can't get away," said Chaffee. "They're hooked. We've got 'em where we want 'em. Now why be hasty about it? There's a jail big enough to hold the crew and plenty of good men for jury duty in due course of law. You want your money back, don't you? You want all this straightened out legally—"

Alki Stryker shook his head, surly and intolerant. "Yore Chaffee, ain't you? How come yore so gentle hearted all of a sudden? Ain't they hazed you from hell to breakfast? Yeah. How much due course o' law did you get? None. Nor will *we* get any by waitin' around. They's just one thing to do and we aim to do it."

The rising undertone of response was like the mutter of some deep, remote disturbance of the earth.

"You've been duped," agreed Chaffee, still amiable. "We can straighten that. It's a big country and there's plenty of time. Take it to court first and see what you can save from the shuffle. Then if it don't suit you—that will be time enough to consider direct action."

"Who paid you to say that?" cried Alki Stryker. "No man that's been hurt like you been can say such a thing less he's in on the profits! Get out of our way! If you ain't got the bowels to knock in some heads we shore have!"

The pressure of the crowd grew against him. The horses moved uneasily and gave ground. Turning an instant he saw Locklear standing in the hotel doorway, a doubtful and stubborn creature who could not forget his measure of authority. And behind him were all those who held to the Woolfridge fortunes. Yet even as he watched they began to retreat from the door and disappear from his sight. He faced the mob once more. "Roaring Horse don't care for massacres, friend. We boys ran this country once. In our own way. We can do it again. But not by lynchings, or by blood."

"You ain't had no luck runnin' it recent," retorted the mob leader. "I'm tellin' yuh for the final time—throw in potluck or get out of the way. We know who yuh are and we're sorry for yore bad luck. But it ain't in the cards to stop us. You can't do it, nor anybody else. Clear the street! We're wipin' them buzzards off the map!"

"We're takin' Woolfridge and we're keepin' him for a jury," was Chaffee's blunt reply. "This is our country. Now stand back and behave while we do it."

He thought for a moment that this change of tone would check them. He saw its effect on the crowd. But, on the verge of following up with a still plainer show of strength, Luis Locklear elected to swing sentiment back to its full fury. The sheriff, now in an alley adjacent to the hotel, played true to his nature to the very last. He was afraid; he would not fight for Woolfridge; he had almost no support behind him. But he could not give; he could not find it in this thick head to compromise or forgive. So he raised a shout.

"Who's askin' you to carry authority in this town, Chaffee? I'm sheriff of this county! You fellows are breakin' the peace! Get off the street or take the consequences! I can send somebody to the grave for this night's work! Clear out!"

The reaction of the mob was instant, and the sudden onward surge almost threw Chaffee off his feet. A gun exploded in his very ear, and the horses began to pitch, pulling away. Chaffee was struck in the neck and hurled from side to side. But he tore free from the clawing arms and beat a path toward the hotel porch, crying up to his partners. "Ride 'em down—block that porch! Block it!" And presently, ripped and battered, he stood in the doorway with half of the old crew ranged around him afoot while the others charged backward and forward with their horses. The mob broke, re-formed, and fought for the door. Then it was split in fragments by the constantly circling horses and the foremost section left high and dry on the porch, threatening the defenders.

"Step back!" warned Chaffee. "We're takin' Woolfridge to the jug."

"Try it," retorted a near figure, and smashed Chaffee's face with a hard fist. Chaffee's head snapped back against the door frame, and a fiery rage came roaring to the surface. After that he almost lost account of his own acts. His gun was out and he knew he felled the man with a sweep of the barrel. Another came on but never reached him; the rest of his partners were using the same tactics. That cleared the immediate neighborhood of the door for a little while.

"We mean business," called Chaffee. "Go on and pull down a few houses if you got to work off steam. But Woolfridge goes to the jug."

Alki Stryker had been swallowed up during the melée, but his voice rose like a rocket now. "Ne'mind—let's get them buzzards which was imported to kill! Let's get Perrine and his outfit! They're going out the back end o' town! Come on—come on!"

That was a rallying cry. The porch almost instantly became deserted. The mob raced along the street and sifted down the alleys. Firing began and the yells came shrilly back, like the sounding of a wolf pack. Chaffee spoke hurriedly. "You fellows close in here. Couple hit for the back way to see they don't try to fool us. I'm going after Woolfridge. Saw him a second ago climbin' toward the sky."

He turned in and walked to the stairway. Looking up he saw Woolfridge standing on the landing and just about to disappear down the hall. It brought him to a full halt, for he discovered a gun in the man's hand and a pinched look on the soft cheeks.

"Come down, Woolfridge. Your skin ain't worth much, but such as it is you owe it to Stirrup S. Step along. We can just make the jug before anybody gets rash."

Woolfridge nodded slightly. "You made a worthy stand, my friend. But was it worth the trouble?"

"I've got to live a long time," muttered Chaffee, "and I don't want you on my conscience. You've bothered me enough as it is. Come down."

"And supposing I don't?" asked Woolfridge in a droning monotone.

"Then I'll come up," said Chaffee.

"Come ahead," grunted Woolfridge, and immediately disappeared from sight.

One of Chaffee's partners left the door. "That means business. He'll get leaded yet before this night's over. Better a couple of us take the back stairs and some more hike up this-away. Mebbe—"

But Chaffee, still watching the landing, shook his head. "It's my play, Mike. He expects me to try it. He's issued the invite. I'm goin' up there alone. Just stay right here and wait."

That drew the puncher's immediate protest. And the rest of the old Stirrup S riders closed in, dissenting. "What for—to get ambushed?" demanded one of them. "Don't be a durn fool."

Chaffee climbed the first step and turned about, face tremendously sober. "Now listen, boys. I've got first call on that gentleman. It was Woolfridge who killed Dad Satterlee, the finest friend I ever had. It was him that bought my ranch out from under me. He was responsible for havin' Mack put out of commission. And it was the same gent who has sent me through all this miserable course of sprouts in the last few weeks. It's my turn. He still thinks he can humble me. He still thinks he's top man of the two of us. What should I do—back down and let him keep on thinkin' it? Not by a jugful. Boys, you let me alone. I am going up there and call his bet. One of us is too proud. Him or me. I aim to find out. Stay here. Keep everybody away from that second floor until you hear one of us sing out."

There was a grumbling disagreement among them, but Chaffee turned and continued on up, gun drawn. His face rose above the landing and he had one swift survey of the hallway, dark excepting for a patch of light coming out of an open door—the door to Gay Thatcher's room. Then he ducked and lunged to the top; a bullet roared in the cramped space and ripped at a post in the railing. Swinging wide he reached the shelter of the wall leading along the back corridor and the back stairs. For a moment he rested silently, listening. He thought he heard Woolfridge shift and breathe somewhere in a room along the main hall.

"Woolfridge—you had better give up and go to jail."

The man's voice, still even but rising to a slightly higher pitch, floated down the corridor. "You will find me in my room. I am waiting for you."

"You won't have to wait long," muttered Chaffee, and without stepping away from his protected spot, shuffled his boots against the carpet. The answer was quick in coming, gun roar following gun roar. Both shots crashed through the flimsy boards of the far wall. "That," said Chaffee to himself, "is three cartridges gone. Three to go unless he's got a supply in his room. I'd better cut this short."

He drew his breath and swung around the corner into the main hall. As he moved he fired point-blank at the black end, raking the left wall where Woolfridge's room was. He had to keep the man humble while he ran the distance; he had to keep the man flinching. There was no time for him to duck, and even if there had been time he would have never thought about it. Jim Chaffee's blood was on the race; all the old, berserk anger swelled his veins and overwhelmed his caution. He wanted to crush, to destroy. He wanted, at that moment, to wipe out whatever lay before. And so he raced past the lane of light, battering the blackness with his gun, and hearing an answering roar match his own. One bullet cut a path across the plastered expanse beside him. Another he felt strike the floor at his feet. There was a third—some cool monitor in the recesses of his brain kept counting the shots—that he thought touched him. Then he was at Woolfridge's door, turning on his heels, poising, plunging through. Immediately he collided with the man and was locked in a hand-to-hand struggle.

The bitterness and the ferocity of Woolfridge's resistance was something he never dreamed the man capable of. That mediocre body with its softness and fashionable grooming was a collection of striking, clawing, twisting muscles. Chaffee wrapped one arm around the man's neck and compressed it with every cruel ounce of strength he owned. He heard the actual snapping of vertebrae, but he could not catch Woolfridge's gun, and his own face and shoulders suffered a constant battering from the weapon's constant slashes. The front sight ripped across his cheek; he felt the blood warming chin and throat. It roused him to incredible fury. He released his grip and freed himself for a terrific sweep at Woolfridge with his own gun. It struck bone. He heard the man whimper. Resistance for the moment ended, and in that moment Chaffee secured another clamping hold on Woolfridge, whirled him around, and smashed him against the edge of the door frame. It revived the last of the man's energy, embarked him on a series of violent, jabbing punches. Chaffee made no attempt to block them. He had Woolfridge out in the hall and was slamming him from side to side like a figure of straw.

The light coming through Gay Thatcher's door fell upon them. At the same instant Woolfridge, crying with a shrillness almost impossible to the human throat, brought his knee into Chaffee's groin and jabbed the thumb of his free hand in Chaffee's eye. It scarcely missed its mark but the pain of the nail's slicing impact was worse than anything that had so far happened. The man was spent, reeling in Chaffee's arms, resorting to all the last and most vicious tricks. Chaffee drew back, struck a slanting blow across Woolfridge's head. The overlord of Roaring Horse went down, sprawled face on the floor, half across the threshold of the girl's room. He was finished, for the time being dead to the world.

Chaffee sagged against the wall, struggling for wind, hearing his partners calling from below. He shook his head, beginning to feel the throb of his slashed face. Then the stairway drummed with boots and a handful of Stirrup S men were crowded on the scene.

"By Jo, yuh give us a scare," said the foremost. "Why didn't yuh sing out?"

"Don't feel much like singing at this precise moment," muttered Chaffee.

"Bleedin' like a stuck hawg," commented another, and walked around the prone Woolfridge. "Dead, or ain't yuh lucky thataway?"

"He'll be all right in a few minutes," said Chaffee. He discovered his gun still in his fist. Holstering it, he wiped his face with a handkerchief. But there was a throb to one arm that he couldn't locate until he skinned back his coat. The last Woolfridge bullet had drilled a neat hole in the fabric and broken skin. One of his partners was sharp eyed enough to discover it and he swore.

"Pinked yuh and scratched hell out o' yore face. The very same dude you was so all-fired anxious to save from bein' sprung on a limb. Mebbe yuh'll get over these fancy notions sometimes. He musta clawed like a woman."

"Pick him up," said Chaffee. "Down the back stairs and through the alley to jail. Got to get him inside before these homesteaders catch wind of it."

They hoisted the inert Woolfridge between them and lugged him along the hall. Chaffee followed, scouted the alley, and then went ahead to the rear jail door. A few minutes later Woolfridge lay on a jail bunk, locked behind the bars with six punchers on guard. Chaffee sat a moment in a chair and soothed himself with a smoke. Outside, in the main street and down along the various alleys, he heard parties of the homesteaders beating around for fugitives; a shot broke through the town occasionally, but it appeared as if the mob had spent its fury and that a certain calm was returning to this embattled town.

"Believe I'll stroll out and see the extent of the damages," said Chaffee, heading for the door. "You fellows stick close, now. I've had enough trouble getting that fellow, and I don't desire to lose any more hide on his account."

"Bein' such a big-hearted guy," retorted one of his partners, "yuh shouldn't mind a little item like that."

He cruised along the walk, finding the homesteaders collected in parties and going about with something like a military orderliness. Apparently they had gotten together and adopted a thorough plan of policing the town; both street ends were blocked by sentries; there was a guard at the hotel now, one at the bank, and a few at the stable. But he saw that the danger of mob action had passed by and their anger cooled to a reasonable determination. They had vented their destructive temper. Arriving at the far end of the street he was met by a party and challenged with an abrupt question.

"Where's Woolfridge?"

"In jail," replied Chaffee.

"Well—mebbe that's the best place for him. He'll hang, anyhow. We been snoopin' around. Got five more for yuh to put in the cooler, includin' Locklear. They's three fellas layin' cold in the stable, a couple bein' them imported gunmen. But we ain't through yet. That man Perrine ain't to be found. While we're cleanin' up this one-horse town we aim to get him."

Chaffee turned back. Abreast the bank he was stopped a second time. Josiah Craib came out of the door, ducking his bald head. He was, as usual, solemn and seemingly bowed by the weight of his thoughts. His gaunt cheeks lifted to Chaffee and he spoke a sparing phrase.

"Jim, gather all gents for me and stay around while I say my say."

Chaffee raised his gun and sent a shot to the sky. Homesteaders tumbled out of the buildings and through the shadows. They collected in front of the banker, eyeing him with a close and not altogether friendly interest. They knew nothing about him, nor had he played a part so far in their tangled affairs. Yet he was a banker and they had seen Woolfridge often talk with him. Therefore he was under the cloud of suspicion. Josiah Craib must have felt that suspicion, but if he did he gave no sign of it. He stood on the steps, watching them group nearer—a clumsy figure conveying the impression of sluggish moving blood. Nobody knew what lay behind the deeply sunken eyes; whether that turning glance concealed craftiness or whether it covered nothing more than the short and colorless thought of one who passed his life without imagination. When they became quiet and he said that which he wanted to say, they still didn't know. Nor did they ever know. But this is what he said:

"Gentlemen, I used to own this bank. It was a good bank in a good country and I made a little money. For my own reasons I sold controlling interest to Mr. Woolfridge, which he wanted kept secret. His business is not my business. I know something of his affairs, but I have no voice in them. I have nothing to do with this land proposition. I sat aside, watched it develop, and fall to pieces. It ain't a homesteading country. It's cattle country. A nice cattle country. I liked it as it was. You boys will never make a penny off it by farmin'. I understand you are broke. What I have to say is that although I am not in any way responsible for what has happened, nor am I able to obligate the bank for any sum of money, I do have money of my own which I will use to straighten out this affair. With homesteaders in the land this bank will go to the wall. With cattlemen in the country it will prosper. It's to my advantage to have cattlemen back and to see you boys on your way to somethin' better. If you'll come in the bank to-morrow mornin' and surrender your rights to me I will pay you whatever sum you have paid Woolfridge. You will be free to go. I will assume the business of clearin' up all affairs, which will take a long time. But the country can get back to its original business again, which is raisin' beef. That's all." And he ducked his bony head and retreated into the bank, closing the door.

A Stirrup S man crowded beside Chaffee. "What's the old duffer mean by that?"

Chaffee shook his head, immensely puzzled. "I don't know."

"He ain't passin' out a lot of coin for nothin'. Mebbe he's doin' it to get hisself in the clear. Why, he don't even know Woolfridge is in jail."

"Don't you think it," replied Chaffee. "He knows everything he ought to know. He sees whatever is going on, don't forget it."

The homesteaders shifted around, talking earnestly. A group of them marched to the bank and tried to get in, but the door was locked. Chaffee started away, thinking of other things. But in passing his eyes caught a light behind the bank cage; under the light Mark Eagle stood, bent over a ledger, black hair glistening. He had on the old alpaca coat, an eyeshade covered his forehead and a pencil lay behind one ear. The Indian had returned to the ways of the white man.

Even that sight, as remarkable and thought provoking as it was, failed to hold Chaffee's attention. He strode down the street, pulled by a more urgent desire. He wanted to see Gay. He wanted to talk to her, now that he was free. Free and poor. Free to speak his heart, and free to offer her a poor man's company. Well . . .

At the hotel he hesitated, reminded that he had one duty yet to perform over at the stable—to see who those dead men were and to lock the prisoners in the jail before any possible recurrence of mob spirit took possession of the homesteaders. So, both impatient and tired, he pressed forward through the shadows. On the verge of crossing the street he heard a man running directly toward him. He didn't know who it was, nor could he make out the fellow's face in the darkness. The unknown one halted, almost touching him, the breath coming in gasps. And he spoke in a sibilant whisper.

"Jim—hey, Jim! For God's sakes, come to Callahan's! They got Luke in the back room—killin' him! Hurry—!"

"Who's that?" challenged Chaffee. But the man was running back. Chaffee raced in pursuit, wishing to call some of the Stirrup S crowd after him. But he was past the jail and he didn't want to draw the attention or the anger of the homesteaders down upon the Perrine gang. There had been too much fighting to start more. So he followed. He heard the unknown one sing out again and drop completely from hearing. Thoroughly aroused, Chaffee struck Callahan's swinging doors with his whole body and knocked them aside. His gun was drawn and he swept the room—to find nobody in it. No customers, no barkeeps, nor even Callahan himself. Yet Callahan's office door was ajar, back of the counter, and a chair went smashing to the floor as he listened, evoking a high and shrill cry of distress Chaffee vaulted the bar and kicked open the door; it swung halfway, struck an obstacle and recoiled. He commanded a partial view of the room and saw nothing; somebody sighed heavily and, throwing aside the last of his caution, he hit the door again and jumped full into the room. The door slammed shut.

Theodorik Perrine, massive and black and sinister, stood against the wall, revolver bearing down upon Chaffee. He had the latter off balance; he had the drop. And he grinned.

"Nobody else here. Just me, Chaffee. I make pritty good sounds o' trouble, don't I? Yeah. Jus' me. My come-on is out in the alley, prob'ly gettin' away from here fast as he's able. God knows where the gang is. Some's dead, some's in the cooler. Rest went yella and hit for other parts. But I'm still here, Chaffee. Yeah, I'm here. It's the end of the trail all right. But I got one more hand to play and I shore wasn't leavin' until I played it. Slip the gun back in yore holster. I got yuh hipped."

"Where's Luke?" demanded Chaffee.

"Not here. It was only a stall to bring yuh over. Put back the gun."

"A trick?" muttered Chaffee. He shook his head, realizing how fully he had fallen into the trap. It angered him. He ought to have known better. Yet he thought Luke was in trouble, and Luke was a partner of his. Perrine's gun was set steadily against him, while his own piece aimed at nothing but a blank wall. Perrine murmured his command again, and Chaffee slid the weapon into its holster.

Perrine backed away until he was at the far end of the room. "Yeah, a trick. Yore pritty clever, Chaffee. Yuh think fast. I had to ketch yuh quick afore yuh had time to think. So it was a trick. But it ain't one now. I never knew the man I had to take advantage of on the draw. I'm givin' yuh an even break. But I want to palaver a minute." His own weapon dropped into its holster. Perrine seemed to relax, yet even in relaxing the mighty muscles strained and rolled along his shoulders. He was still grinning, swart features broken into sardonic lines, narrow eyes half closed.

"Even break," he repeated. "Nobody in the saloon. Nobody out back. Never saw the time I had to have help. Fifty-fifty. One of us walks outen here without hindrance—unless some o' yore centipedes ketch wind of it."

Chaffee turned so that he fully faced the man. Thus they stood, each with his back to the wall, the length of the room between them, the flickering lamp on the table marking a dead line. Across its smoking funnel he viewed Perrine. This was the showdown, the culmination of their years of bitter antagonism, the climax of their hostility. It was in the cards that they should meet and match guns; the prophecy of it had been abroad in the country many seasons. Month by month their paths had approached nearer; now those paths joined and the single trail was too narrow for both to walk along.

"Reckon it had to come," drawled Chaffee. "You said once you'd go clear across America to get me. I said I wouldn't go near that distance. Fact. I could let you alone. It's a big world and plenty of room for all. But you ain't built to let me alone. Top of the pile or nothing for you, Theodorik. I'm not backin' down. Just statin' a fact. But it's a poor play for you. You'd ought to be miles away from Roarin' Horse by now. Don't you know your time is past? Well—I'll wait for you to draw."

"Not for me," said Perrine, growing angry. "I don't have to take odds. Not from any man livin'. Which applies to you, Chaffee." The lamp funnel sent up a spiral of smoke, the glass was clouding with soot. Perrine stared at it, and his body trembled with a mirthless laughter. "Let the lamp decide. It's almost out of oil. When the flame leaves the wick—we draw."

"Fair enough. You're a hand to do things fancy, Theodorik."

"You bet. I make a splash when I jump. That damn' Woolfridge! Yella dawg! With all his fancy airs he wanted to jump the bucket and leave me to play the fiddle."

"He's in jail now," said Chaffee.

"Yeah? He ought to be in hell. He wanted to run. So did his men. So did mine. I ain't runnin'—not till I'm through with you. Here I stand on my hind laigs, too big a man to be budged afore my time. It takes more'n a pack o' homesteaders to pull me down. I'm Theodorik Perrine!"

"And proud of it," murmured Chaffee. There was draught of air coming into this small room. It crossed the lamp chimney and sucked at the light. That light might last five minutes; it might snuff out within the drawing of a breath. Chance—the sporting of the gods. It had always been this way with

Theodorik Perrine and himself. The giant seemed to understand what Chaffee was thinking about, for his grin broadened and his teeth shimmered against the black background of his face. He enjoyed this, or appeared to. As for Chaffee, his nerves were caught by a strange chill and his finger tips felt remote. He was a good and competent hand with the gun, but Perrine's reputation had been a thing of legend and mystery. And Perrine always had fostered the reputation, never revealing his skill in public.

"You bet I'm proud," said Perrine. It sounded as if he spoke against time. "I cover a lot of ground. I cast a big shadder. I can do everything better'n you, which we will prove in another minute. About them hawsses— that was yore luck. It's allus been yore luck to draw meaner brutes than me. I can ride anythin' that wears hair, but I nev' could show on the leather-covered easy chairs they gimme. I don't like you—never did and never will. I'll be runnin' yore name into the ground a long time after yore dead. You been in my way too long. Yuh've hogged the middle o' the stage when it was my place by rights and—*the light's out!*"

The room was a cramped cell of blackness, the stink of kerosene filling Jim Chaffee's nostrils. He heard Perrine's mighty hand slap against a gun butt, and he found himself weaving on his feet, crouched forward like a wrestler; everything was atremble with sound, everything shook under the blasting reports that filled the place. Purple lights flashed and trailed into nothing; there was the spat of bullets behind him. He thought he had fired twice and the belief somehow disheartened him; he felt numb. Then Perrine's breathing came short and quick; rose to a titanic effort and sank to laggard spurts. Perrine was falling; and in falling carried everything around him, like the downsweep of a tree. The table capsized; the lamp smashed and jangled on the floor. Then Perrine was speaking for the last time.

"Never believe yuh—is a better man. Luck. Allus luck." So he died with this faith in himself, going down the corridor of eternity.

Callahan's was of a sudden full of men. Chaffee opened the office door and faced the light. Homesteaders ranged around the walls; Stirrup S men piled through. But when they saw him and observed the bleak gravity of his eyes they stopped.

"Perrine's in there," said he. "I beat him to the draw." That was all he said. He forced a way through the crowd and hurried down the street. During the last half hour there had been a thought and a desire in his head; he had been fighting against interruption. There was nothing now that could stay him, nothing to stop him from going to Gay and telling her what clamored for expression. Behind, he heard a vast upheaval in Callahan's. The saloon was being torn apart, a target for the long suppressed animosity of the Stirrup S men against the headquarters of every disturbing element in Roaring Horse. Another time and he might have turned back to check that, but now only one purpose swayed him; thus he shouldered through the guards and turned into the Gusher. The clerk, discreetly absent during the turmoil, was again in the lobby.

"Have you seen Miss Thatcher recently?" asked Chaffee.

"Not since right after she left the dining room," replied the clerk. "She stayed down here a minute and then went upstairs."

For the first time that evening Chaffee considered the possible significance of her room's open door. The thought sent him up the steps three at a time. The door was still open, the room still empty. He entered, looking about, trying to see if there had been marks of disturbance. But as he peered into the clothes closet he heard a faint murmur of a woman's voice somewhere in the hall. He hurried out, the sound leading him back to the landing, pulling him to the bottom of the rear stairs and across the kitchen to the storeroom. He put his hand to the door, finding it locked; and that isolated fact in all the night's turbulence aroused a hot anger.

"Gay—are you all right?"

"Y-yes, but there's a rat in here!"

He wasted no time on the lock. Bracing himself, he crushed the panel with a drive of his shoulder, ripped the catch clear, and caught hold of her extended arms. He saw instantly the mark of a blow on her temple.

"Who did that?"

"My dear man, don't you eat me alive. Let's wait until I get out of here."

"Soon settled," said he, and carried her back to her room. "Now, who did that?"

"Can it be so bad?" she wanted to know, and went directly to the mirror. "That is a mark of Mr. Woolfridge's affection, Jim. I suppose I should feel honored that he wished to kidnap me. Where is he now?"

"In jail."

She turned and came over. "My poor man! They have hurt you so much more than they've hurt me. Is it all done?"

"All but the judge and the jury."

She made a queer little gesture with her hand. "Then there is nothing for me to do but pack."

"Pack for what? Where are you going?"

"Back home," said she in a rather small voice.

He shook his head. "Not now. Nor any other time without me. Gay—"

Her fine rounding features were pale. One hand crept to her breast, and she seemed profoundly disturbed. He caught the changing expression as he came nearer.

"I can only bring you a bad name," said she quietly. "Only a bad name."

"I ain't interested in that, Gay."

"Oh, you have always been that way! Why don't you ask me about myself? Why won't you let me tell you? Do you think I'd ever come to you with all that's behind me—you not knowing?"

"I know."

"You can't know. How could you?"

"Folks took plenty of pains to tell me during those days in Bannock City."

"Well?"

"They're a bunch of blind fools," he grunted. "Do you figure I believe it? The first time I saw you I knew the kind of a woman you were. I—"

"I ran away," said she, the words rushing out of her, "because home meant only a dad who worked me from daylight to dark and sent me to bed hungry. I ran away because the only man who was ever kind to me in those years helped me to do it. Whatever I am, Jim, I have made myself. That man was nothing but kind. Never anything but that from the time he took me in his rig until the time he put me on a train going east. I have never seen him again. Nobody else ever has. And so the story about me was carried on. Jim, I have been decent—I—"

"Don't need to tell me that, Gay," was his gruff reply. "I don't like to hear you defending yourself. You don't need to. Seems to me I need to do the explainin'. I'm white and twenty-eight. Sound of limb and busted flat. But I think, now that the fighting is over, I can get a job. Always some kind of a job. Some kind of shelter."

"Shelter—Jim, I have never known the security of a home of my own. Never. Pillar to post is the way I have lived. I washed dishes to go to school. Always wandering. Wherever you want to take me—if you want me at all—"

Somebody came up the stairway and turned at the door. Craib's bald head glistened on them as he ducked.

"Oh, Jim."

"Come in, Craib."

But Craib stopped on the doorsill. "Man that rented your place from Woolfridge came to me to-night. I took it over. You're free to go back, Jim. I'll take care of all the details. It ain't mine yet and it ain't yours. But you go back. We'll straighten it out and we'll stock it up. I want no money from you till everything's back to normal. It's just a personal affair between the both of us and I wanted to come and tell you soon's I could. I would like—" and the heavy face changed a trifle, as much as it ever would—"I would like you to consider me a friend."

"Well," began Jim, and found himself looking at an empty opening. Craib had gone.

"There's shelter, Gay," he drawled.

She smiled, and the color came back to her as he closed in. Presently she looked up, the film of tears in her eyes, but still smiling. "You take care of the outside of that cabin, Jim, and I'll take care of the inside."

"Put on a hat," said Chaffee with already that touch of proprietorship which comes to a married man, "and let's go down for a cup of coffee."

THE END

We hope that you have enjoyed
reading this Chivers Large Print Book.
We publish more than 200 new
Large Print titles every year
and maintain an extensive backlist
of titles in nearly every genre.
For more information on other titles
or to receive a complete title list,
please call or write to us
at the address below—
we would love to hear from you!

Chivers North America
1 Lafayette Road
Post Office Box 1450
Hampton, New Hampshire 03842-0015
(800) 621-0182
(603) 926-8744